CROSS MY HEART AND HOPE TO DIE

BY THE SAME AUTHOR

This Way Out
Who Saw Him Die?
Fate Worse Than Death
The Quiet Road to Death
A Talent for Destruction
The Chief Inspector's Daughter
Death in the Morning

CROSS MY HEART AND HOPE TO DIE

An Inspector Quantrill Mystery

Sheila Radley

CHARLES SCRIBNER'S SONS
New York

Maxwell Macmillan International
New York Oxford Singapore Sydney

First American Edition 1992

Charles Scribner's Sons
Macmillan Publishing Company
866 Third Avenue
New York, NY 10022

Macmillan Publishing Company is part of the
Maxwell Communication Group of Companies

Library of Congress Cataloging-in-Publication Data
Radley, Sheila.
    Cross my heart and hope to die: an Inspector Quantrill
mystery/Sheila Radley.
        p.   cm.
    ISBN 0-684-19410-4
    I. Title.
PR6068.0846C76   1992   91–46979   CIP
823′.914—dc20

10   9   8   7   6   5   4   3   2   1

Printed in the United States of America

FOR DOROTHY

1

Their surname wasn't really Crackjaw of course. According to their pension books, the old couple were Zygmunt and Gladys Krzecszczuk. But the derisory nickname, with its rural disregard for the feelings of a foreigner, had been bestowed on Ziggy so long ago that most people in the village assumed that it was his real name.

Even those who knew better, including the sub-postmistress who paid the pensions, found it simplest to pretend that they thought Crackjaw an acceptable pronunciation of Krzecszczuk; and the police, when they were called in, were glad to do the same. After all, neither Ziggy nor Gladys was likely to complain, because they had both disappeared.

Their disappearance caused very little concern among the inhabitants of the Suffolk village of Byland. The Crackjaws lived in isolation at Longmire End, a mile out of the village by road and then another half mile up an unmetalled lane. Ziggy had worked for thirty-seven years at Longmire Farm, and he and his wife lived in one half of a red-brick double-dweller that had been built near the farm in the nineteenth century to accommodate two labourers and their families.

When the Crackjaws first lived there, all three houses at Longmire End had been occupied. Eventually, the tenant farmer had retired and moved away. The Longmire land was now cultivated by a farmer from the next village, and the big old timber-framed farmhouse was empty; so was the other half of the double-dweller. The Crackjaws' numerous children had dispersed and the old couple lived entirely alone, without a telephone, out of sight and for the most part out of mind.

Though Gladys Crackjaw, née Goffin, was Byland born and bred, none of her relatives now lived in the village. Her marriage to a foreign farm-labourer who spoke only a few words of English, most of them not nice, had deprived her of the only friends she had once had, the girls she had grown up with.

'Poor Gladys,' was how they had referred to her at first, with amused contempt. Later – more kindly, taking into account her pinched, anxious face, the clinging toddlers, the many pregnancies: 'Poor old Glad.'

But over the years Gladys's weary expeditions to the village on foot became so infrequent that she slipped from people's memories. Byland grew, and changed. Some of her contemporaries moved elsewhere, some died. By the time the survivors reached their mid-seventies, they had forgotten Gladys so comprehensively that she might as well have been dead too.

Her husband had always been the more visible of the couple. Throughout his working life Ziggy Crackjaw had been a familiar sight in Byland, a rough man in a greasy cap, with broad cheek-bones and thick black eyebrows that met across his nose. Every day after work, and twice on Saturdays and Sundays, he had been seen cycling through the village on his way to the White Horse, and wobbling precariously homewards again when he'd either had a skinful or run out of money.

Ziggy had been tolerated at the White Horse, but never liked or befriended. He was sullen when sober, argumentative when he was drunk, and incomprehensible most of the time. But soon after he reached pensionable age the White Horse changed hands, and Ziggy was forced to change his habits.

The new landlord and his wife, urban refugees, knew exactly what kind of country pub they wanted to run. It looked, in their dreams, exactly like the thatched and heavily beamed Byland White Horse, but cleaned up and renovated, and with the addition of a restaurant. The customers of their dreams were mostly other urban refugees, cheerfully free-spending but rarely drunk and never nasty with it.

Very few of the White Horse's usual customers measured up to the new landlord's standards. The pub was closed for two months while it was being transformed, and afterwards some of the more hygienic regulars were permitted to return in order to provide a little local colour, but Ziggy Crackjaw was not among them.

Too old to cycle to a pub elsewhere, Ziggy took to visiting the village once a week and buying drink for consumption at home. There were two general stores in Byland, one primarily a sub-post office, the other – standing on a rise and therefore known as the top shop – a newsagent and off-licence. Every Thursday, pension day, Ziggy would cycle down through the village to the post office to collect the pensions for himself and his wife, and then return home by way of the top shop where he bought his weekly provisions. These included two litre bottles of vodka, and as many cans of beer as he could pack into the wooden box that he had fastened to the carrier of his bicycle with orange binder twine.

Ziggy continued this practice for some ten years. His shoulders became hunched and stiff, his old legs took longer to push the pedals round, but whatever his health or the weather he made his Thursday morning shopping trip to Byland without fail. And Maureen Norris, joint owner with her husband of the top shop, always had Ziggy's regular purchases – the drink, plus two large wrapped sliced loaves of bread, two large packs of pork sausages, seven large cans of baked beans, half a pound of butter, half a pound of tea and two pounds of sugar – ready and waiting for him.

Then, one Thursday in late March, Ziggy Crackjaw failed to collect his provisions.

It had been a month of gales, and this week was the worst. Winds in Eastern England had been blowing at gale force, on one occasion gusting up to ninety miles an hour. By Thursday the winds had moderated, but they were still sufficiently strong to make Maureen think that the old man must have decided for once to postpone his shopping trip. But although Friday was a relatively calm day, Ziggy still didn't appear.

Saturday was the shop's half day. When Ziggy had not come by closing time, Maureen Norris – as kind-hearted as she was generously built – grew concerned. She and her husband weren't local people, but they'd lived in the village for seventeen years and she knew that Ziggy was married even though she'd never set eyes on his wife. Worried that the old couple might be ill, Maureen – who couldn't drive – urged her husband Vic to go out to Longmire End and see whether anything was amiss.

Vic Norris, a permanently harassed man, refused. It was pouring with rain, and he'd had a hell of a week. Bad enough in fine weather to have to get up every morning at five to sort and deliver newspapers, but wild weather made the job an endurance test.

This week, for four days in succession, he'd driven through winds so strong that they'd sometimes rocked his van, threatening to overturn it. Branches torn from trees had thumped down on the metal roof and he'd felt sure that if the wind didn't get him one of the bigger branches would, crushing him, van and all. It wouldn't be so bad if the customers appreciated what he went through to deliver their papers, but no, they took him for granted. Some of them even had the nerve to moan because he was late!

And now that he'd finished the day's deliveries and thankfully garaged the van until tomorrow morning (Sunday, always the worst day for newspapers, with all those blasted supplements; people didn't read half of 'em, but soon complained if he forgot to deliver a single one) he had no intention of getting it out again.

Besides, he didn't give a damn about Ziggy Crackjaw.

10

The surly old bastard never paid his shop bill in full, always asking for cigarettes and other things as if as an afterthought, and then saying that he'd pay for them 'next time'. And Maureen was soft, she had let the old man run up an account that began to look as though it never would be paid. No, Vic was hanged if he was going to spend a wet Saturday afternoon delivering to the Crackjaws out at Longmire End.

He went eventually, of course. Maureen kept on about 'the poor old couple' and Vic knew there'd be no peace until he did as she wanted. Grumbling furiously, he put on his wet-weather gear again, loaded up the food and drink, and set off.

It was years since Vic Norris had driven up Longmire Lane – not since his early days as a newsagent, when Longmire Farm was occupied and he'd been so eager for custom that he'd been prepared to jolt all the way up there and back seven days a week just to deliver the *Telegraph* and *Farmers' Weekly*. He must have been mad, wasting all that time and petrol, not to mention the wear and tear on the van . . .

The narrow lane had changed during the intervening years. Then it had been bordered by hedges and ditches and overhung by trees, its surface rutted by the passage of farm vehicles in bad weather. But at least the resident farmer had always filled in the worst of the potholes for the sake of his own car.

Since then the hedges and most of the trees had been removed and the ditches filled in so that the fields could be enlarged. The surface of the lane had been churned to battlefield consistency by heavy modern machinery, without regard for any other users. Swearing with vexation, Vic lurched along through mud and rain, his windscreen wipers clacking at full speed.

Ahead, fringing one side of the lane, were the remains of what he could remember as a wood. Some of the trees had been pushed askew by the gales, and broken branches littered the ground, crunching under his wheels. Vic

11

strained forward, watching out for worse obstacles. It'd be just his luck to run into a branch big enough to damage the van –

What he almost ran into, instead, was a whole tree. He rounded a bend in the lane and immediately stood on his brakes because there it was, an ivy-festooned tree-trunk as high as the van, lying slap in his way. Juggling with the steering wheel, skidding on the mud, he managed to stop the van with its offside front wing buried in ivy, just inches away from the barrier of solid oak.

Vic gave a snort of relief, switched off his engine and just sat. His hands were shaking and he needed a few moments to get over the shock. What he felt, though, was doubly thankful. For one thing, he and the van had escaped unharmed; for another, the fallen tree had conveniently put a stop to the whole expedition.

One of his reasons for not wanting to come – though of course he wouldn't admit it to his wife – was that he knew he was no good in emergencies. If he found one of the old Crackjaws ill or injured, he wouldn't know what to do. He was afraid he might panic. But now he had a perfect excuse for not going any further.

Longmire Lane was blocked and there wasn't a thing, Vic told himself, that he could do about it. He didn't know whose job it was to shift the tree, but it certainly wasn't his. He'd more than done his bit. What he intended to do now – when he managed to turn the van – was to go straight back home. If his wife was so keen on helping the Crackjaws, it would be up to her to get the lane unblocked.

Maureen's opinion, when her husband returned and told her what had happened, was that he might at least have tried to get through to the Crackjaws on foot. But she knew she'd be wasting her breath to say so. She had no idea whose job it was to move fallen trees either, but she was an enterprising woman and so she seized the telephone directory.

She began by ringing the District Council offices, but there was no reply. Well, of course, there wouldn't be, on a Saturday afternoon. The directory offered several emergency Council numbers . . . but did she want the Environmental Health Department, or the District Surveyor? And supposing she was asked to leave an answerphone message – what good would that do when two old people were known to be stuck in Longmire End, certainly hungry, possibly ill, possibly injured during the gales? Concerned as she was, Maureen decided that the best thing to do would be to ring the nearest police station at Breckham Market.

Had Vic Norris been a different man, prompted either by compassion or by a sense of responsibility to trudge through the rain and find out what had happened to the Crackjaws, he would have discovered that Maureen's anxieties were unfounded. Had he reported back to his wife that they were no longer at home and that their house was locked up, Maureen would have been happy to assume that the old couple had been fetched by one or other of their family. She certainly wouldn't have bothered to ring the police just to say that the lane was blocked.

But the police, having been called in, were not content to make assumptions. They decided, in view of the advanced ages of the couple and the fact that the Norrises had never known them to leave the village, that it would be advisable to establish their exact whereabouts. And when this proved difficult, a detective went to Byland and began to make further enquiries.

2

The oak in Longmire lane, Byland, was one of many trees in the Breckham Market area that were felled in the March gales. Only the week before, the town itself had lost two great lime trees from the churchyard at the top of the market place. The sudden disappearance of such prominent vertical features had altered the look of the town centre entirely, to the vexation of its more conservative inhabitants.

Among the vexed, those who deeply resented the arbitrary rearrangement of their personal landscape, was Detective Chief Inspector Douglas Quantrill, head of Breckham Market CID. But his annoyance came later. At the height of that week's storm, when the roaring wind brought down a mature walnut tree in his garden, Quantrill had in fact been in no fit state to notice. A large and healthy man, he himself had been laid low for the first time in his life by an attack of bronchitis.

When he first complained of an aching head and sinuses, and tightness in his chest, his wife Molly had tried to persuade him to go to the doctor. Convinced that he was indispensable, he had as usual ignored her and attempted to carry on working. Predictably – though he wouldn't have listened to anyone who had tried to tell him so – this had had the effect of fogging his memory, distorting his judgement and shortening his temper.

It was only when his sergeant, Hilary Lloyd, took the initiative and drove him to the doctor's door that he had finally submitted. Hilary told him that what he did to his health was his own affair, but that she wasn't going to put up with him shedding his viruses all over the office and making everyone's life a misery into the bargain; and he had listened to her because her good opinion mattered to him more than anyone else's.

His former infatuation with her – he sometimes went hot and cold when he thought what a fool he must have made of himself – had been replaced by a slightly rueful affection. His admiration for his sergeant's professional ability had never stopped him from arguing with her about the cases they had worked on, but his personal admiration was boundless. He didn't even think of arguing with her about the doctor. Besides, by that time he felt so unwell that he took the prescribed antibiotics and retired to bed, convinced he was going to die.

When his wife told him, on the Thursday morning, that the walnut tree had been uprooted during the night, Quantrill hadn't been able to take it in. On Thursday evening he had mumbled an enquiry about structural damage to their bungalow, groaned thankfully when he heard there was none, and pulled the sheets over his head. On the Friday he had got up and wandered about in his dressing-gown for a bit, but he was still muzzy-headed and bleary-eyed. Everything in the living-room looked so unfamiliar at first glance that he retreated to the kitchen, drank a little soup, and went back to bed to await the expected relapse.

It wasn't until Saturday, when the antibiotics took effect and his temperature dropped, that he decided he was going to live after all. That was when, shaky but fully dressed, he realized with shock and indignation that the loss of the walnut tree had made a permanent difference to the appearance of the living-room.

The Quantrills' large 1950s bungalow stood in half an acre of garden in one of the best residential parts of Breckham Market. The mortgage repayments were horrendous, but even so Quantrill had no regrets about the move. For the first time in his married life he had enough space round him, and the leafy garden gave him an illusion of privacy, almost of country living. Now, though, the storm had changed his outlook.

Before, the view from the south-facing window of the living-room had featured the handsome spread of the thirty-foot tree. It hadn't darkened the room because there was also a wide window in the west wall, but it had provided interesting patterns of light and shade, giving a particular form and substance to the furniture that the Quantrills had brought to Bramley Road from their previous house.

With the tree gone the room seemed cruelly bright, its worn furnishings exposed in all their shabbiness. And the view from the window didn't bear looking at. The tall Edwardian house next door had previously been hidden and now there it was, dominating the outlook with its purplish bricks and ugly down-pipes. It seemed to have a great many upstairs windows, all of them eyeing the Quantrills' every movement.

'Doesn't it look terrible?' Douglas croaked to his wife.

But Molly, standing in the doorway of the living-room, sounded more relieved than dismayed. 'That's what I've been telling you ever since we came here!' she said. 'I've been really ashamed of that old three-piece suite. Now we shall have to buy a new one, whether you want to or not.'

On Sunday morning, scarfed and tweed-hatted against the cold wind, Quantrill ventured outside to mourn the fallen tree at close quarters.

The walnut lay horizontal, its base still partly anchored at the edge of a great hole in the lawn, its splintered branches tangled among crushed shrubs. In falling, the tree had wrenched out of the ground a massive pad of earth and fine roots, about ten feet across and three or four feet thick. Quantrill peered down into the hole, intrigued despite his regrets by the fact that the walnut, for all its size, appeared to have no large tap roots to anchor it deep in the earth. It astonished him that trees could ever withstand the wind for long enough to reach maturity.

'Good thing it fell where it did, eh Dad?' called Peter as he walked slowly and uncomfortably across the lawn towards his father. 'A bit more to the left and that'd have been the end of your workshop!'

Quantrill told himself that he probably suspected rather than heard a slightly malicious tone of regret in the boy's voice. Feeling in part responsible for the motor-cycle accident that had nearly killed his son, he expected Peter to take every opportunity to have a go at him.

It was fifteen months since the accident, and the boy had only recently been able to walk without crutches or a stick. The old Peter, his father couldn't help thinking, would have loved the fallen tree. He'd have jumped down into the hole, run the length of the trunk, clambered about in the branches. True, the new Peter was older: eighteen now, and beyond the stage of boyish running about. But Quantrill felt a constant guilt as he saw how cautiously his son walked, with trainers on his feet like any other teenager but on legs that had been reconstructed with metal bones and plastic joints. If Peter did take an occasional verbal poke at him, it was surely justified.

'Damn shame about the tree,' Quantrill suggested, by way of conversation.

'That's not what Mum thinks!' said Peter, who had enjoyed overhearing his mother win the long-running argument about the new furniture. 'Gran'll be pleased, too, when she comes back from Aunt Mavis's,' he added provocatively. 'Mum says she was always grumbling that the tree made her bedroom gloomy.'

Quantrill made an uncomplimentary remark about his mother-in-law, and vowed to plant a larger tree even nearer her window. Peter chuckled, and father and son walked more amicably along the length of the fallen tree.

'Can I have some of the wood to season and take to

college?' said Peter. His accident, and the operations that followed, had enabled him to do what he wanted and leave school without any of the academic qualifications his father had previously tried to insist on. His best subject at school had been woodwork, and he had now embarked on a craft design course at Yarchester City College. It wasn't what Quantrill had hoped for for his only son; but at least it kept the boy usefully occupied.

'Have as much wood as you want,' he agreed. 'The rest'll keep us in firewood for next winter. I'll hire a chainsaw and cut the tree up as soon as I'm fit again.'

'No, I can do that!' said Peter eagerly. 'Matthew Pike's Dad's got two or three chainsaws; I'm sure he'll lend me one. I can cut the tree up in the Easter holidays.'

'You can *what*?' spluttered Quantrill, so irritated that his chest tightened again and brought on a fit of coughing.

'Well . . .' Peter's confidence wavered. 'I can have a go at it, can't I? I can cut some of the wood, anyway? Just enough for what I need.'

'Are you out of your mind, boy?' demanded his father hoarsely. 'Of course you can't cut the tree up, not even part of it. Good grief, you've only just started walking without a stick!'

'But I've got to be able to do *something*,' protested Peter. 'Cutting's a standing-up job; I can do that just as well as anybody else.'

'That just shows how little you know about chainsaws! Don't you realize they're dangerous? They're powerful things; you've got to be fit and strong to control them.'

'I *am* fit. I've been doing my exercises, and I'll be perfectly firm on my feet by Easter.'

'So I hope. But I am not letting you loose on this tree with a chainsaw – they're lethal in inexperienced hands.'

'You're not experienced with them!' said Peter hotly. 'I don't believe you've ever used one, any more than I have.'

'Maybe not,' conceded Quantrill. 'But I've seen the damage they can do, and I know better than to run any risks. Just stop arguing, you young idiot, and leave the tree to me.'

What Peter said about his father, as he stumped back towards the bungalow, was a great deal louder and ruder than what his father had said about his grandmother. But Quantrill, who had once seen a principal witness in a murder case kill himself with a chainsaw, felt completely justified and pretended not to hear.

What he heard when he returned to the house some minutes later gave him an unhoped-for pleasure. The front doorbell rang, Molly answered it, and the light clear voice he heard was Hilary Lloyd's.

'Good morning, Mrs Quantrill. I thought it was time I enquired about your patient.'

He loved Hilary for the tactful way she always dealt with Molly, keeping herself at a friendly but deferential distance and never calling him Douglas in front of his wife.

'Patient?' he heard Molly reply scornfully. 'That's the last thing he is! I don't know when he's more difficult, when he's convinced he's dying or when he's getting better . . . He's just bawled out Peter, too. Come in, Hilary, and see if you can talk him into a more reasonable frame of mind.'

Quantrill stood up eagerly as his sergeant entered the living-room, tall and thin and elegant even in casual clothes, a complete contrast to his dumpy wife.

'Morning, Hilary!'

'Good morning, sir. How are you?'

Her coming had done wonders for him, but he remembered to put a croak in his voice. 'Much better, thanks. Should be back at work in a day or two.'

Molly offered coffee, but Hilary refused because she was on her way to play squash. 'I see you've lost your walnut tree,' she said. 'What a shame, it was such a handsome shape.'

19

'Wasn't it just?' mourned Quantrill. 'The place looks all wrong without it, inside and out. I'll replant, of course, but it won't be the same . . .'

'I should hope not!' said Molly. 'That tree was much too big. What I'd like to have there, Douggie, is one of those nice double-flowering pink cherries – '

'Anything interesting happening at work, Hilary?' interrupted Quantrill. He might have lost the argument about the new furniture, but he was damned if he was going to put up with Molly's frilly little choice of tree. And he hated being called Douggie.

As he had hoped, his wife retreated to the kitchen. He and Hilary exchanged wordless grins, and relaxed into their working relationship. She gave him a quick update on their current cases, and then hesitated.

'Something new has come up, and I hardly know whether to take it seriously or not. An old couple, late seventies, living in squalid isolation on the other side of Byland, seem to have disappeared. The husband didn't collect their usual groceries on Thursday, and when one of our patrol men went to their house on Saturday he found it empty. They've not been taken to hospital, or moved out by the social services, and the shopkeeper is fairly certain they've never been outside the village during the past eighteen years.'

'Any suspicious circumstances?'

'Not really. The house had been left locked, and I found their pension books on the mantelpiece so it seems that they intend to return. But I feel uneasy about it.'

'Any family?'

'Eight children, apparently. All adult now, of course, and none living locally. I've made contact with two of them so far, but there doesn't seem to be much in the way of family feeling or communication. Their surname's Polish, by the way. Don't ask me to pronounce it.'

Intrigued, Quantrill scratched his chin. 'What do they say about their parents, the two you've seen?'

'Not seen, telephoned. The eldest son, a single man,

works offshore on a North Sea gas rig. He goes to see his parents occasionally, and says he's been trying for long enough to persuade them to move into the village. He doesn't seem too worried about their disappearance. They were reasonably well when he called last Monday, he says, and he thinks one or other of his family must have fetched them for a visit.'

'Sounds a bit wishful to me,' said Quantrill.

'That's my impression. He feels a responsibility, and he's thankful to be relieved of it. But the only sister I've been able to contact, in Peterborough, knows nothing about them. She says she isn't in touch with her parents except to send them a card at Christmas, and she's doubtful if any of the others do more than that. I really think we need to be concerned for their welfare, Douglas. A Press appeal for information, do you think?'

Quantrill agreed. 'No cause for alarm, but we'd certainly like to know they're all right. What's your next move, Hilary?'

'If I haven't discovered anything before tomorrow afternoon, I'm going to Byland again. The son's coming off the rig to meet me.'

Quantrill sat up. 'D'you mind if I come with you?' he asked hopefully. 'Not to interfere, just for the ride.'

'You're still off sick,' Hilary reminded him. 'And what would Molly think?'

'You heard what she said, she'll be glad to get me out of the house. Besides, I'm interested. If the old couple really are missing, I want to know what's happened to them.'

3

The obstruction in Longmire Lane had been cleared, and Sergeant Lloyd was able to drive her Renault up to the gateless gap in the broken-down garden wall that fronted the old couple's home.

'Good grief . . .' said Chief Inspector Quantrill, easing himself reluctantly out of the passenger seat and turning up the collar of his coat. The wind was sharp, he still didn't feel fully recovered from his bronchitis, and their destination was more uninviting than he'd imagined.

The landscape was not picturesque, but even so the dilapidated building made a blot on it. The site of the two adjoining houses – a double-dweller, in Suffolk parlance – was at an elbow of the lane, where the surface of churned mud was differentiated from the cultivated land by a remnant of hedge and one or two scrubby trees.

Immediately surrounding the houses was a piece of garden ground, long overgrown, with a few old fruit trees, one of which had been pushed at an angle by the gales. Surrounding the whole was an expanse of arable land, striped green by row upon row of emerging sugar beet. The only relief for the eye was a couple of hundred yards up the lane, where an old farmhouse stood on a rise, sheltered by stag-headed oaks.

'Is the farm occupied?' Quantrill asked.

'No, it looks as though it's been empty for some years. A great shame, because it's a fine old timber-framed house. It needs a lot of work doing now, but I should think it's had money spent on it in the past. Which is more than you can say of this pair.'

The mean little double-dweller had been thrown together at a period when the cheapest materials, instead of being fittingly local, were Midland bricks and thin Welsh slate. The front elevation had a door at either end, and four windows, one up and one down for each house. In the centre of the roof was a shared chimney.

After a hundred years of neglect, the building seemed to be on the point of disintegration. Slates were slipping off the roof, guttering hung loose, cracked brickwork was green with damp, windows and doors were rotting. There was, though, a difference between the two houses. The one on the right was unoccupied, its windows blackly empty behind broken panes. The one on the left was shabbily curtained, and a plaster Alsatian dog ornamented the window sill.

'It's unfit for human habitation,' pronounced Quantrill.

'Wait until you see inside,' said Hilary.

They could hear the sound of an approaching car and presently a Jaguar XJ6, several years old but obviously cherished, nosed cautiously up the lane towards them. The driver, a man in his early forties, was smoking a cigarette but he civilly dropped it in the mud as soon as he stepped out of the car. He was long-legged, athletic-looking, husky in a thickly padded bright blue windcheater.

Hilary introduced herself and the Chief Inspector, and apologized for not having known how to pronounce the man's name when she contacted him.

Krzecszczuk laughed. 'We're known hereabouts as the Crackjaws,' he advised, 'but I gener'ly answer to Andrew.'

His appearance was eye-catching. He had a shock of prematurely greying hair, thick black brows that met in a straight line over the top of his nose, and very wide cheekbones; a Slav with a Suffolk accent, very much aware of himself, and of Hilary, but pleasantly wry when she failed to respond.

'Any news of the old folks?' he asked.

'I'm afraid not,' said Hilary. 'The only other member of your family I've been able to contact is Sonya, and she couldn't tell me anything about them.'

'Our Sonya?' He shrugged: 'I'm not surprised. She's never bothered with them, hasn't been here for years. Still – no news is good news, eh?'

The detectives made non-committal noises.

Andrew gestured defensively at his parents' home. 'Look, I know what you're thinking,' he said. 'I shouldn't have left them to spend their old age in a place like this, should I? But I've done my best to persuade 'em to move to one of the council bungalows in the village, and they won't budge.'

'Old people get stuck in their ways, you can't force them to do things for their own good,' Quantrill reassured him. 'D'you think it's possible they went off under their own steam, though?'

'Not a chance. Mum's poorly on her feet, she'd never have got beyond the gate. Besides, if they wanted to go anywhere they'd have told me when I came over at the beginning of last week.'

'Have they lived here long?' asked Hilary.

'All their married lives. It suits them, they like to keep to themselves. I don't manage to get here as often as I should, but at least I know they're contented. I'm certain they'd never have gone away, even for a few days, if somebody in the family hadn't insisted. Did you find the door key, by the way?'

'No, they must have taken it with them, so we forced an entry. We needed to be sure they weren't lying ill.'

Andrew pulled a face. 'Oh God, you've been upstairs then . . . I haven't done that for years. I s'pose it was in a terrible state?'

'I've seen worse,' Hilary said diplomatically, as she unpadlocked the temporary fastening on the front door.

They walked straight into a jumbled living-room that stank of wet rot, mice, mouldering wallpaper, old clothes and a lifetime of greasy dinners. The cheap furniture had long ago been battered into submission, and over everything was a fingermarked fuzz of ripening dust. The room was saved from complete squalor only by the fact that the table had been cleared and the worn vinyl floor-covering had recently been given a sketchy wash.

Andrew went on the defensive again. 'It hasn't been easy for Mum out here, with no water laid on or anything. She's always done her best, she's just too old to cope.'

'She's kept trying,' said Quantrill generously, 'we can see that.'

'Have they anything to live on, apart from their State pensions?' said Hilary.

'A few pounds put by, I daresay, but nothing in the way of income. I don't s'pose they left their pension books behind, did they?'

'As a matter of fact they did.' Hilary went to the mantelpiece and took the two books from where they were lodged behind a tarnished looking-glass. She flicked one of them open, and showed Andrew the post office date-stamp on the most recent counterfoil.

'The 23rd – when was that?' he asked.

'Last Thursday. I've talked to the postmistress, and she says your father drew both their pensions in the morning just as usual. He didn't say anything to her about going away.'

'No reason why he should, I s'pose . . . P'raps he didn't know himself, at the time.'

'But if he didn't know he was going away, why didn't he collect his groceries as usual? That's what's puzzling us.'

Andrew Krzecszczuk's eyebrows knotted over his nose. 'That's a rum 'un, that is,' he agreed slowly. 'I dunno . . . unless whoever came to fetch them drove him to the post office first, to collect the pensions before they went.'

'That's possible,' said Hilary.

'More'n likely, I'd say.' He brightened. 'The main thing is that they didn't take their pension books with them. The

25

next docket's dated the 30th, this coming Thursday, right? That must mean they're intending to come back this week to collect their money. So what are we worrying about?'

'It's our job to be concerned when anyone goes missing,' said Quantrill. "Specially when they're as old as your parents. Look, if they've been fetched by one or other of your family, that's fine by us. We don't want to interfere, we just want to be sure they're all right.'

"Course they're all right!' said Andrew confidently. 'Sure to be. Somebody in the family'll be looking after 'em.'

'Not according to your sister Sonya,' said Hilary.

'Oh, you don't want to take any notice of *her*. She never visits, so she wouldn't know who does. M'sister Cathy's the likeliest, she was always Mum's favourite.'

Hilary reached behind the looking-glass again and produced a discoloured Christmas card, on the back of which a shaky hand had written a number of names and addresses.

'This is how I found you and Sonya,' she said, 'but I can't make contact with any of the others.'

Frowning, Andrew studied the card. 'Oh well, this is an old list . . . Cathy's been divorced and remarried since then, I know that. Mum did tell me her new name, but I've forgotten. No idea where she's living now, or any of the others come to that. Mum's prob'ly got a more up-to-date list somewhere.'

'This is the only one I've been able to find. There don't seem to be any family letters about, either. Are you absolutely sure you can't remember Cathy's new name?'

'Sorry,' he apologized handsomely. 'In one ear and straight out the other. I like to be independent, I've never bothered with keeping in touch except to see Mum once or twice a year. But don't you worry, somebody'll be looking after the old folks.'

He paused and gave a wry grin. 'Well, it stands to reason. They couldn't have gone off on their own, and let's face it – who else but family would want to have 'em?'

*

26

Andrew Krzecszczuk drove off in the direction of Yarmouth and the helicopter that would return him to his North Sea gas rig. Quantrill, whose breathing hadn't been improved by the atmosphere in the Crackjaws' house, decided that he'd just as soon take the remains of his bronchitis home. But on their way back through Byland he agreed to wait in the car while Hilary had another word with the sub-postmistress.

The village shop and post office, a substantial late-eighteenth-century building in local grey brick with a roof of dark blue pantiles, stood in a prominent position beside the green. Byland was a growing village, favoured by commuters who worked in either Breckham Market or Yarchester, and the shop looked well maintained and relatively prosperous.

The business had evidently expanded over the years and now occupied much of the ground floor of the house. The original private front door remained, together with two downstairs windows and all the upper windows, but the shop itself had a modern commercial façade. On one side of the building was an iron gate leading to a garden, and on the other big double gates stood open to reveal an ageing Vauxhall estate car in a yard surrounded by outbuildings.

Hilary had discovered on her previous visit that the post office was situated at the back of the shop, where a room in the original house had been opened up to accommodate it. Customers stepping through the doorway found themselves in a small waiting area in front of the post office counter. On the wall hung a rack of official leaflets, and below it was a writing table. A pen was provided for the use of customers, but it was prudently attached to the table leg with string and sellotape.

The counter was fronted by a screen that stretched across the width of the room. The centre of the screen, the service area, was constructed of security glass, with an access door at one side. The remainder of the screen was made of hardboard and displayed official posters, but its chief function seemed to be to provide some privacy for the postmistress, Miss Thacker.

Her domain immediately behind the counter was business-like, with a large safe, and scales and filing cabinets and reference books and folders stuffed with forms. But evidently the room also served as a private office because the far end, glimpsed through the glass screen, appeared pleasant and comfortable. Bookcases lined the walls, and on a table in the window – barred for security, but with a sunny outlook over the garden – stood a word processor.

Miss Thacker, working at the keyboard, looked up irritably as Hilary approached the counter. Then, recognizing her visitor, she donned a smile as she came forward. 'Ah, Sergeant Lloyd again! What can I do for you?'

She was a stocky woman of medium height, forty-ish, round-faced, with a high complexion, dark bobbed hair, and watchful brown eyes under a fringe flecked with grey. There was no trace of an accent in her voice, though she was unmistakably a younger version of the elderly Suffolk woman who was serving in the shop.

'Sorry to bother you again, Miss Thacker – '

'Janet, everybody calls me Janet. Any news of the Crackjaws?'

'Afraid not. I'm still hunting for information, and I'd appreciate your help.'

'Surely. Only I can see customers heading this way – we usually get a bit of a rush about this time, so you'll have to bear with me. Look, why don't you come and wait round the back while I get rid of them?'

She unlocked the door in the screen and beckoned Hilary through into her private office. 'I wouldn't normally do this,' she said, 'I have to be very security-conscious. But I reckon the post office money should be safe enough with a CID sergeant!'

The area beyond the counter was even more comfortable than Hilary had realized, a private sitting-room with a carpet, a radio-cassette player and an armchair with a

28

resident cat. An electric kettle and the makings for tea and coffee stood on a corner table.

With a detective's insatiable curiosity – and shamelessly taking advantage of the fact that Janet Thacker's back was turned – Hilary looked round the room. From the books that were piled on the table beside the word processor it appeared that the postmistress was interested in local history and topography; possibly writing a book of her own. From her briskness with her customers it was apparent that she was only too anxious to get back to it.

If kindly, gossipy, old-fashioned village postmistresses still existed, Janet Thacker was not one of them. Hilary watched and listened as she disposed of a small surge of customers, most of them pensioners. True, she addressed them by name and either enquired after their health or commented on the weather, but she rationed the conversation to the exact time it took her to pay out their pensions.

Janet Thacker worked to a programme: accept the proffered pension book, and check that the week's docket had been signed; date-stamp both docket and counterfoil with two firm thumps; tear out the docket; take the money it represented from the cash dispenser, and count it out in front of the customer; push book and money under the security screen, add the docket to others on a bulldog clip, thank you and goodbye.

Not all her customers were so easy to deal with. Not all transactions were so straightforward. Hilary heard her being helpful to someone in a muddle, sarcastic to a smart-alec, and giving short shrift to a man who came in to have a row with the nearest available representative of Authority. Hilary knew that she herself would chafe in such a job, and she was amused by the placard that Janet Thacker displayed on her private side of the screen.

ALL VISITORS BRING JOY TO THIS OFFICE.
SOME WHEN THEY ENTER,
OTHERS WHEN THEY LEAVE.

29

'I love your placard,' she said when the last customer had been served. 'I must make a copy for our Station Sergeant.'

'Oh well, it helps to keep me going,' said Janet Thacker with a slightly embarrassed grin. She swivelled her stool away from the counter and revealed that she was dressed entirely for comfort, with a touch of the eccentric: jogging trousers, old tennis shoes, and a fisherman's slop, its pockets jangling with keys.

'It must be very frustrating to be stuck behind a counter all day,' said Hilary.

'It is. But then again, it's a lot more congenial than the Civil Service job I used to do in London. Besides, I shan't be stuck here for the rest of my working life, thank God; I'm lucky enough to have prospects.' She reverted to official briskness: 'You said you need some information – ?'

'About old Mr Crackjaw, when he came for his pension last Thursday. Did you notice anything different about him, Janet? Was he wearing better clothes than usual, or was he better shaved?'

The postmistress looked blank. 'Good lord, I don't know . . . I didn't take any notice of the man, I never do. He just grunts when I say "Good morning", and again when I hand over the money, so I don't waste my breath on him. I couldn't swear to it, but I don't *think* he was any different.'

'What we're wondering', explained Hilary 'is whether one of the Crackjaw children might have collected their parents, and stopped here for the old chap to draw their money first. But of course you can't see any comings and goings from here, can you?'

'No – but Mum probably saw him as he came through the shop. Let's ask her.'

Mrs Betty Thacker was undoubtedly her daughter's mother. She was a stout white-haired woman in her sixties, with Janet's brown eyes and round cheeks and high complexion. She wore an overall and bustled about uncomfortably on swollen feet that looked as though they

30

were killing her. The relationship between mother and daughter seemed slightly fraught, an old-established compound of affection and exasperation.

She greeted the detective warily, with a note of belligerence in her Suffolk voice. No, she hadn't noticed whether Ziggy Crackjaw came on his bike last Thursday, she had too much to do to stand gawping out of the window at people. No, she hadn't taken any notice of him as he came through the shop, he never bought anything so she always ignored him. Come to think of it, though, she didn't b'lieve she'd seen him last Thursday at all –

'You must have been out in the warehouse, then,' said Janet. 'He was here at the usual time.'

Mrs Thacker sniffed. 'I'm sure I don't know what his usual time is. I didn't see him, that's all I can tell you. But if I *had* seen him, I wouldn't ha' noticed him.'

She stumped off to serve a customer, and Janet walked with Hilary to the shop door. 'Sorry we can't help,' she said.

'What about the Crackjaw children? I'm in contact with Andrew and Sonya, but I can't locate any of the others.'

Janet Thacker's voice took on an irritable edge. 'It's no use asking me, I haven't the faintest idea where any of them live.'

Hilary persisted: 'I wondered whether you might perhaps have noticed letters going from the old couple to one or other of the family.'

'How could I? We don't handle the mail at this post office, it's all done from Breckham Market now.' She made an effort to control her irritation. 'Look, the Crackjaws have always been outsiders. I'm sorry, I'd help if I could, but I really know nothing about them at all.'

4

So far, Sergeant Lloyd's most useful informant in Byland
had been Maureen Norris, wife of the newsagent at the
top shop, who had alerted the police to Ziggy Crackjaw's
non-appearance. Maureen's own acquaintance with the
Crackjaws was confined to Ziggy. But she was able to
point Hilary in the direction of Miss Edna Griggs, an old
lady who had for many years been headmistress of the
village school and would no doubt remember the Crackjaw
family.

Whether Miss Griggs could be expected to have any
notion of their present whereabouts was another matter.
But Hilary's Press appeal for information about the old
couple had met with no immediate response, and so she
went to see Miss Griggs the following morning.

The old lady lived in a 1930s pebble-dashed suburban
house at the far end of the village. Her front garden
consisted of cement paths and a few disciplined shrubs.

Miss Griggs, nearing eighty and neatly cardiganed, was
small and thin with grizzled hair. There was very little of
her, but what there was seemed reinforced with wire. She
held herself stiffly upright, and though one of her eyes
watered weakly her voice was stern. But she seemed not
displeased to have a visitor, and invited Hilary into a
formal dining-room, chilly with disuse but meticulously
dust-free.

They sat on either side of the table and she listened to
what Hilary had to say. She agreed that she had taught

the Crackjaw children, though she couldn't resist correcting her visitor's pronunciation.

'Kreck-chuck,' she instructed. 'The name is Polish. There was a Polish army unit at Byland during the war, billeted in the Hall. Afterwards, Krzecszczuk found work at Longmire Farm, and married a rather simple local girl.'

She paused, her thin blue-tinged lips soundlessly rehearsing her next remark. Then she said, 'I should be sorry if you were to imagine that Krzecszczuk is in any way typical of his countrymen, though. The Poles shared our social evenings in the village, early in the war, and most of them were charmingly well-mannered. And wonderfully brave – '

For a moment, Miss Griggs had softened. Unexpectedly, Hilary caught a glimpse of a young woman who, it seemed, forty-odd years before, had found Polish soldiers gallant in both war and love.

'But Mr Krzecszczuk wasn't like that?' she prompted.

Miss Griggs snapped back to the present.

'No, he was always uncouth, a heavy drinker. I haven't seen him for many years, but I've no reason to think he has changed. He used to visit the White Horse regularly, even though he had eight children to support. And when he was drunk he could be violent.'

'Against people, or property?'

Miss Griggs hesitated, as though anxious to be strictly fair. 'My own knowledge is limited, of course. But he did burst into the classroom on one occasion and threaten me because he'd had a visit from the school attendance officer. He smashed a chair and tore up some books. But the caretaker had seen him coming and sent for the village policeman, so he was arrested before he did too much damage. It was a very unpleasant episode.'

Hilary murmured sympathetically. Then 'Tell me, Miss Griggs, how did he treat his own family?'

Another careful pause; Miss Griggs mopped her eye with her handkerchief and struggled with her conscience.

'The children sometimes came to school with visible

injuries,' she said eventually, 'though of course I can't say how they got them. But in those days, you know, when children misbehaved, it was expected that their parents would punish them. And the young Krzecszczuks were very wild, I often had to punish them myself.'

'Did you see much of Mrs Krzecszczuk at that time?' asked Hilary.

Miss Griggs didn't hesitate. 'Very rarely. She'd made a foolish marriage and she kept out of sight of the rest of the village. There was gossip about the number of children she had, but I've always made a point of ignoring gossip.'

She rose to her feet, but not dismissively. 'Would you care for a cup of coffee, Sergeant? I usually have one at about this time.'

There was a great deal more that the old lady could say if she would, Hilary was sure of it. She accepted the offer of coffee, waited patiently while it was made and brought in, and then enquired whether Miss Griggs had any information about where the Krzecszczuk children were now living.

'None at all.' She took a slow drink of coffee, holding her cup in both veined hands, and then seemed to come to a decision. 'But I can tell you of someone in the village who does know all about the Krzecszczuks. She and her parents used to live next door to them at Longmire End.'

'At the farm?'

'No, in the other half of the double-dweller.' Miss Griggs dabbed her eye again. 'They live now at the shop in the middle of the village. Her widowed mother, Betty, looks after the shop, and Janet is the sub-postmistress.'

Hilary paused in mid-sip. Then, 'Oh, yes, Janet Thacker,' she said casually. 'I had to call at the post office, so I've met her already. I imagine it's some time since they lived in Longmire End, though?'

'Ten years, possibly . . . But they lived next to the Krzecszczuks for twenty years, at least. Janet grew up there, with the Krzecszczuk children. She left home for

London, but then about ten years ago Mrs Thacker senior had heart trouble – '

'Mrs Thacker senior?'

'Betty's mother-in-law, the owner of the shop. She must be in her nineties now. When she was taken ill, Betty moved in to look after her, and Janet came back to Byland to join them. Our previous sub-postmaster was about to retire, so Janet applied for the job and transferred the post office from his house to the shop. Though I really can't imagine', Miss Griggs added severely, 'why she should want to return to Byland.'

Hilary thought it was plain enough. Janet had said she had prospects, and presumably she was counting on an inheritance; though her grandmother was certainly making her wait for it. But that had nothing to do with the present inquiry.

'Miss Griggs,' she said, 'I'm still not clear why you think Janet can tell me anything useful about the Krzecszczuks, after all this time.'

The old lady's voice rose high. 'Oh, I think you'll find that she was well acquainted with one of the Krzecszczuk family! I'm sure she'll be able to tell you whatever you need to know.'

There was a tremble in her hands, a flush on her mottled cheek, a glitter in her good eye. And the cause of it all was, unmistakably, a long-pent indignation directed at Janet Thacker.

Edna Griggs was aggrieved, and intent upon airing her grievance.

She had devoted her life, she told Hilary, to the education of the village children. It had been an uphill task, and one for which she had rarely been thanked, but her reward came from the achievements of the children she had educated.

Her star pupil had been Janet Thacker. Recognizing the child's promise, Miss Griggs had done everything in her power to encourage and coach her, opening her eyes to the existence of a world beyond the village and far beyond rural Suffolk. As a result, Janet had been the first child to progress from Byland school, via Breckham Market grammar school, to university.

The girl's achievement had given Miss Griggs a great deal of pride. Pleasure, too, though with a mixture of sadness. Janet had never visited her after leaving the village school, nor even sent her so much as a Christmas card. If they happened to meet, Janet always made some excuse to hurry away. It hurt Miss Griggs deeply, and puzzled her because she had never shown the girl anything but kindness; but she had long ago learned to practise a stoical acceptance.

Her pride in her pupil remained. Miss Griggs herself, she told Hilary, had never had the opportunity to go to university, but putting Janet on the right road was a kind of fulfilment. She had been delighted to hear from Betty Thacker that after graduation Janet was going to make her career in London, surrounded by cultural opportunities she herself could only dream of.

Janet's subsequent return to Byland had been a great disappointment to Miss Griggs. The role of village sub-postmistress was trivial, requiring no qualification at all beyond a good character. Miss Griggs felt that everything she had done to widen Janet's horizon had been rejected, if not thrown back in her teeth. And Janet was so abrupt with her when she went to the post office that she had gladly accepted a neighbour's offer to collect her weekly pension.

Hilary tried to be patient as Miss Griggs unburdened herself. Her own interest in Janet Thacker was limited to the woman's knowledge of the Krzecszczuk family, and as she made what she hoped were soothing remarks she looked covertly at her watch. It seemed to her that Miss Griggs was being over-sensitive. Janet Thacker was brisk with everyone; she had been Byland's sub-postmistress for ten years now, and it was high time the old lady swallowed her disappointment.

'Thank you for listening,' said Miss Griggs. 'You're the only person I have told this to, and I assure you that it's less irrelevant than you think. You see, when she was living in London, Janet wrote an autobiography covering her years in Byland. It deals in detail – distasteful detail – with her relationship with the Krzecszczuks.'

'Has it been published?'

'Not as far as I know. At least, not the whole book. But a chapter of it was published in an anthology called *Writers of East Anglia*. I borrowed it from the library without realizing that Janet's work was in it. She'd used a pen name, and she'd also changed the names of the villagers, but what gave her away was that she used the name Crackjaw. As soon as I saw that, I knew it was Janet's work.'

'What did she say about the Crack – the Krzecszczuks?'

'Nothing significant, in the published chapter . . . That's in the rest of the book.'

'Which you've read?' suggested Hilary.

The old lady's cheeks went a defiant pink. 'Without Janet's knowledge,' she admitted. 'I told Betty Thacker how much I'd enjoyed the published chapter. She had read it and was proud of it, without realizing that it was a small part of the whole. She looked among Janet's books, found the original typescript, and lent it to me. The names in it are real, including mine – '

'Do you think Janet would let me borrow it?'

'Don't ask her, please! She'll wonder where your information came from, and I don't want her to know, for her mother's sake as much as mine. Betty was most anxious that Janet shouldn't get to hear about the loan. Not that Betty knew what's in the book – she couldn't have read it herself, or she would never have lent it to me. It's full of indiscretion and unkindness . . .'

The old lady declined to say any more, and Hilary rose to leave. Miss Griggs followed her to the front door.

'I must beg you, Sergeant,' she said earnestly, 'not to mention my name to Janet when you ask her about the Krzecszczuks.'

'Of course. Don't worry.'

'But please don't think I'm being vindictive towards her. I feel no ill-will, though I admit to being hurt and disappointed. You see – '

Standing on the doorstep, frisked by the cold wind, the old lady shivered her cardigan round her. Her lips framed her words before she spoke.

'You see, Janet makes it quite clear in the book that she disliked me as a teacher. She says she found my lessons boring. Oh, one doesn't expect to be remembered with affection or gratitude by one's pupils. But an acknowledgement of one's help, a little respect for one's life's work – surely that isn't too much to ask?'

Sergeant Lloyd drove straight to Bramley Road, Breckham Market, and called on Chief Inspector Quantrill. She found him, with his wife safely out at work, enjoying his convalescence with a mid-day can of beer and the video of a football match.

'Feeling better?' she suggested.

'Not too bad,' he said guiltily, switching off the television. 'I went to the doc this morning and he says I can go back to work tomorrow.' He offered Hilary a drink, sherry, coffee or whatever, but she said she was too busy to linger.

'What's been happening, then?' he asked. 'Any news of the old couple, the Crackjaws?'

Hilary told him what she had gleaned from Miss Griggs. 'Well, we know Ziggy drinks,' she added. 'We've seen the empties in his house. But it's the violence that's interesting, isn't it? Perhaps he hit his wife, with or without intent, found that he'd killed her, disposed of her body, and took off.'

'Now hold hard,' said Quantrill. 'That doesn't sound like the contented couple their son told us about.'

'Family solidarity?' said Hilary. 'Or perhaps they're on their best behaviour on the rare occasions when Andrew's at home.'

'Maybe . . . It's an interesting possibility, I agree – but there isn't a scrap of evidence for it. Is there?'

'What about their living-room floor, with the conspicuously washed patch near the hearth? We all assumed that Mrs Crackjaw had cleaned it. But perhaps it was Ziggy who had to do that, to get rid of bloodstains before he left?'

'Ah!' said Quantrill, clicking back into top gear. He was tempted to issue an instruction, but remembered just in time that his sergeant was in charge of the case, and she was touchy about being told what to do. 'Right, then, Hilary, what's your next move?'

'I'll send the scenes-of-crime team to search for evidence at Longmire End,' she said. 'And then I'm going back to Byland post office, to find out why Janet Thacker pretends to know nothing about the Crackjaws.'

5

Later that afternoon Sergeant Lloyd drove to Byland and spent some time sitting in her car beside the village green, from where she had a good view of the Thackers' shop. She kept an eye on the number of people who approached it, and deliberately chose to enter the premises at a time when the post office was busy.

Janet Thacker was at her counter trying, between customers, to check a pile of dockets and list them on a calculator. She was not at all pleased when Hilary approached. She hadn't time to talk, she protested. The mail was due to be collected shortly, and there were official forms that she had to complete and send to head office today without fail.

Hilary assured her that she was in no hurry, and didn't in the least mind waiting. And as she had hoped, Janet Thacker unlocked the counter door and invited her – though ungraciously – into the private part of the office.

'Thanks very much. D'you mind if I look round your bookshelves while I'm waiting?' Hilary asked.

Janet tossed an answer over her shoulder. 'Help yourself,' she said absently.

It took nearly half an hour for the postmistress to complete her forms, deal with customers' complications, and book out the official mail. As soon as the mail driver had cleared the post-box and driven away, the office went quiet.

'Phew – ' Janet Thacker slumped on her stool, pushing her greying fringe out of her eyes and blowing out cheeks that were redder than usual with concentration. She was dressed more conventionally that afternoon, in sweater, skirt and casual shoes, though her bunch of keys was attached to her belt with a length of string.

'Sorry to keep you so long,' she told Hilary. 'There's never an even flow of work in this job, you're either bored silly or rushed off your feet.' She went to the corner table and switched on the kettle.

'At least you've got your word processor to stave off boredom,' said Hilary. 'Are you writing a book?'

'I'm working on a social history of this area: rural life in the twentieth century. I do a bit of freelance journalism, too: I'm the Byland correspondent for the local newspaper. They pay me 35p a line, and you'd be amazed how much I find to report!'

'Have you had any books published?'

'No such luck. I wrote one years ago and sent it to half the publishers in London, but they all sent it back . . . Cup of tea? Mum and I reckon to have one as soon as the mail goes.'

Hilary declined; she could hardly accept the woman's hospitality when she was about to question her truthfulness.

Janet Thacker made two half-pint mugs of tea and carried one into the shop. 'Any news of the Crackjaws?' she said as she returned.

'None at all. I've been making enquiries in the village, though, and I was surprised to hear that you once lived next door to them. I wondered why you hadn't mentioned it when I was here yesterday?'

For a moment Janet seemed to freeze, but a customer came in and saved her from an immediate reply. By the time she had dealt with a telephone bill and a savings bank transaction, she had relaxed again.

'Longmire End?' Hilary prompted.

'Oh yes – you wondered why I hadn't told you we lived

41

there,' she said easily. 'Well, I suppose it was all so long ago that it never crossed my mind. And even if I'd remembered, I couldn't have told you anything that had any bearing on the Crackjaws' disappearance.'

'You could have told me about their habits,' said Hilary. 'That Ziggy was a drinker, for instance.'

'Everybody knows *that*,' said Janet. 'I thought you'd have heard it from the top shop, where he gets his supplies.'

'And that when he's drunk he can be violent?'

Janet Thacker shot her a dark look. 'I don't know anything about that.'

'Oh, come on,' said Hilary. 'You must have known whether or not he hit his children.'

'Well, yes . . . yes, he used to give them good hidings. They were little devils, the lot of them, they usually deserved it.'

'What about his wife? Did he hit her?'

'I don't know. I have no idea what went on in their house, apart from a lot of shouting.' She frowned at Hilary. 'What are you getting at?'

'We're wondering whether Ziggy might have hit his wife a little too hard.'

'*Killed* her, you mean?'

'It's one of the possibilities.'

'Good Lord . . .' Janet's high complexion intensified. Then, 'Oh no,' she said vigorously. 'No, I don't believe that for a moment. If he'd been going to kill her, he'd have done it long before now!'

'Perhaps,' said Hilary. 'Tell me, when did you last see any of the Crackjaw children?'

'At least twenty years ago . . .' The postmistress was beginning to grow irritable. 'I wouldn't know them now if I did see them.'

'You'd know Andrew, by his eyebrows.'

Janet hesitated, controlling her irritation. 'Ah, well, yes – I have seen Andrew once or twice, when he's been over

42

here visiting his parents. But as for the rest of the family – '

'When did you last see Andrew?'

'He came to the post office one day last week. I think it was Monday – early in the week, anyway.'

'Did he say anything about his parents?'

She shrugged. 'I said, "How's your Mum?" and he said, "Not too bad." '

'And that was the extent of your conversation?'

'Yes. That's how long it took me to sell him a book of stamps. You must have noticed that I don't encourage customers to linger.'

'I'd have thought it might be different with Andrew,' said Hilary, pushing her luck. 'After all, you grew up together.'

Janet was annoyed. 'What's that got to do with it? We never liked each other, we never had anything in common. We exchange a civil word on the rare occasions when we meet, but that's all.'

Hilary sat still, looking at her but saying nothing. Janet produced an exasperated smile. 'Look, Sergeant Lloyd, there is nothing more I can tell you about the Crackjaws. Not even if you sit in my office until closing time – '

Hilary took the hint, picked up her briefcase and went.

There was rain overnight, and the lane outside the Crackjaws' house at Longmire End was soon churned to a brown porridge by the vehicles of the scenes-of-crime team. Among them was Chief Inspector Quantrill's large Rover.

When Sergeant Lloyd arrived, the noise and activity from the empty half of the double-dweller – the Thackers' former home – suggested that its rotten woodwork was being taken apart. Hilary changed from driving shoes to wellies, turned up the collar of her trench coat, hoisted her golf umbrella against the residual drizzle and went in search of the chief inspector.

She found him beside the big apple tree that had been blown at an angle by the gales, surveying what had once been the gardens of the double-dweller. He was impervious to the weather in a waxed waterproof, a fishing hat and outsize wellington boots, but with a woollen scarf by way of acknowledgement that he'd just recovered from bronchitis.

He greeted his sergeant with even more appreciation than usual.

'You were absolutely right about that washed patch on the Crackjaws' living-room floor,' he said. 'The lads have found a smear of blood. There was more on the iron fender in front of the fireplace, and a few grey hairs as well, so it looks as though the old lady might have hit her head in falling. How she came to fall is another matter, but we're working on the likelihood that she's dead.'

'No sign of the body, though?'

'Not so far. It's not in their own house, and it doesn't look as though it's going to be found next door. It's not in any of the old sheds, or the privies, and it can't be buried out here because the ground hasn't been disturbed for years. I've walked all over it. It's matted with weeds and couch grass, there's no newly dug earth anywhere.'

Quantrill kicked at the base of the leaning apple tree, where some of its roots had been partly heaved up out of the soil. It was the only sign of disturbance in the whole garden, and attributable solely to the force of the wind.

'Anyway,' he concluded, 'Ziggy's an old man, he wouldn't attempt to dig a grave. I reckon he's much more likely to have dumped the body somewhere.'

'He couldn't have carried her far,' said Hilary. 'Andrew told us his mother was slight, but even so – '

'You know what I think?' Quantrill took the handle of her umbrella so that they could walk together to her car, and never mind what interpretation the nosy scenes-of-crime team would put on it. 'Ziggy could have moved her by putting her over the cross-bar of his bike and wheeling her up to the old farm. He's bound to know the best hiding-places among the barns and sheds. If we draw a blank here, I reckon that's the next place to search.'

'But meanwhile', said Hilary, 'where's Ziggy himself?'

'Ah, yes. That's more difficult. He didn't leave here on his bike, that's still in the shed. If he'd walked to the village to catch a bus, we'd have heard about it. So he must have hitched a lift, which means he could be anywhere.'

'Another Press appeal?' suggested Hilary. 'This time national, and for Ziggy on his own?'

'Yes – nothing to cause alarm, we just want to talk to him.'

They sploshed up to Hilary's car, and Quantrill sheltered her with the umbrella while she changed out of her muddy wellies.

'Did you see the postmistress yesterday?' he asked. 'Did you find out why she wouldn't tell you anything about the Crackjaws?'

Hilary laughed. 'Yes, I saw Janet Thacker, but I got nothing out of her. I didn't expect to. So I helped myself to the information I wanted – literally helped myself, I mean. I walked out of her office with the typescript of her autobiography in my briefcase.'

'Without her knowledge? You've got a nerve!'

'Of course without her knowledge. It was no use asking her to lend it to me, was it?'

'Depends what's in it, I suppose – '

'I've already flicked through it,' said Hilary, 'so I've a good idea. It tells us a lot more than Janet was prepared to say about the entire Crackjaw family. Also, Andrew's name seems to crop up quite often. By the time we've read the book, I think we may take an entirely different view of the old couple's disappearance.'

The Drop In

by Janet Thacker

Chapter One

'Teacher's favourite . . . get you after school!'
But I knew better than to hang about waiting to be got. As always, I legged it for home.

Bolt out of the playground and down the long hot road, summer sandals tacky on melting tar. Off the road and along our lane, slipping now on winter mud while brambles trip and clutch me. Quick look back and here they come, Andy Crackjaw leading; I try to run faster but my feet are clogged with great boots of wet clay and I flounder past Spirkett's Wood, slowing, slowing. 'Gotcha,' jeers Andy, making a grab, but I can see the roof of our house through the trees and I yell, 'Dad, Dad, Dad!' and fight off the brambles and the boys as they pull me down in the mud until Dad from miles away says, 'It's all right, my lovey, you're dreaming that's all,' and he strokes my head with his long cool fingers and soothes and murmurs me awake.

'What were you dreaming about, Janet?'

'I forget.'

'Don't you ever have nightmares, Dad?' I once asked.

'Not me,' he said, 'mine are all daymares.' And he laughed so I thought he was joking, but now I'm not so sure.

'Don't waste time brooding over anything that happened in the past,' he told me when I was a teenager. 'And don't think you'll always be stuck with things as they are, either. Your life's going to be different, our Janet. You've got prospects for the future. You can do anything you put your mind to, and you must make the most of your chances.' And then he'd talk about

47

the time when I'd have finished my education, and I could leave our isolated little house in the middle of sugar-beet country and get a well-paid job in a town where there were people to make friends with and no end of interesting things to do, where there would be hot water on tap and telephones and public transport, and I'd at last be able to join the twentieth century.

I don't know why my nightmares about being chased by Andy Crackjaw went on for so long after I left the village school. So long after that now, nearly nineteen as I sit here writing this down to get it out of my system, I can't even remember whether Andy ever did chase me all the way home or whether my dreams were just the result of his classroom threats: 'Get you at playtime!' 'Get you after school!'

It wasn't my fault either, it was old Miss Griggs's. She was the head teacher, very strict and old-fashioned, with stiff white whiskers on her chin and hands as hard as bread boards. If you played her up she'd set about slapping, not on your palms but on the soft inside of your wrists. It hurt. Even the big boys, the elevens, sometimes cried.

I didn't get slapped more than once. It wasn't that I liked her, or wanted to be her favourite, but I didn't see any point in asking to get hurt so I kept quiet in the hope that I wouldn't be noticed.

The village school was gloomy, with high church-shaped windows you couldn't see out of, and the days there went on for ever. From the time we were nine it was all spelling and sums and eleven-plus tests until we were sick of it. School bored me just as much as it bored the others, but I'd discovered that I liked reading. I passed the time by reading the books that came on the library van and the others passed it by playing up the teacher, seeing how far they could go before she lost her temper. Most days it was no distance at all.

Miss Griggs liked me just because I kept quiet. But she didn't need to make it public, she didn't need to shout at the others and slap them and then turn to me and say sweetly, 'Now Janet, how are *you* getting on?' No wonder they took it out on me at playtime.

Andy Crackjaw was always the worst. He lived next door to us, with no other families within a mile, and he tormented me just to prove to the rest of the school that we weren't friends.

'Don't you dare tell on me,' he used to say in the playground

48

while everybody crowded round to watch him give my arm a Chinese burn, 'else I'll *really* get you!'

I yelped, but quietly so as not to draw the teacher's attention, and made my promise.

If anyone had warned me when I was nine that I should still be at school when I was seventeen, I'd have run away from home. Except that I loved my home and family too much to think of leaving.

Home was marvellous when I was at the village school. Later, when I went to a town school and found out how other people lived, I was ashamed that our house at Longmire End was so primitive. But then, before I was eleven, it was the only way of life I knew.

We were a happy family, just the three of us. Mum often used to snap and grumble, and bang the pots and pans about to relieve her feelings, but she and Dad hardly ever quarrelled. Not like the Crackjaws next door. Mr Crackjaw isn't at home much, he's either working on the farm or drinking at the White Horse in the village, but whenever we see or hear him come wobbling home on his bike we know that a row's about to start. They're always arguing and shouting and swearing, we can hear them at it through our shared wall.

Mum says that Gladys used to be one of the prettiest girls in the village, but she has to be joking. Mrs Crackjaw looks a hag, with her scrawny face and straggling hair and her front teeth missing. Still, it can't be much of a life for her, with dirty old Ziggy and all those kids to look after. Andy's the eldest, a few months younger than me, and then there's a girl and two more boys, and after that I gave up trying to keep count.

Mum and Mrs Crackjaw are quite friendly, which is just as well because the only other people living in Longmire End are the Vernons up at the farm, and all we get out of Mrs Vernon is a gracious wave as she zooms past in their big car. So Mum and Mrs Crackjaw are glad to have each other for company, though they don't go into each other's houses. They usually meet down by the gate, at the pump where we get our water. I used to think it was coincidence that they met there so often, but then I realized that Mrs Crackjaw would go out as soon as she saw

Mum, fetching a bucket of water whether she needed it or not for the sake of having a chat.

Mrs Crackjaw has always been a clumsy woman, forever tripping over things or walking into doors, bumping and bruising herself. 'She's fallen downstairs,' Mum said sharply, hustling me indoors, when I once asked why the side of our neighbour's face had turned such a peculiar colour. I couldn't understand why she wasn't more careful, until the day I happened to be at the pump with Mum when Mrs Crackjaw came hobbling towards us with one hand clutching her hip.

'Oh, Bet,' she said, in a snuffly voice, 'I'm black and blue, black and blue.'

Mum made a clucking noise that wasn't entirely sympathetic. 'You'll have to take more water with it, Glad,' she said. It was what Mum said about Ziggy whenever she saw him toppling off his bike on his way back from the White Horse, so I realized then that Mr Crackjaw wasn't the only one in that family who drank.

I often wished I weren't an only child, but living next to the Crackjaws must have put Mum off, with all those bristle-headed boys popping up like peas. 'If there's more to come, they'll come,' I once overheard Mrs Crackjaw say; I couldn't tell from her voice whether she was vexed or just resigned, but it certainly sounded as though she believed it. Their name isn't really Crackjaw of course, it's some fantastic Polish concoction, all 'k's' and 'y's' and 'z's'. No one ever tries to pronounce it except old Miss Griggs at school. I've sometimes collected Mrs Crackjaw's family allowance from the post office when she hasn't been feeling well, and her signature practically covers the page. She has to copy it from the cover of the allowance book to be sure of spelling it right.

When Dad and I were at home we didn't see much of the Crackjaws. We heard them all right, but we preferred to keep ourselves to ourselves. Andy would sometimes pull faces at me if we happened to meet at weekends or in the holidays, but he was usually going off to meet his gang and took no notice of me.

There was one occasion, though, not long before we both left the village school, when he started being nice to me.

'I've got something to show you,' he said.

'Where?'

'In Spirkett's Wood. It's a secret. I'll show you on the way home.'

But I ran off on my own as usual. I'd had enough of Andy's Chinese burns. Lynn Baxter and Susan Freeman went with him instead, and they came back to school next day with the giggles.

'You ought to have gone, Janet, you'd have liked it.'

'Not interested.'

They fell about laughing. 'She don't know what it was! She don't know what it's for!'

'Don't want to know. Don't care.'

They kept prancing about the playground, taunting me, but I pretended not to mind. Then Andy ran up and kicked my ankles, so I knew that things were now back to normal and on the whole that was how I preferred it.

I couldn't ever tell Dad about Andy. Partly because I'd promised not to and I knew that if I did tell, Andy would find out and make things worse for me. And partly because I knew that Dad wouldn't be able to do anything about it, anyway.

Dad was tall and thin and pale, with wavy ginger hair and a modest chin, always very soft-spoken and gentle. He never ever smacked me, no matter what I did. There was none of the 'you-wait-till-I-tell-your-Dad' routine from Mum that Mrs Crackjaw went through with her lot. Generally she didn't tell Ziggy, but when she did the Crackjaw kids were really for it, we could hear their howls through the wall even though we turned the telly up full blast. In our house, though, if I deserved a smacking I got it from Mum on the spot. Dad wasn't even much good at telling me off, so it wasn't likely that he'd have had any influence over Andy.

Not that I often gave him cause to be cross with me, I loved and admired him too much. I was always Dad's girl. It may sound silly to say so, but it's the truth. I used to spend all my time with him when he was at home.

'Bloddy kid, always somewheres around,' grumbled Mr Crackjaw in his thick foreign voice when I followed Dad into the rubbishy next-door garden to take some carrots Mum had promised Mrs Crackjaw.

'Just ignore him,' said Dad afterwards. 'You're my girl and you can come with me whenever you want.'

Dad was a wonderful person to be with. He never went to the White Horse but spent his evenings and weekends pottering about usefully at home, telling me what he was doing and showing me how it was done. He made a swing for me and a hutch for the rabbit and a kitchen cupboard for Mum, and a toboggan for me and hutches for all the baby rabbits and a kitchen cupboard for Gran Thacker because she grumbled that he didn't look after her. That wasn't true, he was always doing things for her, but she liked to keep him on the run.

Dad was a good cook too. He was once a cook in the Merchant Navy. 'He's got real pastry hands,' said Mum grudgingly. Her own hands are broad and red and heavy, and her pastry's so tough Dad could use it to mend the roof. She's never liked cooking, and she was only too glad to let us get on with the week's baking on Sunday mornings, but you could tell from the way she grumbled that it made her feel redundant. She always reckoned that Dad was extravagant with fats when he was cooking, and complained that we didn't do the washing-up properly afterwards. Well, I did sometimes skimp over the washing-up, but it's difficult not to when you have to heat every drop of water first. A kettleful of hot water goes nowhere.

Dad wasn't just a handy carpenter and a good cook. He used to make up stories to tell me every evening, giving each character a different voice and making me laugh so much that Mum would finally snap at him to give over or she'd never get me to bed. I used to sit on his knee and watch his Adam's apple bobbing up and down as he spoke, and admire his long pale eyelashes and his green eyes and orange hair.

There was even a time when I was convinced that I'd grow up to look like him because I loved him so much. Just my luck to take after Mum's side of the family instead, straight dark hair and brown eyes and round cheeks, a plain healthy everyday country girl, and still dressed like one even at seventeen. We were allowed to wear our own clothes in the sixth form, but I stuck to my uniform skirt and blouse and cardigan. Actually I hadn't got much else to wear except my best skirt and my jeans and one or other of Mum's shapeless hand-knitted jumpers. It wasn't that I didn't like clothes. I desperately wanted a pair of knee-length fashion boots, and a red cowl-neck sweater, and a long list of other things. But I knew that until I could leave school and earn some money of my own I'd just have to go on wanting.

Chapter Two

Dad was thrilled when I passed the eleven-plus and went to Breckham Market girls' grammar school. Mum was pleased too, but with reservations; she was afraid that grammar school might put ideas into my head. They bought my uniform and games equipment and a satchel and a second-hand bike, and I rode down to the village every morning and left the bike at the shop while I went to Breckham Market on the bus.

I thought I would probably like the new school, once I made some friends and stopped losing my way in the long corridors. The best thing of all was not having Andy Crackjaw there. But Mum was right, it certainly put ideas into my head. Before, I'd never stopped to think whether we were rich or poor. Well, obviously we were poorer than the Vernons up at the farm, but people like that are so different that you don't make comparisons. Most of us in the village lived in more or less the same way, but at the grammar school nearly all the others were town girls, and I soon realized that they were living in a different century.

Of course I envied them. And I hadn't the sense to realize that it wasn't a good idea to go home and say, 'Why haven't we got a bathroom?' and 'Why can't we have a car?'

Mum was furious. 'I knew how it would be, spend good money and deny ourselves to send her to grammar school, and she turns out a snob. If this is what education does for her she can leave as soon as she's old enough and work for her living, same as we had to.'

But Dad knew it was no use shouting at me. That evening he sat down and took out his biro, borrowed a sheet from my rough notebook, and gave me a lesson in home economics. On one side of the paper he wrote down his weekly bring-home pay, and on the other side he wrote down our expenses. Half of them I'd never heard or thought of: rent and rates and coal and electricity and shoe repairs and television licence, not to mention food, and my school clothes and dinner money. He told me to have a go at balancing our budget myself. I just couldn't do it, there wasn't enough money to go round.

'That's your answer, then,' said Dad. 'We couldn't manage as it is if your mother didn't grow our veg and keep the hens and rabbits, and go out to work as well. We can't afford anything else.'

When Mum found out what he was doing she let rip even more. I must have been about twelve at the time and from the way she carried on you'd have thought he'd been telling me the facts of life.

'You've no business to let her know what you earn, Vincent Thacker! It's not right, at her age.'

'She's a sensible girl,' said Dad. 'If I hadn't told her she'd think she was hard done by. Now she'll know better.'

Naturally I had a few bright ideas, such as why didn't Dad get a better-paid job? Mum exploded again, I'd never seen her so mad with the pair of us. Dad sighed, but patiently.

'Think about it, our Janet. What well-paid job could I get round here?'

I thought hard about what other children's fathers did for a living, but the fact is that there's not much choice of jobs in the village. Some do farm work, like Mr Crackjaw, but Dad said their wages were no better than his. Some men drive lorries, but Dad couldn't drive. As long as we stayed in the village, it looked as though he would be stuck with his job at the shop.

'Couldn't Gran Thacker pay you more?'

Mum snorted. 'That'll be the day.'

'Mother pays me the regulation wage. And this is her house, she lets us have it cheap because it isn't modernized. We're lucky to pay so little rent.'

'Well, couldn't we move to Breckham Market? You could get a good job there.'

'Not without any qualifications, I couldn't. Besides, if we lived in town we'd have to pay so much rent that we'd be worse off than we are here.'

I'd almost run out of helpful suggestions. There didn't seem to be any way round the problem, not while they were keeping me at school. But at that stage I was still finding the grammar school bewildering: I hadn't got used to changing for PE and doing my homework on time, and I dreaded maths lessons. 'I'll leave school when I'm fifteen,' I said willingly. 'Once I'm earning we'll be all right for money.'

'Oo-oh – sometimes you talk real daft,' Mum snapped, and she started banging plates about to demonstrate her aggravation.

'What's wrong with that?' I asked Dad.

'What good will it do?' he said. 'Use your sense, Janet. If you leave at fifteen with no qualifications you'll be stuck here, same as we are. Education is your way out. You're one of the lucky ones, you've got the chance of a lifetime. You must stay at school as long as you can, pass all your exams, go on to college. If you better yourself, you'll be able to get a really good job. People with college degrees can get a thousand a year as soon as they start earning.'

Mum stopped slapping the crockery. 'Never!' she said, thunderstruck.

'It's right, I've seen adverts in the paper.'

'Well there must be a catch in it,' Mum declared. 'Who'd pay a fortune like that to beginners?'

I was awed into doing some mental arithmetic. A thousand a year . . . that was twenty pounds a week! Nearly twice Dad's wage, for a start. If my staying at school would make us rich like that I was all for it.

'In that case,' I said generously, 'I don't mind putting up with things a bit longer. If *you* don't mind, that is,' I added, but it was too late. I'd seen their faces as they glanced at each other and for the first time I realized that they weren't just my Dad and Mum, they were two separate people and they weren't very happy either.

'Oh, *we* don't mind. We're used to putting up with things,' Mum said, and her voice was as raw as a nettle. 'We haven't had much choice in *our* lives.' Dad didn't say anything, but he looked shrunken and bleak although the room was warm. I felt suffocatingly embarrassed.

'Can I have scrambled egg for breakfast in the morning, Mum?'

'No, you can't,' she snapped, 'you'll have a boiled egg as usual and like it.' And things seemed back to normal, but it must have been then that I started to grow up.

*

There isn't any regular work for women in or near the village. We're fourteen miles from Breckham Market, and the earliest bus, the one I took to school, is too late for the factories. So Mum's work has always been outdoors, casual field work, on and off according to the season.

She used to take me with her on the back of her bike when I was still too young for school. I can remember helping her pick strawberries and currants in summer, and getting told off for eating too many, and in autumn I used to huddle under a hedge while she lifted potatoes in wind and rain. Mum always grumbled that her back would break in the fields and at the end of every job she swore she'd never go again, but apart from needing the money she enjoyed the company of the other women. Despite her grumbles she always looked forward to the start of each season, setting off in her outsize jeans and sweater, wellies and a woolly hat, with a bag containing her plastic mac, sandwiches and thermos hanging from the handlebars of her old bike.

But not long after I started at the grammar school, a rumour went round the village that a turkey-processing business was going to be set up on the old airfield a couple of miles away. Mum was really excited, thinking that she'd be able to get a regular job at last.

There was an American Air Force base there when I was small. A left-over from the war, Dad said. I often saw the airmen driving jeeps through the village when I was on my way to or from school. At playtime, the older girls would giggle and encourage us little ones to shout through the railings, 'Got any gum, chum?' and the men would throw sweets or money to us, and Miss Griggs would rush out and tell us off for letting down England.

Then the Americans went, and the airfield returned to agriculture. So much of it was covered in concrete, though, that the farmer went in for pigs rather than barley. Then he tried turkeys, and a year or two later we heard that he'd sold the old airfield to a big turkey-processor from out Saintsbury way. And that was when the excitement started, because Mum's youngest sister Brenda lives not far from Saintsbury and likes to let us know what wonderful jobs she and her husband have both got at the turkey factory there.

'It'll be marvellous to have their new factory built practically on our doorstep!' said Mum. 'Won't it be marvellous if I can get a job there, Vince?' She hardly ever asked Dad's opinion about anything, in fact they didn't talk to each other much at all, which I suppose was one reason why they didn't quarrel.

'You don't like working indoors,' said Dad.

'But eight pounds a week if you do the full day shift, our Brenda says! It'd make all the difference. And they send a bus round the nearby villages to pick up, free. And free overalls an' all. It's a wonderful chance.'

'Well, I wouldn't fancy it meself,' said Dad, pulling a squeamish face. He was always very fastidious, forever washing his hands and scrubbing his fingernails on account of handling food in the shop. It's always Mum who has to do the killing and preparing when we eat any of our livestock. 'Standing on a production line gutting turkeys all day . . . no thanks! But there, you must suit yourself.'

'I shall do,' said Mum triumphantly. 'Oh, it'll be marvellous . . . And you'll be glad enough, Vince Thacker, when I bring home eight pound a week, regular!'

'I shouldn't count on it if I were you,' said Dad. 'Not until the place is built and the jobs are advertised.'

'Oh, you streak of misery!' said Mum. 'Just keep your ears open in the shop and let me know as soon as they start building.'

She went on being excited for weeks after that, singing to herself as she worked about the house and in the garden. I was excited too, thinking what we could buy with all that extra money we'd soon have. Even Dad looked a bit more hopeful than usual. But then, one evening in late spring, he came biking home from work with a very long face.

"Fraid I've got some disappointing news for you, Bet,' he said as he came into the kitchen where Mum was frying bacon for his tea. 'They've started work on the old airfield – but it's not going to be a processing plant after all. What they're building is just rearing sheds. They're going to rear all their turkeys here, and take them to Saintsbury for processing. There'll be a few jobs for men, but nothing for women at all.'

Mum's round red face sagged like a deflated balloon. She thumped down on the kitchen chair, still holding her cooking fork, and burst into tears. I'd never seen her cry before, and I didn't know what to do. Dad didn't seem to know either, but he gave her shoulder an awkward pat.

'Don't take on so, Bet,' he said, and I'd never heard him speak to her so tenderly. 'It's not worth crying over a mucky job like that.'

'But the money,' wailed Mum. 'I'd got that all planned out and we could have lived real well.'

'Never mind about the money,' said Dad, 'we'll manage. Anyway, they say Bartrum's going to start hoeing his sugar beet at the end of the month.'

'Is he? *Is* he?' Mum wiped her eyes with a torn scrap of sheet that she was using as a hanky and, wonderfully revived, returned to the frying pan. 'Well, thank the Lord for that! All right, let them keep their stinking turkeys over at Saintsbury. I'd sooner scrub floors for Mrs Vernon than do that job.'

For Mum, that says the lot. She's permanently fed up with her own housework and she hates the idea of doing it for anyone else. Her own mother, Gran Bowden, left school when she was twelve, before World War One, to work as a kitchen maid in a big house. She kept at it until she married and as soon as her children were at school she was at it again, doing other people's housework as well as her own. She died when I was eight, and until a month before her death she went scurrying out every morning wearing a felt hat, with an apron under her coat, to spend the day scrubbing other people's floors. It's something Mum would never do, and she's never forgiven Mrs Vernon for asking her.

I was at home when it happened, one Saturday in March not long after Gran Bowden died. There had been no field work for weeks and Mum was getting fractious, so Mrs Vernon couldn't have chosen a more likely time to pick her way down from the farm in a camel-hair coat and a silk headscarf, towed by a large dog, to enquire whether Mum would care to give her a little help in the house three mornings a week.

'No thank you,' said Mum, putting on her poshest voice to compensate for her baggy old clothes and the enviable fact that even at eleven in the morning Mrs Vernon smelled as sophisticated as the toiletry counter at Boots.

Mum had answered so promptly that Mrs Vernon assumed she'd misunderstood. 'Well, of course, I should pay you, Mrs Thacker.'

'I'm not in need of money, thank you, Mrs Vernon.'

There was an awkward pause. I knew that Gran Bowden

would have asked the visitor in and apologized for the untidiness and dusted a chair for her, but Mum stood blocking the doorway. She replied nicely, firm without being rude, but her ears and neck were red and her behind shook with indignation.

'A little extra money is always useful, though, isn't it?' coaxed Mrs Vernon. 'Say three and six an hour . . .?'

Mum swallowed, tempted but not won over. 'Not for double the money,' she said grandly.

Her opponent knew when she was beaten. 'Then I'm sorry to have bothered you, Mrs Thacker.'

'Not at all, Mrs Vernon.'

The farmer's wife retreated up the lane, leaving Mum chuntering away to herself on the doorstep. I stopped listening, until she said something about being thankful that ours wasn't a tied house.

'What's a tied house?'

'One that's part of the farm, goes with the job, like the Crackjaws'. If you're tied, you can't afford to offend your employer or you might lose your job and your house as well. Not that poor Gladys needs to worry, Mrs V.'s not likely to ask *her* to do any cleaning.'

I was puzzled. 'But why does next door belong to the farm, when our house belongs to Gran Thacker?'

'They all belong to Gran Thacker. Mr Vernon's a tenant farmer. He rents the Crackjaws' house from her, same as he rents the farm. Gran Thacker owns the lot.'

This bit of information was so fantastic that I stood and boggled at her. 'Gran *owns* all three houses? The whole of Longmire End?'

'And more. Old man Thacker owned half the village at one time. He was a dealer as well as keeping the shop, he bought and sold anything he could lay his hands on, and farms were cheap enough before the war.'

'Then Gran Thacker must be rich?'

'Tidy,' agreed Mum.

This idea took some getting used to. Gran Thacker certainly didn't look or behave rich. She was a dry little old thing, tough as the leather bootlaces that hung like sticks of liquorice above the shop counter. She hardly ever went out of the shop, and she bought her clothes from the drapery traveller and they never fitted properly, so she looked a bit of a freak. But Mum always said that she was sharp as a needle, and you'd have to be up very early to get the better of her.

I'd always assumed that Gran Thacker made her living out of the shop, and it was difficult to start thinking of her as a property owner. But when the idea sunk in, I couldn't resist bragging about it in the village school next day.

'My Gran's rich,' I told anyone who would listen. 'And when she dies, we'll be rich too.'

I suppose it got back to Mum through the Crackjaws. Anyway, a couple of days later I was for it.

'Don't you *ever* say that again.' Mum wasn't just furious, she seemed to be in a panic. 'Don't you dare say another word to anybody about Gran Thacker dying and us being rich. If she gets to hear it, she could ruin us. And don't let your Dad hear it, neither.'

'But Mum . . .'

'That's enough. One more word from you and you'll get the good hiding you're asking for.'

So I shut up, though I couldn't see why. But thinking about it, I realized that Gran Thacker's being rich hadn't made any difference to her or to us in the past, so it wouldn't now. And when I looked at her, I could see that she hadn't any intention of dying for a very long time to come.

Fortunately Gran Thacker never did get to hear what I'd said. I don't know what she'd have done about it but she's a real old terror when she's roused. She never seemed to like any of us, or any of her customers come to that. She didn't speak to anyone if she could avoid it, but sat in her back room doing the accounts and interviewing travellers and giving her orders while poor old Dad rushed about trying to please everybody.

Mum kept me out of Gran Thacker's way as far as possible when I was small, and always told me to mind my manners when we did meet. With Gran Bowden it was quite different; she made a great fuss of me, and if Dad's mother had been the same I'd have been spoiled to death. As it was, she was so snappy and disapproving that I never felt bold or affectionate enough to call her Gran to her face.

I was cheeky to Gran Thacker just once. As soon as I spoke, I knew that I'd chosen the wrong person to cheek. She whipped round on me faster than I'd ever thought she could move and spat out the words; literally, I could feel the drops spray on to my face, but I was too frightened to wipe them off.

'Don't you dare be pert to me, Miss, or you and your mother will be sorry!'

I mumbled some sort of apology and nipped off home, and I didn't tell anyone. After that, I really did mind my manners with her, but the knowledge of her disapproval didn't worry me. I never felt that she counted as one of our family. As I saw it there were just the three of us: me and Mum, who does her best for me even though she drives me mad in the process, and my wonderful Dad, the nicest father in the whole world.

Chapter Three

A November evening at home. Me, seventeen, supposedly doing some schoolwork, Dad reading a detective book from the library, and Mum knitting away like a machine-gun, rattling out a stream of socks and scarves and sweaters in horrible shades of mauve and yellow wool that Gran Thacker had bought from a traveller because it was cheap and then couldn't sell to her customers at any price.

'Beggars can't be choosers,' said Mum, measuring me for a bilious cardigan, and though I'd die if anyone saw me in it I'd be glad enough to wear it in bed over my pyjamas. None of our doors and windows fit properly and there's always ice on the inside of the panes in bad weather.

I just didn't hear Mum next time she spoke. I admit that there are occasions when I do hear and don't bother to answer, but that night I was well away. Mrs Bloomfield had lent me a paperback of seventeenth-century poems and I sat with the book on the table and my head in my hands, absorbing open-mouthed. Before, I'd read only the censored poems in school anthologies, and this was a revelation. It sent my temperature soaring.

TO HIS MISTRIS GOING TO BED
Come, Madam, come, all rest my powers defie,

Until I labour I in labour lie . . .
Licence my roaving hands, and let them go,
Before, behind, between, above, below –

No wonder I didn't notice Mum until she thumped the table so
hard with a rolled-up copy of *Woman's Weekly* that I jumped and
knocked over my cup and the cold tea dregs drooled over the
tablecloth.

You'd never guess from the way she carried on that the
tablecloth wasn't purest linen. Just because she happens to have
a genuine old-fashioned best tablecloth tucked away upstairs,
she has an obsession about spillages. I don't think we'd had the
linen cloth out more than once. It's too big for our table and I
can remember sitting under it as though it was a tent when we
had a houseful of people to tea after Gran Bowden's funeral. We
weren't even allowed to dirty the cloth out after this ceremonial
airing; Mum had it whipped off the table and into the wash and
back upstairs before you could say Bottom Drawer.

But even though the tablecloth we actually use is guaranteed
wipe-down-fresh-as-a-daisy plastic, Mum still behaves as
though it's linen. I just lifted my book out of the way –
fortunately it wasn't touched – and carried on reading while she
ranted away as usual. 'I can never keep a clean cloth in this
house . . .'

O my America! my new found lande,
My kingdom, safeliest when with one man mann'd,

'Work all day but I can never keep anything nice.'

My mine of precious stones, my Emperie,
How blest am I in this discovering thee!

'And what thanks do I get? Never a civil word from either of
you, always got your silly heads stuck in a book. I've a good
mind to pack up and clear off, then you'll both be sorry.'

To enter in these bonds is to be free,
Then where my hand is set my seal shall be.

It takes something drastic to interrupt me when I'm reading but Mum eventually remembered the solution. She reached over and switched off the telly, and the sudden silence shocked us both into attention.

'Hey,' Dad protested. He usually read while the telly was on but that didn't mean he wasn't following the programme.

'It's ten o'clock and that's your lot,' snapped Mum. 'You're to go to bed, our Janet, I won't have you up half the night reading. The trouble I have getting you up in the mornings, and no wonder.'

'In a minute,' I said, as a matter of principle. But the spell of the poem had been broken and I was ready to leave it.

'Ah well,' said Dad. He got up, sighed and stretched, and went outside. I carried the cups to the kitchen while Mum lifted the kettle of hot water from the living-room fire. She obviously felt better for having a good grumble. She doesn't mean any of it but she enjoys getting it off her chest every now and then. She was quite cheerful as she gave her face a bedtime wipe at the sink, and I apologized silently by sponging her plastic tablecloth.

'You go on up,' I said. 'I want a wash.'

'"Night, Janet,' said Dad, padding across the living-room to the stairs door in his mauve socks. He made a fuss when Mum first knitted them, but she said her piece about beggars and I persuaded him that they looked positively trendy. I was glad enough to borrow a pair in winter to wear as bedsocks.

Mum finished pottering and said, 'Get on with it, then. I want you in bed by half-past. And don't forget to bolt the door and put the lights out and turn off the paraffin.'

'Have I ever forgotten?'

'There's always a first time.' She shut the door behind her and I heard the stairs creaking under her weight. Thank heaven I'm not her size, even if I do look like her.

Back in the kitchen I got busy with the Vim and the dishcloth on the blue plastic bowl. We use the one bowl for everything: washing the dishes, washing ourselves, washing clothes, washing hair, peeling spuds, the lot. Cleaning the bowl before I have a wash uses up half the hot water, but it's worth it.

Stripping off is an ordeal in our kitchen in winter so I washed in bits, keeping my clothes on as long as possible. Even with the paraffin heater on, the kitchen is a clammy place; the walls run with wet and the towels are permanently damp. It must be fabulous to live in a house with a bathroom.

When I'd finished washing I refilled the kettle from the bucket of water, stealthily made up the fire and put the kettle on it. Then I switched off the light and went up to bed, deliberately creaking the stairs so that Mum should hear me.

She slept in the front bedroom and Dad and I shared the room at the back. He had partitioned it so that we each had a very small room, but it was only visually private. We could hear each other cough and turn over in bed. I think he knew that I sometimes had a late night, but he didn't interfere because he knew that it was all for the sake of my future.

I put on my pyjamas and lay on top of my bed, under the eiderdown. I didn't dare get between the sheets in case I fell asleep. Dad was breathing lightly on the other side of the partition, though I could hardly hear him for the thunderous snores that came intermittently through the wall: Ziggy Crackjaw, drunk again.

I tried hard to ignore Ziggy, and also to forget John Donne's poem and all its implications, concentrating instead on the essay I had to write before morning. Within half an hour Dad's breathing deepened, and I slid out of bed. I had to take a chance with Mum; I couldn't tell whether she was asleep or not so I had to hope she couldn't hear as I sneaked downstairs in my old gym shoes.

Long practice had made me crafty with the creaking stairs and with the loose knob on the living-room door. Once I had shut that behind me I was pretty well safe. I poked up the fire under the kettle, put on my raincoat as a dressing-gown and made a cup of Camp coffee to keep me going. Gran Bowden's old grandfather clock was just jerking up to eleven. I pulled the books out of my school satchel, headed the paper with the quotation about human rights that was the subject of the essay, added the all-embracing injunction, 'Discuss', and got stuck in. I used plenty of historical illustrations, from medieval Peasants' Revolts to Hitler's persecution of the Jews, and brought it up to date with the American Civil Rights movement; and I threw in quotations from Locke, Thomas Paine, Karl Marx and Martin Luther King. It was a very long essay.

I'd got into the habit of sitting up late whenever I had an essay to write. I always hated the thought of essays, and put them off and put them off until they were due the next day. It was my final term at school but they'd given me a year's worth of work to keep me occupied, and it wasn't easy to do it in our living-room, the only heated room in the house.

I'm not making excuses about the telly. I did watch it quite a lot when I should have been working, but whatever the pro-gramme I'd as soon have it on as not. We all would, because it drowned the other noises. There was nearly always some kind of ruction coming through the wall from next door, but on the rare occasions when the Crackjaws were quiet we were con-scious of our own noises. Mum clicked her knitting needles and sniffed and sucked loud sweets; Dad's tummy rumbled; accord-ing to Mum I had an irritating cough. If we hadn't had the telly on we'd have driven each other mad with all the clicking and sniffing and rumbling and coughing. But there's no doubt that the telly wasn't conducive to writing essays, and I found it much easier to concentrate late at night.

Even then, the room was full of small noises. The coal shifted and settled in the grate. The old grandfather clock that used to belong to Gran Bowden ticked very loudly, and at two minutes to each hour it wheezed and whirred, gathering energy for the strike which, when it came to the hour, never came. A mouse scrittered about somewhere behind the skirting board. I wrote steadily, once I got a start, because I'd already made all the notes I needed. Sometimes I stopped to look up a reference, and sometimes I got up to put another lump on the fire, and once I went to the pantry and cut myself a slice of cake, being careful not to leave any crumbs to encourage the mouse.

By half-past two I'd had enough. The essay was finished, apart from the final paragraph which I'd have time to do in school. The fire had died out, and I was cramped and cold. I packed my books and papers in my satchel and then went to the kitchen for Dad's bicycle lamp. This was the bit I always hated. I opened the back door quietly and peered out.

At least it wasn't raining, so I didn't need my wellies. The moon was bright and the long brick path glittered with frost. I shivered, but there was no help for it, and I nipped tiptoe in my gym shoes down to the bottom of the garden.

Inside, the lav was familiar and friendly enough by the light of the lamp. Dad kept it well scrubbed out and whitewashed, and emptied the bucket regularly, and at least we had proper

65

paper. Gran Bowden wouldn't hear of such extravagance when she was alive; she used to tear old newspapers into neat squares and string them up on a nail behind her lav door. Newspapers don't do a good job. Besides, they scratch.

At that time of night I could at least be sure that there was no one next door. The two lavatories were just a brick hutch with a single-brick dividing wall, and you could hear everything. We tried to make a point of not going down there when we knew that one of the Crackjaws was temporarily in residence, but they didn't bother to do the same for us.

Gran Bowden once told a story – not to me, but I happened to be holding a pow-wow with her cat under the tassels of her plush table-cover at the time – about when she was a girl and lived in one of the old yards in the village. Pulled down years ago, council houses now. The lavatories for all the houses in the yard were built on the same principle as ours. Little Gran Bowden went skipping out there after dark one night, and as she sat there she heard the old chap from next door. He was moaning and groaning and she thought, 'Poor old Billy, he is having a bad time, it must be something he ate.'

Next morning young Billy, his son, found him in there, hanged from the rafters by his braces.

It wasn't a pleasant story to recall but it was difficult not to remember it out there late at night. Fortunately I could see a cluster of stars through the serrated gap at the top of the door. I always liked the stars. Dad had told me, when I was very small, that they were friendly twinkling eyes guarding over me. It was a helpful thing to tell a child who lived at the end of a lonely country lane; starlight made life pleasanter in winter, and helped me to forget about old Billy.

In the kitchen again, I bolted the door, blew out the paraffin stove, washed my hands and cleaned my teeth, filled a hot-water bottle with what remained in the kettle, and crept upstairs. I was dead tired, but before I got into bed I had to kneel down and say my prayers.

It wasn't that I was religious. It was more of a superstition really. Gran Bowden, who was Chapel, had taught them to me and after she died I carried on with them out of sentiment and affection for her. By the time I stopped believing that a venerably bearded God was giving ear to them in person, the habit had stuck and I felt that it would be bad luck to break it. I didn't know whether there was a God or not, but it seemed advisable to keep in with him just in case.

The ridiculous thing was that at nearly eighteen I still said my prayers just as I had learned them from Gran Bowden when I was four: Gentle Jesus meekanmild look upon a little child, pity mice implicitee, suffer me to come to Thee Amen; and God Bless everybody I could think of including Gran herself and Joey her fat cat, dead before her. I gabbled the prayers, but at three o'clock in the morning that ought to be excusable.

I crawled wearily into bed, but couldn't go straight to sleep for thinking of John Donne's poem. It didn't fit in with the 'pity my simplicity' bit, but after all Donne was a parson, so that ought to be excusable too.

Chapter Four

I don't know how many times Mum came to the foot of the stairs and shrieked at me, but I didn't wake properly until Dad put on the light and shook me.

'Come on, Janet,' he said anxiously. 'Here's a cup of tea, only you'll have to get up right away. You'll never catch the bus, it's half-past seven already.'

The bus went from the village at eight. If I missed that there wasn't another until half-past ten.

I pulled on my clothes, swallowed the tea standing and hurtled downstairs.

'You'll put your feet through that woodwork!' Mum hollered. 'Why can't you get up when you're called?'

I ignored her, and charged down to the end of the garden. When I got back to the kitchen Dad stood aside from the sink, shaving soap all over his face, so that I could wash my hands and wipe the sleep out of my eyes with the family flannel. Mum shoved a bowl of cereal at me. 'I don't know why I bother, I'm sure. At your age you ought to be out earning, not idling your time at school and having me waiting on you hand and foot.'

I slurped down a couple of spoonsful, grabbed my satchel and shot out to the shed for my bike. It was still dark. I know the lane backwards but it's difficult to go fast by the wobbling light of a lamp. The frost had hardened all the ruts and pot-holes and I jolted up and down with the heavy satchel banging on my back.

As I swerved out of the lane on to the road, I could see the distant lights of the bus coming up the rise past Boundary Farm. I did a snappy free-wheel, changed gear, and hammered at the pedals, head down. Good job nothing was in my way. Then I could hear the bus coming up behind me, snorting up my rear wheel as the driver slowed for the stop just outside Gran Thacker's shop. Made it! I threw the bike against the wall for Dad to rescue later and fell up the steps into the bus, breathless.

'Late again,' said the driver as he clipped my weekly school ticket. 'Don't know what keeps you young girls up so late at nights . . .'

If I'd known it was Joe Willis driving I wouldn't have killed myself to get to the stop. He was a regular on our route, had known me by sight ever since I'd been going to the grammar school. If he passed me on my way to the stop he'd always wait for me, but the trouble was that I never knew which driver it would be.

I flopped on the nearest vacant seat and drew in a few lungsful of air. It was well-used air, fusty with early-morning people and cigarette smoke and vinyl seat-coverings, but it helped. Recovering, I tidied my clothes and combed my hair, sat up and took a cautious look round. It didn't do your dignity as a school prefect any good if the juniors saw you rushing about like a human being. There were two of them on the bus so far, but they were sitting at the back with their heads together and they didn't seem to have noticed me.

It's a horrible feeling when you don't have time to clean your teeth after breakfast. I tried to suck them clean, regretting the slimy combination of milk and cornflakes and hoping that nothing had lodged visibly between any of my front teeth. I wanted to look my best at the stop in the next village, just in case.

Polite as always, he got on last. And stood there at the front of the bus, as well-thatched and dazzlingly blue-eyed as Robert Redford, looking for a vacant seat. It was my daily prayer that he would come and sit next to me, but even if no one else took the seat first he always found somewhere else to sit. This morning, it was on the other side of the gangway. I peered round the frontage of the large woman beside me and admired his profile and wondered if he read John Donne.

His name was Mark Easton. He was about my age, a prefect at the boys' grammar school, and working like me for university entrance. With so much in common it ought to have been natural for us to be friends, but however hopefully I looked at him he didn't seem to get the message.

It was easy for girls who had brothers, or who lived in town. They met boys all the time, and some of them were paired off before they were sixteen, but I didn't know any except my old tormentor Andy Crackjaw. There were formal get-togethers between the two grammar schools several times a term, but that wasn't much help to me because I was always Cinderella, having to rush off to catch the last bus.

But at least I had university to look forward to. Everything would be wonderful when I got there. Mark and I might even end up at the same one. I leaned forward to look at him again, but he sat with his eyes closed and his pocket transistor clamped to the side of his head. The woman next to me thought I was looking at her magazine and rattled it crossly, so I got a book out of my satchel and read up the economic consequences of the Dissolution of the Monasteries.

The headmistress had her 'engaged' sign up when I went to her room, as summoned, prompt at ten o'clock. There was no one about in the corridor so I leaned against the wall and had a good yawn while I waited. I was feeling dopey from insufficient sleep and the day seemed too long already.

Presently the 'knock and enter' light flashed, so I did, and stood looking respectful. Miss Dunlop was small and neat and grey, with a precise, finicky Scottish accent: 'gerrls' was how she invariably addressed us, and she called me 'Jennet'. Her standards were so high that we'd have had to dislocate our necks to measure up to them. She was an expert at making life uncomfortable for rebels, and as I didn't believe in looking for trouble I always humoured her and kept my thoughts to myself.

Another girl, Caroline Adams, was also trying for Oxford entrance, and Miss Dunlop gave us each an individual grilling twice a term. I could see my last week's essay lying on her desk, but her greeting didn't suggest that she'd been bowled over by its brilliance.

She picked it up and looked at me through her gold-rimmed spectacles. 'Length in itself', she said severely, 'has no merit. You must be more selective, Jennet. Write less, and think more.'

So much for all the midnight hours I'd spent on it. So much for last night's essay, which was even longer.

'Yes, Miss Dunlop,' I said.

She told me what else she thought of the essay and then devoted the next few minutes to a brisk rummage through my mind. She treated it like a free lucky dip, holding up an occasional find for qualified approval but for the most part throwing out the rubbish. I hated this process, it always left me floundering. And I liked most of the rubbish. I could see why she thought I ought to get rid of it, but I determined to sneak it back later.

'Now, Jennet – ' She took off her glasses. That meant she'd finished with my work and was about to have a go at me personally. 'You're beginning to look very short of sleep. What time did you go to bed last night?'

'Half-past ten, Miss Dunlop.'

She looked as though she didn't believe me, but I'm a good liar and I looked back at her without a blink.

'This final term is an important preparation for your academic life,' she said. 'I know how great the social temptations are, but you can gad about – ' she pronounced it *ged* ' – after the end of term. As long as you're still at school, your work must take priority.'

Social temptations? Gadding about? What kind of life did she imagine we led, in deepest Suffolk? Ah yes, there was bingo in the Coronation hut once a week in winter, and a whist drive once a month, and it was high time the Women's Institute held another jumble sale. It was all go in our village.

'Yes, Miss Dunlop,' I said patiently.

Then she dropped the headmistress act and became friendly, almost anxious. 'I haven't seen you since you took the Oxford entrance papers. How did you find them? I thought they were very fair.'

Miss Dunlop had been at Oxford, some time in the Middle Ages, and every year she did her best to push some of us there as well. Caroline and I were thoroughly confused about university entrance, so we did as we were told and put down Oxford as our first choice, even though it meant staying on at school for an extra term to take the entrance exam. Mum was vexed about the extra term, but Dad was so impressed by the idea of my going to Oxford that he was all for it.

I would just as soon have taken the place I'd already been offered at one of the London colleges on the strength of last term's A-level results. University was the passport I needed to get out of Longmire End, and whether I went to London or Oxford – neither of which I'd ever visited – was incidental. But I agreed to do the extra term because it meant that I'd be able to leave school at Christmas, get a temporary job, and use the money to buy some much-needed clothes before I took off for civilization next October.

I gave Miss Dunlop an edited version of what I'd thought of the examination papers. I really didn't believe I'd done well enough for the college to want to interview me.

'If they do, you should soon hear from them,' she said. 'But keep working while you're waiting. And don't forget, Jennet: *more sleep.*'

She showed me her teeth, which meant that she'd finished with me. I said, 'Thank you, Miss Dunlop,' and went out. The buzzer had already gone for break, and I was eager to get at the apple that Mum had pushed into my satchel before I left home.

Caroline came over as soon as I appeared in the sixth-form common room. She was an enviably pretty girl with a good figure and shoulder-length straight fair hair.

'How did it go with Miss Dunlop?' she asked.

'Much as usual. She said she was tempted to call my essay meretricious.'

'Is that good?'

'Not the way she said it. Got a dictionary?'

Caroline looked it up while I munched my apple. 'What else did Miss D. go on about?' she asked. She was due for the next session with the headmistress.

'"More sleep, Jennet,"' I mimicked.

She considered me critically. 'You do look as though you could do with it.'

'Well, you know how it is.'

She gave a sexy sigh in agreement.

We'd never been close friends, but because we were taking

the same subjects we spent most of our time in school together. Caroline's father was production manager at one of the factories on the Breckham Market industrial estate, and they lived in a large detached house near the golf-course, and they had two cars, one of which she was learning to drive.

Caroline had always had boy-friends. That was something else we didn't have in common. But I wasn't going to let on that I'd never had one, so when she talked about hers I half-invented one of my own. It was no use trying to pretend that it was Mark Easton, because she knew him. But she'd never been anywhere near Byland, and as Andy Crackjaw had grown into a not-bad-looking man I'd found myself describing him.

Andrew, I'd told her, was a neighbouring farmer's son: six feet tall with rather dramatic dark eyebrows that almost met across the top of his nose, tremendously romantic on account of having European blood in his ancestry, unswervingly faithful, unflaggingly ardent, but so gentlemanly that he was always prepared to take 'No' for an answer. Andrew was the answer to a maiden's prayer, and Caroline was so impressed by my steady relationship with him that she sometimes came to me for advice.

She looked carefully round the common room, leaned towards me and began to whisper. Her hair fell over her nose and a strand of it fluttered about with every breath.

'Richard asked me if I would, last night.'

I was still brooding over my meretricious essay. 'Would what?'

'You *know*.'

'Oh.' I realized what she was talking about. 'Did you?'

'No, of course I didn't. Not like that, in the back of his car. But I'm seriously thinking about it. Should I?'

I knew the answer to that one because I read it in Mum's *Woman's Weekly*. 'He won't respect you if you do.'

'That's what my mother always says. But Richard's so *persistent*. Besides, it's such a temptation – '

'Don't I know it!' I said.

We sighed together.

I longed to have a real boy-friend, and anyone would do, temporarily, just so that I could chuck my imaginary one. I'd built up a complex of implications, half-truths and downright lies during my time at the grammar school, and I was sick of the whole business. It was such a drag trying to keep it all up.

Once I got to university, I intended to abandon the entire

edifice. I'd have achieved something then, and I'd be able to start my life afresh. I'd be my own person, and it wouldn't matter if everybody knew what a primitive way of life we'd led at home.

It sounds horribly snobbish, I know, but I was ashamed that we lived in a damp poky little farm cottage miles from anywhere, with no bathroom and an outside pump and a bucket lavatory at the end of the garden, and that my mother worked in the fields and my Dad was a shop assistant. I wasn't ashamed *of* them, I was ashamed *for* them.

No, that's not honest either, because the only time Mum came to school for an Open Day, wearing a terrible straw hat with cherries on and saying all the wrong things in a stupid mincing voice, I was so ashamed of her that I could gladly have strangled her. But I know she couldn't help it, she'd never had a chance to mix with different people and see how they lived. I was getting the chance, and making the most of it; no point in having an education if you stay exactly the same as you were when you started.

It didn't take long, when I first went to grammar school, to see that the girls were divided into those who came from ordinary homes like mine, and those who were different. The different ones fascinated me. They were so much more confident, so enviably relaxed, and they made me feel inferior. I knew that I was awkward and anxious, and I wanted to acquire some of their confidence, so from my first week at the school I watched and listened and copied.

There was so much to find out, beginning with how to use a flush lavatory without being afraid that the chain would break if you pulled it too hard. At school dinners I learned not to hold my knife like a pen, and to put my knife and fork neatly together on my plate when I'd finished. And I worked on my Suffolk accent, shortening the broad vowels that would otherwise give me away as a country girl.

I didn't tell too many lies about my background. No need. I said that our house was right out in the country, and if anyone chose to imagine that it was large, attractive and permanently covered in roses, that was up to her. If the subject of our fathers' jobs came up, I said that mine worked in the family business. When school trips abroad were planned I wouldn't admit that

73

we couldn't afford them, but said I had so much fun with Andrew-the-boy-next-door that I preferred to stay at home.

Fortunately I lived too far away to invite any friends to tea, and the only girls from the village at grammar school were either several years older or several years younger than me, so I got away with it. By the time I was fifteen I was accepted as one of the middle-class girls, the confident ones who had a future.

It's only subsequently that I've wondered whether any of the other girls were in fact keeping up the same pretence as I was. When you know you're a liar, and feel guilty about it, you imagine that everyone else is always telling the truth.

Chapter Five

The only person at school I did confess to was Sally Buckle. She was my best friend for four years. She lived in the town and I went to her house several times. Her Dad worked on the railway and they lived in a small terraced house near the station, and the first time she invited me home, because I'd missed my usual bus, we surprised her mother out in the back yard, shabbily dressed and with her hair in rollers, unpegging some corsets from the washing line.

I don't know which of us was most embarrassed. Their kitchen was in a terrible muddle, just like ours on wash day, and Mrs Buckle couldn't have been more apologetic if Sally had brought Miss Dunlop to visit her. Poor Sally was squirming on her mother's behalf, and I didn't know what to say until it occurred to me to tell the truth.

'My Mum would be green with envy if she could see your kitchen, Mrs Buckle – inside tap and hot water and everything. We have to fetch our water in buckets and heat it up in the copper on washdays. You are lucky.'

She relaxed immediately. Obviously she'd been fooled by my carefully polished accent and thought that Sally had brought home somebody from a posh family, and you could see how chuffed she was at the thought that we were ordinary people and not as comfortably housed as they were. After that, we got on very well together and I had a standing invitation to go there whenever I missed my bus.

Sally was the best friend I've ever had. We spent all our time at school together, and during the Easter and summer holidays we'd cycle to meet each other for a sandwich and apple picnic at least once a week. But then the railway junction at Breckham Market was reduced to an ordinary main-line station and Sally's Dad was made redundant, so they had to move to Ipswich. We wrote to each other every week at first, but it's difficult to keep up the same sort of friendship just by writing and our letters tailed off. I missed her tremendously, though. Still do.

Another person who knew, or guessed, about the act I was putting on was Mrs Bloomfield, the deputy headmistress. She arrived at the school at the beginning of my last term, ready to take over as headmistress when Miss Dunlop retired at the end of the school year.

We'd got so used to Miss Dunlop and the rest of the middle-aged teaching staff that when word went round that the new deputy head was a widow we expected someone solemn and grey-haired. Mrs Bloomfield, when she arrived, was a revelation: about thirty-five, we estimated, tall and very slim with ash-blond hair which she wore swept up into a knot, and fabulously dressed. We were all dazzled by her sophistication, and her widowhood gave her an added glamour because it was rumoured that her husband had been killed flying with the Royal Air Force.

Mrs Bloomfield taught English, and Caroline and I had weekly tutorials with her that term. She made a point of treating us as students, not schoolchildren, which I suppose is why she lent me the book of uncensored poems. She was cool, detached and amused, and I really looked forward to those tutorials, partly because she made English literature so fascinating, but chiefly because I hoped that some of her confidence and poise would rub off on me. Well, no harm in hoping.

At our second tutorial, Caroline was a few minutes late and Mrs Bloomfield had suddenly said to me, 'I believe you come from Byland. I was born in Suffolk too. My father was a farm worker, we lived at Ashthorpe.'

I had been astonished. I probably sat there gaping, unable to believe that anyone so stunning could have emerged from a background similar to mine. 'I'd never have known, from your accent,' I'd blurted out, and she had laughed. 'I worked at it,' she said. 'Did you have to work at yours?'

But then Caroline turned up, and that had put an end to the conversation. I was always hoping for an opportunity to continue it, though, and I had one to look forward to on that particular day.

It was my turn to be one of the dinner-duty prefects. At least, it would have been my turn in ten days' time but I knew that Mrs Bloomfield was going to be on staff duty so I'd fiddled the rota. It was a spread-out school so there wasn't really much chance of seeing her as we patrolled round, but it was worth a try.

The first job, after school dinner – fish pie with mashed potato topping, followed by lemon sponge pudding – was to make sure all the girls went outside. Fresh Air and Exercise was one of Miss Dunlop's manias. In winter all the layabouts tried to hole up indoors, but since we'd done exactly the same thing when we were their age, we knew where to look. I took the old building and Sandra Pell took the new wing and we flushed the kids out.

'Must we, Janet? I've got a terrible cough.'

I knew her, young Wendy Barnes from the Lower Fourth, a cheeky little monkey. She was making heartrending coughing noises, but spoiled them by laughing.

'Go on with you,' I said. 'Get some nice fresh air and exercise, it'll do you good.'

'But it's terribly cold. I'll die of exposure.' Her friends had already run off ('And don't run in the corridors,' I'd called after them, too late) and she was lingering for the sake of it.

'Only if you stand still. Go on, I want to get outside myself.'

'Are you going to play hockey?'

'Certainly not, at my age. Out you go.'

She grumbled and dragged her feet but I refused to encourage her any further.

'See you outside, Janet?'

'Not if I see you first. And don't run in the corridors.'

I put on my raincoat for warmth and started the outside patrol, keeping an eye on what was going on. There was hockey practice on the sports field. I'd been in the second eleven for four years, which must have been a school record because usually you either made the first team or were dropped to third.

But I was too useful to be relegated – all that running home from school for fear of Andy Crackjaw, and then biking up and down the lane, must have strengthened my leg muscles. I was an accurate hitter, and I'd found that haring about the hockey pitch swiping at a ball was a good way of getting grievances out of my system. I packed it in as soon as compulsory games stopped in the sixth form, but I still sometimes joined in a practice. I watched the players wistfully, feeling rather old.

Sue Larter, the second-eleven captain, saw me and trotted over in her tracksuit, looking madly healthy.

'Like a bash, Janet?'

'I'm on duty.'

'It's the only time you come out here these days. All that sitting about in the common room doesn't do you any good, you're not nearly as fit as you used to be.'

'Ah well, I've got other interests . . .'

'So I've heard. But are they as good for you?'

Sue was a clown, always bouncing about full of cheerfulness and fresh air. But her offer of a hockey stick was tempting. I looked round. There seemed to be no crises that demanded my immediate attention so I slipped off my raincoat, borrowed the stick and waded in.

A fast ball skimmed past and I ran, trapped it, dribbled round an opponent and whammed it across the centre. Lovely stuff. I felt fourteen again, easy and irresponsible. I was just glancing round to see who was in what position when the wretched ball, slammed straight back at me by some hefty young idiot, cracked me hard on the side of the foot. I howled, and hopped, and said a word that I knew I knew but had never before been sufficiently provoked to use.

Sue bounded over. 'All right, Janet?'

'Yes, fine.' My foot felt as though it were broken in six places.

'Still playing?'

Some junior ghouls were gathering and my one thought was to get off the pitch and nurse my foot in peace. I shook my head. 'Better not – I'm supposed to be on duty anyway.'

I hobbled to the bench where I'd left my raincoat, and Sue hustled her troupe away. I'd just eased off my shoe and was having a tender exploratory feel of my foot when a cool, amused voice said from behind me, 'I didn't know you went in for these rough games.'

Mrs Bloomfield, of course. It would be.

'That was positively my final appearance,' I said, hoping that my cheeks weren't as red as they felt.

'Is your foot all right?'

'Perfectly.' I rammed on my shoe and regretted it, but I didn't want to make myself look any more of a fool than I had done already. She strolled round to the front of the bench, casual but elegant in a sheepskin jacket and the kind of knee-high boots I'd have given my back teeth for.

'Well, you know the rules,' she said. 'All injuries must be reported to the member of staff on duty. I ought to put it in the incidents book.'

'Please don't.' I thought she probably didn't mean it, but I couldn't be sure. 'I'm not hurt, truly.'

Mrs Bloomfield laughed. 'I'll take your word for it. Let's walk, then; it's too cold to stand about.' She strolled away with her collar turned up and her hands deep in her pockets, and I hobbled after her, eager to resume our personal conversation.

'Did you come to this school from Ashthorpe?'

'No, we moved to west Suffolk and I went to Saintsbury High School. But I like this area. I was very happy in Ashthorpe, and if I can find a house in the village I'd like to live there.'

'Would you really?' I couldn't imagine myself ever wanting to go back to Byland to live, once I managed to get away. I was just going to say so when a junior came running towards us, full of anxious importance.

'Please Mrs Bloomfield, Julie Binns has been sick behind the pavilion.'

We exchanged resigned, adult glances. 'Is anyone with her?' Mrs Bloomfield asked the girl. 'Good. You run off and fetch her a glass of water, and I'll be along in a minute.'

'I'll go,' I offered. 'I expect it was the fish pie, I had my doubts about it.'

'I'd better go myself, thanks. I have to remember the incidents book.' She began to walk purposefully towards the pavilion and I stayed where I was, disappointed that our conversation had been cut short. But Mrs Bloomfield beckoned me to join her.

'What I wanted to ask you', she said as we walked, 'is whether there are any buses out of Byland on Sundays? Can you get to Yarchester?'

I didn't really know. Going all the way to Yarchester on a

Sunday was unheard of. 'There's a Sunday afternoon bus to Breckham Market,' I said, puzzled. 'I'm not sure whether it goes on to Yarchester, though.'

'Good enough. Are you doing anything this coming Sunday? Because if you're not, I'm going with some friends to an evening performance of Britten's *War Requiem* in Yarchester Cathedral. There's a spare ticket, and I wondered if you might like to come? If you can't get a late bus back, I'll drive you home.'

I was flabbergasted. I'd never been to a concert in my life, never been out on a Sunday except to visit relations, never had an adult invitation to anything. I stammered my assurances that I wasn't doing anything else, that I'd love to go. Her next words deprived me of speech completely.

'Why not come to tea first? About five, if that fits in with your bus? 12 Riverside, the new block of flats just past the town bridge. Know where to find it?'

I nodded. I'd no idea where it was, but that hardly mattered. All I could think of was that I was going to get a foretaste of civilized living at last.

'See you on Sunday, then.' Mrs Bloomfield disappeared round the back of the pavilion and I turned away, elated.

I wanted to run, punching the air like a goal-scoring footballer, the length of the hockey pitch. But it wouldn't have been a cool thing to do, so it was just as well that my foot hurt too much for anything more than a dignified limp back to school.

Chapter Six

Saturday mornings I worked at the shop. I'd have liked to work there most of the holidays too, but Gran Thacker would only pay me for one morning a week.

I started biking down to the shop with Dad on Saturdays just as soon as I was big enough to be useful. I thought of it as helping him, and I didn't mind what I did, fetching and carrying at a run all morning. It didn't seem like work and I looked forward to the Saturday shilling he gave me and the bar of chocolate Gran Thacker handed me grudgingly as I left, though

I usually had cause to feel guilty because I'd already nibbled some currants or a sliver of cheese when no one was looking.

As soon as I was fifteen, though, Dad said, 'That's it, our Janet. You're of working age and you're not coming to work at the shop unless Mother pays you properly.' He did his best to make his chin look determined. 'I shall speak to her about it.'

The next Saturday Gran Thacker beckoned me into her little office behind the shop. I always hated going in there. She had a paraffin heater on full blast, and the windows were kept tightly closed whatever the weather. There was a permanent smell of stewed tea and old ladies' woollens.

'You're wanting to get paid, I hear.' There was no doubt that she wasn't in favour of it.

'Yes, please,' I said. It was rather like visiting the headmistress at school, so I was very quiet and respectful. Gran pawed through the papers on her crowded roll-top desk, muttering and clicking her false teeth. Eventually she produced an official Wages Council leaflet and ran her finger along the columns of figures.

'How old are you?'

'Fifteen. Gran,' I added for extra politeness, but she looked at me as sharply as if I'd been cheeky.

'Full-timers at your age get three pounds fourteen and six for a forty-two-hour week,' she announced with disapproval. 'No wonder there's no profit in shopkeeping! Well, Miss, what's that per hour?'

Questions like that always floor me. Instead of trying to work them out in my head I just stand there saying to myself, 'How on earth do I know?'

'I'll get a pencil and paper,' I offered.

'Don't bother,' snapped Gran, 'I'll do it myself. Staying on at school, are you? Need to, by the sound of it. No proper schooling these days . . . One and ninepence an hour, as near as I can make it. Saturday mornings only, half-past eight to twelve, take it or leave it.'

'I'll take it, please.' I couldn't work that one out in my head either and I was anxious to get it down on paper.

'And I expect real work for it, mind. No idling about. A good morning's work for a good morning's pay, and if I catch you eating any of the stock there'll be trouble. That's theft, and it's a crime.'

80

I hoped she wouldn't notice my blushes.

'What's she paying you?' Dad asked when I went back into the shop.

I scribbled the figures on the back of a cardboard price-ticket. 'It'll only come to just over six bob,' I concluded, disappointed. I'd expected at least ten for a morning's work.

'That's about what I thought.'

'It isn't very much.'

'Well, now you see why you've got to stay on at school and qualify for a really good job. Still, six shillings is better than nothing, eh?'

It certainly was. By the time I was seventeen I was earning eight shillings a week at the shop, and that money was my lifeline. Most of the others in the sixth form at school had ten bob just given to them as pocket money, and some of them even had an allowance for buying their own clothes, but I knew that our family budget didn't run to such luxuries. Dad slipped me something extra whenever he had it to spare, and Mum bought me whatever I needed in the way of basic clothes out of the money she earned in the fields.

My main job in the shop was filling up the shelves. Once or twice, when Dad was extra busy, I'd tried to help him by serving behind the counter, but I hated it. It was very difficult to remember the prices of everything and I was hopeless at adding up in my head. I had to write it all down in a long wavering sum on the back of a price ticket, and even then I was liable to get flustered and make mistakes, while some of the customers made sniffy remarks about my being so bad at arithmetic when I was supposed to be so clever. I was the only one from the village, girl or boy, who'd passed the exam for the grammar school for several years, and I had to put up with a lot of needling on account of it.

So what with one thing and another I didn't much enjoy serving the customers. Anyway, Dad knew their habits, and what they wanted. 'My usual, please,' some of them would say. Or 'A piece of cheese,' and when I asked which sort and how much of it, they weren't sure: '*He* knows what I have,' they said. So it was really easier all round if I left the serving to him.

Instead, I dusted the two long mahogany shop counters, the grocery side and the drapery side, and I lugged cases of baked beans and sugar and cornflakes from the outside warehouse to the stock-room at the side of the shop, and I emptied the cases and checked the contents for damage. Then I filled up the shelves behind the grocery counter, being careful to rotate the stock as Dad had taught me and put the new things at the back and the earlier tins and packets in the front. In winter I carried the customers' paraffin cans out to the yard and filled them from the big tank. I swept out the stock-room and tidied the warehouse, and dusted the things we didn't have much sale for, and shook the creases out of the drapery goods and changed the window displays and tried hard to avoid Gran Thacker, though I was always respectful to her when we did meet.

It was an old-established village shop, going back 150 years at least, one of the properties bought by Dad's father in the 1920s. It must have been old-fashioned then, and it couldn't have changed much since except that Dad usually spent his holiday fortnight repainting the woodwork while Gran grumbled away doing the serving.

Dad longed to be able to modernize the shop to appeal to the younger customers. He wanted to get rid of the counters for a start, but Gran wouldn't hear of it. I overheard them once, arguing about whether Gran should buy a deep-freeze cabinet.

'The customers want frozen food,' said Dad. 'They see things advertised, and if they can't buy them from us they'll go elsewhere. We've got to move with the times.'

'Frozen muck's no good to anybody,' snapped Gran. 'And I don't hold with all that advertising, putting ideas into people's heads. Customers were thankful in the war to take what was offered. Your father always sold fresh food, and what was good enough for him is more than good enough for you.'

Acutally, though, she did give way over the deep-freeze, and fairly quickly, because her rival Mr Timpson at the top shop installed one and Gran's customers started making loud comments about how handy it was to be able to get frozen food in the village, and how good Mr Timpson's bacon was. That really upset Gran because she prided herself on her bacon. She never let Dad prepare it but always boned and rolled the sides herself. She couldn't bear the though of losing any of her bacon customers to Mr Timpson, so she ungraciously gave Dad the money to buy a second-hand deep-freeze, and within a couple of weeks she was eating fish fingers like the rest of us.

I agreed with his ideas about modernization. Counter service was hopelessly inefficient, because customers had to stand about waiting to be served while poor old Dad was run off his feet trying to keep them all happy.

The older customers were very patient; quiet, respectable countrywomen who believed in keeping themselves to themselves, who managed on very little money, never asked for credit and never complained. They called Dad Vincent, because they'd known him all his life. There were some customers, though, those who'd been at the village school with Dad, who always called him Ginger. It was understandable, with his hair, but they managed to say it in rather a sly, unpleasant way as though they were making fun of him.

'Come on, Ginger,' they'd say, 'hurry up, don't keep the ladies waiting,' and they'd snigger while Dad blushed. I wished that I could defend him in some way, but I didn't know how. Even their kids called him Ginger, and that made me mad. I'd been brought up to call their parents Mr and Mrs and I didn't see why they shouldn't be equally polite to my father.

Saturday was the shop's early-closing day and the morning was always busy. Dad was often harassed to death, particularly when any of his least favourite customers happened to be in there, chivvying him and making obscure jokes at his expense. If I were Dad I'd have thrown them out of the shop, but he just went on patiently serving, pale and quiet. And as if the customers weren't enough there was Gran Thacker, forever calling out to him from her office regardless of whether or not he was busy.

'Vincent! Did the tinned pears come in?'

'Vincent! Have we got any children's socks left?'

'Vincent! Did you hear me?'

It was a real madhouse in there sometimes. But every now and again things went quiet, and some customers who came in during these quiet patches would settle down to talk to him, taking it for granted that he had nothing else to do. One of the most persistent was Mrs Marks, a recent incomer with a sharp London accent who always wore high heels. She trotted into the shop every day, to buy cigarettes if she wanted nothing else, just for the sake of having somebody to talk to, and Dad behind his counter was a captive audience.

You could almost feel sorry for the Markses. They'd paid an astonishing price for one of the few bungalows in the village, but if they'd imagined it would be worth it to retire to the peace of the countryside they were soon disillusioned. Mrs Marks kept complaining to Dad how noisy Byland was, with tractors and haulage lorries roaring about at all hours, cockerels waking them at five, and church bells spoiling their Sunday morning lie-in. She said the village stank of pigs, which is true when the wind blows from Mill Farm, and she was always grumbling about the price of vegetables and saying how much fresher and cheaper things were in London. As Dad could have told her, except that he was too polite, food in the country is fresh and cheap only if you grow it yourself.

Someone else who didn't understand that was Mrs Hanbury. Her husband was a retired army officer, and they were both tall and thin with very superior voices. They'd moved into the village a few years ago and taken charge of everything from the Parish Council to the Women's Institute. They loved organizing things, and to be fair, which is difficult, they did a good job. But that didn't mean we had to like them.

The Hanburys had bought a tumbledown old house in the centre of the village to renovate in advance of their retirement. It was a big timber-framed building with a roof of mouldering thatch and cracked plaster walls, and over the years it had been divided into two or three rented dwellings. When the Hanburys bought it, it was empty except for old Fred Wainwright who lived in one end.

Fred was over eighty at the time, and though the Hanburys told him he would be provided with one of the bungalows the council were building for old people over at Horkey, he didn't want to move out. There wasn't a bungalow immediately available anyway, but the Hanburys couldn't wait. They sent in the builders, and Fred was so upset by the dust and disruption and noise that in the end he was glad to be given a place in the council old people's home, the great red-brick building on the turnpike that used to be the workhouse. A neighbour said that after the man from the Welfare had told him he was going away, Fred sat for two days and nights with his coats and shirts bundled and tied, and by the time the ambulance came to fetch him he thought he was ploughing with horses again, and sat calling to his team across the kitchen table.

The Hanburys certainly did a good job on the old house. By the time they'd finished spending money the place was unrecognizable, gutted and plumbed, with new thatch and plaster, new dormer windows, and carriage lamps outside the front door. According to a signboard it was now called The Glebe, but the Hanburys always referred to it as 'the cottage'. You can always tell townspeople from country people because they insist on talking about their cottages. Houses, we call them.

Mrs Hanbury did most of her shopping in Breckham Market, but every now and again she'd call in at Gran Thacker's to give us the benefit of her patronage.

'Oh, Vincent, good morning to you. I want a dozen fresh eggs, please. No no no, not *prepacked* eggs! I mean genuine fresh ones, free range. You don't have them? Really, how absurd it is to live in the country and to be offered eggs from battery hens . . . No, thank you!'

Then she spotted me, as I passed her loaded with a case of dog food, and smiled at me benevolently.

'Ah – Janet, isn't it? The Colonel tells me you're hoping to go to university! Now which one, I wonder?'

I was going to say London, but Dad chipped in eagerly, trying to show me off, to tell her that I'd just taken Oxford entrance.

Mrs Hanbury had very thin painted eyebrows and they rose up to join the wrinkles on her forehead. '*Oxford*? My goodness, how very ambitious. But of course things are so very different these days, aren't they? What I want, Vincent, is just an ounce of whole almonds. I want them for the top of a cake, so they must be unbroken. Well, could you pick out the unbroken ones for me, please? I am a nuisance, aren't I? Thank you so much. And *well done*, Janet.'

Mrs Hanbury was someone else I'd have liked to throw out of the shop. It wouldn't have done the takings any harm, either.

Our least favourite customer of all was Mrs Farrow. She'd married a Byland man, but you could tell from her voice that she'd been brought up in a town a long way from Suffolk. She was big and noisy and pushy, and she hadn't any time for village respectability. She didn't mind what she said to anybody, in fact she enjoyed causing disruption and embarrassment.

'Well, Ginger, what are you giving away today?'

She always started off like that. There wasn't a polite reply, so Dad just said, 'Good morning Mrs Farrow.' Then she hustled him along, changing her mind and complaining about quality and price as though he were personally responsible.

'What? A tanner each for them miserable little oranges? Never, I could grow 'em bigger meself. You keep 'em. I'll have a tablet of Lifebuoy soap. The biggest. *How* much? Not bloody likely, I'll take the small. They'll have to make it last. I'm not paying that for flaming soap. And a double Andrex toilet roll. Blush pink, eh, Ginger? Hey, that reminds me – '

Mrs Farrow cackled and shoved an elbow into the ribs of the person standing next to her. It happened to be Mrs Cantrip, one of our nice elderly customers, a regular chapel-goer who was obviously shocked by Mrs Farrow's language. She stood with a splotch of red on each thin cheek, holding her limp shopping-bag in front of her with both hands, and at Mrs Farrow's nudge she started and drew in her hands and her lips, retreating as far as she could without actually moving her feet.

'Well,' went on Mrs Farrow, enjoying herself, oblivious of poor Mrs Cantrip's embarrassment, 'I was in the top shop last week and I meant to ask for a double Andrex. I dunno what my lot do with it, anybody'd think I fed 'em rhubarb every day, the rate they use up paper. Well, anyway – ' she looked round the shop, gathering her audience – 'do you know what I said? I said, "Morning Mr Timpson, I'll have a double Durex." Double Durex! You should have seen his face! He must've thought I was going to have a good time . . . Laugh, I nearly cried!'

I didn't see what was so funny, and I'm not sure that Mrs Cantrip did either, but she closed her eyes tight and made herself even more thinly concave. Mrs Keysoe, one of Dad's contemporaries, spluttered with amusement and then pretended she hadn't. Susan Freeman, who used to be at the village school with me, shook with laughter behind her hand. Old Mrs Dillon, resting on the shop chair, nodded and smiled but she's deaf anyway, she always nods and smiles.

Dad, trying to add up Mrs Farrow's bill, kept his head well down. But she wasn't going to let him get away with that so she leaned across the counter to prod his arm.

'How about that, then, Ginger? Good job I didn't ask you, I bet you don't stock Durex! No call for it, eh?' She choked with laughter again, and had to wipe her eyes.

Then I saw that Dad was blushing. His skin was so fair that he blushed very easily. He looked reprovingly at Mrs Farrow and nodded in my direction, but I knew how to be a diplomatic shop assistant. I grinned enough to show Mrs Farrow that I appreciated her joke, but not so much that I might offend Mrs Cantrip.

'Ah, you needn't worry about young Janet,' Mrs Farrow chortled. 'Look at her, she knows what it's all about!'

'Fetch us some tins of custard powder, Janet,' said Dad urgently.

'Oh, go on with you,' Mrs Farrow said to him with scorn. 'You've got a shelf full of custard powder, you old woman.' But I was already half-way out of the door. Poor Dad had to stay put behind the counter but I could always find a job to do in the store shed.

Chapter Seven

Shortly before my finishing time at twelve, the telephone rang in Gran's office. She treated the telephone casually and never minded using it, but she always assumed that it was deaf.

'Sounds like an order,' said Dad, and presently Gran called him in.

'Old Miss Massingham,' he reported when he returned with a short list. 'We haven't seen her all week, seems she's not well. Do you mind getting these things up for her and taking them on your way home?'

It was an odd sort of order for a week's groceries, but Miss Massingham was a bit of an oddity herself. Not that I really knew her except by sight, but she was one of the village characters. I packed her order in a cardboard box: 400 cigarettes, half a pound of cheese, a packet of water biscuits, three small tins of soup, six boxes of matches and twelve large tins of cat food. People always said she lived on cat food and I began to think it must be true.

When I went to Gran's office to collect my wages it was still a few minutes to twelve.

'You're off already, Miss?'

I pointed out that I was going to take Miss Massingham's order.

'I don't pay you to ride about the village,' retorted Gran, but she gave me my eight bob. 'And mind your manners with Miss

Massingham,' she added, 'don't forget she's a lady. Only don't leave the goods unless she pays you, or we'll never get the money out of her.'

Miss Massingham lived about a mile outside the village, in the opposite direction to Longmire End, up a quiet road that passed the fields where Byland Hall had once stood. That was where Gran Bowden had worked when she was young, when the Massinghams had been important people in the county. But the family had all died off except Miss Massingham, and the Hall had been burned down in the Second World War when Ziggy Crackjaw and his Polish army mates were billeted there, so the old lady lived alone in what had once been their gamekeeper's house.

It had rained during the morning, and I cycled gingerly along the tree-lined road, the box of groceries balanced on my handle-bars, trying not to skid on wet leaves. I hadn't been in that direction for years. The gamekeeper's house, when I came to it, was smaller than I'd remembered, but even so it was bigger than ours and the Crackjaws' together. It stood by the roadside, overshadowed by trees, and it looked gloomy and damp. I'd imagined it was genuine Tudor, with its mossy tiles and half-timbering, but now I could see that the timbers were too regular, and the initials H.P.M. and the date 1879 were picked out boldly in coloured plaster above the front door.

No one in our village, except probably the newcomers, uses front doors, but I wondered whether Miss Massingham might on account of being a lady. But her front door, like ours, had plastic fertilizer bags propped against the sill with bricks to keep out the driving rain, so I decided that even a lady might prefer not to use it. I propped my bike against the garden hedge, pushed open the gate with my elbow, and carried the box along a muddy path, past various outbuildings, to the back door. There was an old sack lying in front of it as an outdoor doormat, just as we had at home, and when my knock was answered with a creaky 'Come in' I was careful to make use of the sack first.

'Good morning, I've brought your groceries.'

It was a superfluous remark, since I was standing there clutching them, but I had to say something. Miss Massingham usually did her shopping mid-week and I hadn't seen her for some time, so I was shocked by the change in her appearance.

She never looked like a lady. I remembered her as a large

vigorous woman, grey hair flying, dressed any old how, riding through the village on an ancient bike with a basket on the front for her shopping. She always called a cheerful greeting when she passed anyone in the street, and often she could be heard whistling.

But now a change had come over her. She seemed to have shrunk in height as well as in width. Her hair was limp, her cheeks sagged. She wore a long dressing-gown, mangy with age, and she looked old and ill.

All I got by way of acknowledgement was a fit of coughing. Miss Massingham had a cigarette stuck in one corner of her mouth and the smoke obviously caused her extreme discomfort. She stood in the centre of the room, peering at me through the haze and breathing harshly.

'From Mrs Thacker's,' I added. Miss Massingham grunted, and cleared a space among the unwashed crockery on the table so that I could put the box down. Her kitchen was larger and more comfortable than ours, with a small fire and a wooden armchair in front of it, but otherwise it was almost as antiquated as ours and every bit as untidy.

She began to unpack the box. An assortment of cats immediately materialized from various sleeping quarters about the room and began to purl round the skirts of her dressing-gown, tails up. Miss Massingham got busy with the tin-opener. I didn't like to ask for the money for the groceries, but I didn't dare leave without it. I tried a polite cough, but it was overpowered by her own. She forked several separate dollops of cat food on to a big baking-tin, put in on the floor and watched the chomping cats affectionately. Their tails gradually subsided as they concentrated their energies on the food, and she turned to raise an eyebrow at me through the cigarette smoke.

'You're waiting for the money, I suppose?'

'Oh no,' I said, 'it doesn't matter. But I'll take it if you want me to.'

Miss Massingham fetched a wallet from a drawer. 'How much?'

I offered her the bill.

'Good Lord. Nearly six quid for a few tins of cat food!'

'There's almost five pounds' worth of cigarettes,' I pointed out defensively. She barked with sudden amusement, started coughing again and thumped her chest. I tried not to look disapproving.

'I can see you take the view that I shouldn't smoke,' she said, throwing her cigarette butt into the fire. 'Well, I take the view that I shouldn't have a cough.' She gave me some banknotes. Dad had provided me with some loose cash and I carefully counted out the change and wrote, 'Paid with thanks, J. Thacker,' at the foot of the bill.

'Thank you for bringing the things, anyway,' she said. 'The doc won't let me out for a bit.' Wheezing, she pulled a packet of cigarettes and a box of matches from the pocket of her dressing-gown, lit a fresh one and shifted it to one side of her mouth. 'Who are you, by the way?'

'I'm Mrs Thacker's grand-daughter, Janet.'

Miss Massingham looked at me doubtfully, and then her face relaxed in recognition. '*Now* I've got you! Of course, Betty Bowden's daughter. Well, well.' She put her hands on my shoulders and turned me towards the light from the window. It was uncomfortable, standing so close to her cigarette, but I didn't like to break away.

'Haven't had a good look at you since you were a nipper,' she said. 'Yes, I can see the resemblance to your mother.'

I don't know whether I looked agonized but I certainly felt it. Mum must weigh all of twelve stone. Miss Massingham dropped her hands but didn't move away, looking at me and reminiscing.

'Young Betty Bowden's daughter, eh? When *she* was a nipper, her mother sometimes brought her with her when she came to work at the Hall. Jolly little kid – I always liked Betty. Such a pity . . . she could have made something of herself if only she'd had the confidence, instead of just letting things happen to her. And poor Vincent Thacker . . . He did at least get away from the village, but then he came running back as soon as his mother sent for him. Well, I hope you've inherited some guts from someone, young Janet. Not going to spend *your* life stuck in Byland, I hope?'

The smoke from her cigarette was making my eyes water, and I didn't like the look of the grey caterpillar of ash that was waggling at its tip, threatening to drop on to my anorak. Fortunately Miss Massingham noticed it and moved away to tap it into the fireplace, and I took the precaution of putting the table between us before I answered.

'I'm going to university next October.'

'University, eh?' She said it eagerly, not patronizingly. 'That's more like it! Yes, I remember now, Vincent told me how well you were doing at school. He's very proud of you. I hope your mother's pleased, too?'

'I don't know about pleased, but she doesn't object. Only I cost a lot to keep at school.'

'It'll be worth it. You tell her from me. She made mistakes, poor girl, but it'll be different for you. I can see that. Get away from the village, that's the thing. Good education, new friends, a career, a different life. That's the stuff!'

She was so enthusiastic that she started coughing again, spluttering through the smoke. I shifted uneasily towards the door, but she beckoned me back.

'Here.' She took out her wallet again, produced two pound notes, folded them small and pushed them into my hand. I stammered and protested but she closed my fingers over them.

'Just a present. Old friend of the family, you know. Good luck – oh, and remember me to your mother.' She almost pushed me to the door, and closed it behind me before I gathered wit enough to thank her properly.

I rode crazily back to the village, singing aloud. Two pounds, especially coming unexpectedly like that, was a fantastic present. There were so many possibilities that I couldn't begin to decide how to spend it. Good old Miss Massingham!

Poor old Miss Massingham. I sobered up, thinking of her. Obviously she wasn't well, and from all I'd ever heard of her she hadn't had much of a life either.

The church stood just at the turning where the road joined the village street and on an impulse, remembering that the Massinghams were buried there, I propped my bike against the wall and went in.

In Byland, most people who are religious enough to go to services are chapel-goers, as Mum and I were expected to be when Gran Bowden was alive. There's a service in St Mary's only once a month, and then the parson has to come from another village. But Dad's family were Church when he was young, and he'd heard that when the Massinghams lived at the Hall, St Mary's had been full every Sunday. He took me in once, just before I left the village school, to see the Massingham memorials, and now I wanted to look at them again.

The Massinghams weren't an old-established family in our village. Dad said they were originally Breckham Market people, innkeepers and brewers, and they'd made their fortune out of beer in Victorian times. And then Horace Percival Massingham, Miss Massingham's grandfather, had decided to set himself up as a country gentleman. He'd bought Byland Hall, which was then quite a small place, pulled it down and replaced it with a massive great mansion, all towers and turrets. Gran Bowden used to have a framed photograph of the Hall on her sideboard, with the assembled servants including herself posed in front of it. She was very proud of her connection with the Hall, though as a chapel-goer she didn't approve of the way the Massinghams had made their money. She used to say that the Hall was built on beer barrels, and it was a long time before I realized that she didn't mean it literally.

So the Massingham memorials in the church go back less than a hundred years, and most of them aren't very interesting. The commemorative stained-glass windows are downright ugly, in lurid reds and yellows just like Gran Thacker's cheapest boiled sweets, the popular assortment at a shilling a quarter. But what Dad had wanted me to see were the more recent memorials.

First there was the marble reclining figure of Gwendolen Rose Massingham, wife to Arthur Reginald, the old man's grandson. She had died in 1916, in childbirth, aged twenty-eight. The figure was lifesize, but small and fragile. The features were completely beautiful.

When Dad first showed me the figure on the tomb, I'd thought that it was in fact Gwendolen Rose's body, petrified. Now, though I knew it was only a sculptor's handiwork, I still approached it with reverence. I knew that the face was too beautiful, too much idealized, but twenty-eight didn't seem very old to die. I traced my fingers over the cold forehead and the gently swelling cheeks and lovely lips, and wondered whether her husband had ever had the opportunity to come in alone and do the same. The air inside the church was mustily cold, but the shiver I felt was one of sadness, because poor Arthur had had very little time to mourn. A memorial tablet on the wall above his wife's tomb recorded his death in action at Passchendaele in 1917.

Miss Massingham, Dad had said, was Arthur's only sister. She had been left to bring up a little orphaned nephew and there he was, commemorated on another tablet: Major John, died of wounds in Burma in 1943.

I sat in a pew and tried to grasp the full extent of Miss Massingham's tragedy. Bad enough to lose her brother and her sister-in-law, but to bring up their child only to lose him in another war, and then to have her home taken over and burned down, and to move to an isolated gamekeeper's house and grow old and ill alone, was desperately sad.

But what I hadn't noticed when Dad first showed me the two memorial tablets was the text at their foot. I didn't see how anyone with that load of loss could keep any kind of religious faith, but the fact was that Miss Massingham wasn't miserable or sorry for herself. Ill as she was, she'd been cheerful and full of enthusiasm and encouragement, and I could see that the text made the memorials uplifting instead of depressing. I didn't know whether I believed it myself, but if Miss Massingham did, then she wasn't in need of any sympathy from me.

I read the text over again, aloud: '*I know that my Redeemer liveth.*' Then I patted Gwendolen Rose on the cheek, and went home for my dinner.

Chapter Eight

Saturday dinner was always fish and chips. Mr Jessup's van came bumping up the lane, chimney puthering, soon after one o'clock, and the smell of frying fat clung round the hedgerows long after it had passed. Mum reckoned to buy a piece of cod and sixpennyworth of chips for each of us, and to give Mr Jessup a cup of tea by way of thanking him for coming.

Mrs Crackjaw had to budget more carefully than Mum, but she always took a big enamel bowl out to the van and had it filled with chips covered in salt and vinegar for herself and the younger kids. She bought a piece of fish for Ziggy, to be reheated at whatever time he came home from the White Horse, and if any of her older children happened to be at home she bought fish for them as well. That wasn't very often, because their household wasn't the kind that even the Crackjaws wanted to linger in any longer than they had to. Andy had left home to work on a construction site somewhere near Yarmouth. He reappeared occasionally, but if we happened to meet we just ignored each other.

Dad didn't get home from the shop until nearly half-past one, so Mum kept his fish and chips hot beside the fire. When he'd sat down to his dinner, I told them about Miss Massingham. They were both very impressed when they heard about the two pounds she'd given me.

'You're sure you didn't beg it off her, though?' said Mum.

Some of the things she says make me want to jump up and down and shout rude words at her. But then I remembered that I'd told Miss Massingham that I cost a lot to keep at school, so I felt a nag of guilt.

'She said it was because she was an old friend of our family,' I snapped. 'And she asked to be remembered to you.'

'Did she?' Mum was chuffed. 'Well, my poor mother worked hard enough for the Massinghams when she was alive, and that's a fact.'

I'd have liked to find out what Miss Massingham had meant when she mentioned Mum's mistakes, but I thought I'd better not ask. Then I remembered something that had puzzled me in the shop that morning.

'By the way, Dad – what's a double Durex?'

He nearly choked over his fish and chips. 'A what?' said Mum, thunderstruck.

'A double Durex,' I repeated. 'Mrs Farrow was making a joke about it in the shop.'

Mum's ears and neck went so red they were practically humming. 'That woman! She would!'

'What is it, Dad?'

He looked unhappy. 'Well, it's the same as Andrex. Only more durable.' He shovelled chips into his mouth.

'It can't be, I'm not that stupid. Come on, what was the joke?'

He shook his head and pointed apologetically to his bulging cheeks. 'Never you mind,' said Mum. 'You'll know when you're old enough.'

That did it. With a remark like that from Mum, it was obviously something to do with sex. I was doubly furious, with them for refusing to tell me and with myself for exposing my ignorance.

'I *am* old enough,' I yelled. 'I'm seventeen, for heaven's sake stop treating me like a kid! Everybody else knows these things, you just don't care whether I look a fool or not.'

They both kept their heads down, munching, and I pushed away from the table and slammed out to the kitchen. The walls were so thin that I could hear what they were saying just as well as if I'd stayed in the room.

'You ought to tell her,' said Dad reproachfully.

'You're the one she asked. Tell her yourself.'

'How can I? It's your place.'

'And a fat lot I know about it, don't I?' said Mum bitterly. She scraped back her chair, and I dodged away to the cupboard and busied myself by getting out the cups and saucers.

It was no use hoping for any information from my parents about anything to do with sex. Not that I could expect it from Dad, and of course I wouldn't have badgered him about Durex if I'd known there was any connection. But Mum was ultra-respectable. She seemed to think that sex was something that wouldn't appear if you didn't encourage it, so she'd never attempted to explain anything. The start of my periods in my second year at the grammar school seemed as much of a surprise to her as it was to me.

'There now! I was going to tell you about that, lovey,' she'd said, when I showed her why I needed a clean pair of pyjamas in the middle of the week. I was bewildered and a bit frightened, but when the only explanation she offered was, 'You'll be like the big girls now,' I realized that at least it wasn't anything I'd have to go to the doctor with.

'Oh, I know all about it,' I said airily. 'We've done it at school in biology.' That wasn't true, we'd only got as far as rabbits and even then I didn't understand how the buck actually set about fertilizing the doe, but I wasn't going to let on to anybody.

Even with my best friend Sally, in and out of school, I'd never talked about sex. We were too friendly. It would have been easier to talk about it to someone I didn't like. Sally did once say, embarrassed, that it must be an advantage to be a country girl because you saw animals mating and producing their young, but either I was completely unobservant or our livestock waited modestly until I wasn't there, because I never saw a thing. As far as I knew, our rabbits and hens bred by way of spontaneous combustion.

In the sixth form, of course, we discussed the subject frequently, but on a global scale: over-population and the pill, abortion and the Pope. We didn't mention the practical details, and I didn't see much chance of finding out about them until I got away to university. Roll on October!

Meanwhile, it was a waste of time to row about it at home, so I shut up and made a pot of tea.

We liked to be idle after Saturday dinner. There were always plenty of jobs that needed doing, particularly when Mum was on field work, but we didn't believe in rushing at them. She'd been out lifting carrots that week, and had spent Saturday morning doing the bedrooms and washing the sheets, but the day was too damp to dry things out of doors so the bedlinen was now draped over the clothes-horse, steaming away in front of the fire. The living-room and kitchen both needed a good clean, but we all wanted a break before we started, so we lingered at the table over the debris of fish and chips and jam tart and cups of tea, reading. Dad read the *East Anglian Daily Press*, and while Mum lapped up the local weekly paper I took the opportunity to read her *Woman's Weekly*.

I wouldn't admit to enjoying the magazine, of course, but it was perfect relaxation after a week of schoolwork. It's full of exciting knitting patterns and recipes for happy family meals, and powerful new serials about doctors and nurses and their misunderstandings before he takes her in his arms for the first time and proposes marriage before he kisses her. It's entirely pure and cosy, so no wonder the problem page is filled with bleats from girls whose boy-friends have turned out to be neither. Their problems make fascinating reading, but it's pathetic that they feel the need to pour out their troubles to a magazine. I felt a bit sorry for them, but I couldn't understand how they let themselves get into such stupid messes in the first place.

'The bingo report's in,' said Mum, pleased as anything. She loves reading her own name in the paper. 'Listen – "*At a bingo evening held in the Coronation Hut, Byland, on Saturday last, the prizes were won by Mrs G. Firmage, Mrs V. Thacker –* "

We could hear a car coming up the lane, and we assumed it was going to the farm, but instead it slowed to a stop. Mum interrupted herself: 'Who's that?'

'Andy Crackjaw, I suppose,' I said absently. I'd just got to the bit in the serial where the doctor's firm mouth comes down on

96

the nurse's and she wonders why her senses are in such a tumult. 'He seems to be doing all right these days.'

'He was home a couple of weeks ago,' said Mum. 'It's not like him to come again so soon.'

Dad, who was nearest the window, got up to look. 'Oh, no – ' he groaned. 'It's your Brenda and her family. They must've bought a car and come to show it off.'

Mum and I rushed to the window. Sure enough, there was her youngest sister, with a small girl on her knee, peering and waving from the front passenger seat. Two older boys were jumping up and down in the back.

'Ooh, that little devil Brenda . . .' Red-faced with vexation, Mum struggled out of her disreputable cardigan and shoved it out of sight under the cushion of her easy chair. 'Fancy them coming unexpected, and us in our dirt! Get that table cleared quick, oh, what a mess this place is in.'

Dad and I hadn't waited to be told. I was already ferrying the dirty crockery out to the kitchen. He bundled up the plastic tablecloth, still with the pepper and salt pots and all the crumbs inside, and shoved that and the scattered newspapers and a couple of pairs of slippers on to the stairs, and shut the door on them. Mum lugged the laden clothes-horse into the corner behind the door. By the time Brenda and the children had made their way up the front path and round to the back, Dad and I were washing up and Mum had covered her old blouse and skirt with a more or less clean nylon overall.

'Well, our Bren,' she said as she stood holding the door open, smoothing down her hair with the other hand, 'what a lovely surprise, we are glad to see you. Come in, you must excuse the mess, hello Darren, hello Lyndon, what big boys you are, and little Samantha, I haven't seen her since she was a tiny baby and she must be nearly two, come to your Auntie Betty then, what a little dear she is.'

Mum hurried them through the kitchen, Brenda vexingly slim in a tight skirt and high heels, the little girl pretty in frilled nylon, the boys overdressed in miniature suits with long trousers and bow ties. Dad and I, mumbling greetings with inane grins on our faces, stood side by side to hide the dirty crockery as they passed the sink. Brenda's seedy-looking husband slouched after them and I said, 'Hello Ray,' as brightly as I could.

'How do, Janet.' He sounded thoroughly fed up. 'Vince.' The two men nodded at each other coolly and we all crowded into the living-room. There weren't nearly enough chairs so we stood looking at each other while Mum chattered wildly, trying to distract attention from the unswept floor and the dust. When she'd said, 'This *is* a nice surprise,' three times running, and paused for breath, Brenda got a word in.

The sisters weren't a bit alike, though you could see from the roots of Brenda's blond bubble-curls that she'd been born as dark as Mum. She and Ray lived near Saintsbury and both of them, with help from Ray's mother in looking after the children, had good jobs at the turkey factory there. We didn't see much of them, thank heaven, partly because they always seemed to be working overtime, but also because they hadn't been mobile until now.

'We were just out for a run in the car,' said Brenda grandly, 'and Ray said, "Why don't we go to Byland and see your Bet?"' Ray looked indignant, but she bored on before he could deny it. 'So I said, "What a lovely idea," I said, "it would be nice to see them again." Sorry to take you by surprise, we'd have phoned if only you'd got one. It makes all the difference, having a phone.'

'Oh, we like unexpected visitors,' said Mum. 'A real nice surprise.'

We all stood about wondering what to say next.

'How do you like the car, then?' said Brenda.

'Very nice, I'm sure,' said Mum. Brenda insisted on our going out to look at it, so we all trailed outside, Mum carrying the little girl to keep her white shoes out of the mud.

'Is it new?' Mum asked as we stood looking at the car. It was a typical Mum question, everybody knows they haven't made those bulbous two-colour cars for years. Anyway, you could see rust at the bottom of the doors.

'Nearly new,' said Brenda.

'Looks in good nick, Ray,' Dad offered, but Ray ignored him and rubbed at a splash of mud on the bonnet.

'Not with your hanky,' snapped Brenda. 'Here, there's a duster in the glove compartment.' She opened the front passenger door with a flourish and we peered dutifully inside. The two boys pushed their way on to the driving seat, showing off, and one of them thumped the horn. Ray ordered them out. I glanced

98

at next door, and saw several bullet-headed little Crackjaws at their window, gaping.

'Have a sit in it,' Brenda urged Mum, but she wasn't keen on playing the poor relation.

'I've sat in cars before,' she said.

Brenda nudged Ray. 'And been taken for a ride, an' all,' she murmured, but Mum was too busy talking to Samantha to hear. Dad and I both declined to sit in the car, and we all trailed back to the house.

'Can we stay out and play?' asked Darren, the seven-year-old.

'Not in your best,' snapped their mother.

'When's tea, then?'

'You wait until you've been invited,' growled Ray.

'Well, of course you're invited,' said Mum, looking worried. I could see her mentally reviewing the contents of the larder and I knew as well as she did that we hadn't got enough to go round.

'Oh no, don't bother about tea for us!' Brenda sounded shocked at the very idea. 'We wouldn't dream of putting you about.'

'It's no trouble. You're ever so welcome, you know that. A lovely surprise – '

'The match is on at three,' said Ray, cheering up. 'You watching it, Vince? No, you wouldn't be . . .' He pushed his way over to the television set. 'Bloody hell, you've got a real museum piece here.'

Mum was vexed. 'Do you mind, Ray Lummis! That was our poor mother's telly, given her by the last lady she worked for.'

'I wonder that old set still goes,' said Brenda, sitting in Mum's chair with Samantha on her knee and the boys perched one on each of the wooden arms. 'We've got a twenty-four-inch slim-line, don't take up half the room.'

I almost expected Mum to say, "Beggars can't be choosers," but that was obviously for family consolation only. 'It does us very well,' she snapped.

Ray turned up the volume, and settled himself in Dad's easy chair. 'Got any beer, Vince? No, you wouldn't have. Go out to the car, Darren, and fetch us a couple of bottles from the boot.'

Looking defeated, Dad made up the fire and sat on one of the hard chairs at the table. Mum nodded at me meaningfully: 'You did say you were going to the village this afternoon, didn't you, Janet?'

I took the hint. I couldn't go round to Gran Thacker's back door for groceries on her half-day, she'd have bawled me out, but Mr Timpson at the top shop was always open on Saturday afternoons. 'Yes, I'm going to see a friend,' I said for Brenda's benefit.

She wasn't deceived. 'You mustn't get anything special for us,' she cried above a roar from the crowd at the football match.

'No, I shan't,' Mum mouthed, 'you must take us as you find us.' She followed me out to the kitchen and we had a rare moment of unity as we grumbled about our unwelcome visitors. 'I'm ever so sorry to send you out again, lovey.'

'Doesn't matter, I'd rather go than stay. What am I to get?'

Mum opened the door to the larder under the stairs, and did a quick check. 'A big sliced loaf, for a start, and half a pound of butter. I've got a small can of fruit for our tea tomorrow but it won't be enough for today, better get a big can of peaches. And a jar of salmon spread.'

'What about cake?' I opened the tin and estimated the size of what was left of a swiss roll. 'This'll never go round eight of us.'

'See if he's got any of them individual fancy cakes, then. Just get half a dozen, we shall have to eat small. Here's my purse, there should be enough in it.'

'I've got the money Miss Massingham gave me, if it's any more.'

'Thanks, lovey, I'll pay you back later.'

The door opened and Brenda put her head into the kitchen. Mum and I both started guiltily.

'If Janet's going out, would she mind taking the boys for a walk? They get fed up watching telly.'

''Course she won't mind,' said Mum, but I certainly did.

'I'm going on my bike.'

'Well, you can just walk for a change,' Mum snapped.

'It's going to rain. They'll get wet,' I threatened, but the women ignored me. Brenda called the two boys and pushed them into their anoraks.

'You're going to go for a walk with your cousin Janet,' she said. The bigger boy burped aggressively. 'Don't *do* that, Darren. How many times do I have to tell you?'

'Bless them,' said Mum indulgently, thankful to see the back of them. 'Janet will buy you some sweets. Buy them some sweets, Janet.'

'Only if they behave,' I said, putting on my own anorak. 'Come on, then, if you're coming.'

'I want to go to the toilet,' said five-year-old Lyndon, so I took them both down to the end of the garden. Darren came out holding his nose. *'We've* got an upstairs bathroom,' he said.

'So've we,' I said, 'but we don't let other people use it.' And I walked so fast to the top shop that they had to trot to keep up, scuffling about behind me all the way.

Chapter Nine

I'd never gone to the top shop before. There was no reason why I should. Apart from drapery, which his shop was too small to stock, Mr Timpson sold the same things as Gran Thacker did, so we were rivals.

A few people, like loud-mouthed Mrs Farrow, didn't mind which of the two shops they went to, but in general Mr Timpson had his customers and we had ours. This segregation had nothing to do with convenience. It went back to a village feud all of fifty years ago, when the Thackers and the Timpsons fell out and the rest of the village took sides. As a result, some people would go without food sooner than darken Gran's doors, and others would be so fixated on going to Gran's that they'd walk past the top shop even in pouring rain, so it was a real embarrassment for me to have to go to there.

The shop was full. It would be. When I arrived with the boys there was a great stirring of interest and a nudging among the waiting customers.

'Looks as if you've got unexpected company, Janet.'

'Five of them, Mrs Yaxford,' I agreed, trying to indicate that it was a greater invasion than any family could reasonably be expected to cater for without notice.

'Ah, that'll be your Mum's sister Brenda.' Nosy old woman. I just nodded, and tried to interest Darren and Lyndon in a poster advertising cat food.

'Soon be leaving school, Janet?' That was Mrs Jermy, nudging Mrs Yaxford as she said it.

'At Christmas.'

I knew what was coming next. They all knew perfectly well what I was going to do, it had been chewed over in the village for long enough, but now they'd got me cornered they meant to embarrass me as much as possible.

'You'll be getting a job at last, then?'

'Just a temporary one.'

'Janet isn't going to do an ordinary job,' said Mrs Yaxford, mock-impressed. '*She's* going to college.'

'Well, I never!' said Mrs Jermy, mock-surprised. 'And there's our Julie, younger than her, getting married next summer. And been out earning for three years.'

'Ah, it's nice when they're out earning. Got plenty of independence, mine have, like yours. Don't want to sponge on their parents any longer than they can help.'

'Mind you,' Mrs Jermy conceded, 'it takes all sorts. I dare say some are brainier than others.'

'That's true. Though wherever Janet gets it from, we know it can't be the Thacker side of the family.'

The two women sniggered behind their hands, overcome by their own wit. Lyndon hauled at my skirt. 'I want a lolly.'

'You'll have to wait,' I snapped, taking my irritation out on him. Mrs Yaxford must have thought she'd gone too far because she turned to me quite graciously. 'Seeing as you've got company, Janet, you can go ahead of me.'

Mrs Jermy agreed, and I was certainly grateful. I didn't want to be there any longer than I could help. I thanked them, and moved up to the counter as soon as the previous customer left. Unfortunately, Mrs Yaxford and Mrs Jermy were now standing behind me with their ears flapping, and I felt defensive on behalf of Mum's housekeeping because I knew my order would sound as though we hadn't any food in the house at all.

I wished Mr Timpson a polite 'Good afternoon,' and keeping my voice as low as possible asked for half a pound of butter.

He smirked. 'I expect you'll want the best?'

I'd forgotten that he wouldn't know which brand we had. We always bought the cheapest, but I wasn't going to say so in front of that lot.

'What about our sweets?' interrupted Darren.

'Wait a minute! Yes please, Mr Timpson – and a large sliced loaf.' I worked my way through the tea menu while the boys worried at my heels. The fact was that I daren't commit myself to buying them anything because I didn't know how much there was in Mum's purse, and I'd just remembered that I'd left Miss Massingham's two pound notes on the mantelpiece. I was afraid I wouldn't have enough money and I couldn't possibly ask Mr Timpson for credit, especially with the two women listening.

'Have you any fancy cakes, please?'

Mr Timpson pointed to a tray at the far end of the counter. He bought his cakes from a baker in the next village but Gran Thacker wouldn't have them in her shop, she said the bakehouse was full of beetles. The cakes were sticky, bright pinks and yellows and greens decorated with shreds of coconut and whorls of artificial cream. I thought it might shut the boys up if I let them choose their cakes, so I lifted Lyndon. 'Which one would you like for your tea?'

'This one,' he said, and poked his finger in the cream. I dropped him and he set up a howl so I pushed his creamy finger into his mouth.

'My turn,' yelled Darren. He stood on his toes to peer at the cakes but he wasn't quite tall enough. I held him under the armpits and hauled him up. 'Get on with it, then,' I puffed.

'This . . . no, this . . . no, this . . .'

I plonked him on his feet. 'I haven't got any cream,' he shouted indignantly.

I raised my voice. 'Six cakes, please, Mr Timpson. Any of them. With the one he touched, of course.'

Darren thumped Lyndon, and their wails filled the shop. 'Hope you didn't leave your kettle on, gal,' called Mrs Jermy to Mrs Yaxford.

Mr Timpson scowled at the boys and added up my bill on a paper bag. 'That'll be eleven and a penny,' he said. I delved in Mum's purse, scraped up eleven and threepence, and paid it thankfully.

'Let me have a lolly,' sobbed Lyndon.

'I can't buy you one,' I hissed.

'You promised us.'

'I know, but I forgot my own money.'

'You'll have to shut them up somehow,' said Mrs Yaxford. 'Get them some penny gum,' she advised.

Mr Timpson silently offered me two twists of bubble gum, and I handed back the change he had given me. 'There,' I said brightly, distributing them to the boys, 'now let's go home to tea.'

'We'd rather have sweets,' said Darren.

'That or nothing, and if you don't shut up I'll take it away.'

We got home at last, the boys trailing and wailing. Brenda came out to the kitchen to take off their anoraks.

'What ever are you chewing?' she asked Darren.

By the way of an answer, he blew a large pink bubble. Brenda was furious. 'That filthy stuff, you know I won't let you have it!'

'We didn't ask for it,' he said indignantly. 'It wasn't our fault. We wanted sweets. *She* made us have it.'

Mum was even more furious. 'Why ever did you buy them that rubbish, our Janet?'

'Because it seemed a good idea at the time,' I snarled, and stalked out to get a jug of water from the pump.

The football match was still on, and when I went into the living-room to put the kettle on the fire all five of the Lummises were watching it, filling the room. We had to keep stepping over their feet as we got the tea ready. Dad and I moved the table to a different position so that we could all squeeze round it, and Mum opened the stairs door to go up and fetch her linen tablecloth. There was an immediate slither and a bump as two pairs of slippers, a pepper and a salt pot, a plastic tablecloth, some newspapers and a shower of crumbs fell into the room.

'Well, I never,' said Mum, 'how did that lot get there?'

Dad fetched down a chair from each bedroom, and somehow wedged them all round the table. It was only when he'd irretrievably blocked the sideboard that Mum hissed at me, 'Get the best cups out.'

The best and only tea set, a wedding present unused from one Christmas to the next, lived in the sideboard.

'I can't get at them with the chairs there,' I hissed back.

'You'll have to, else we shan't have enough to go round.'

Fortunately the sideboard had sliding doors, and by crawling under the table I could reach between the chair legs for the china. As I surfaced with the first pile I could see out of the corner of my eye that Darren was aiming a kick at my behind, but I mouthed, 'You dare!' at him and he stuck out his tongue instead. I was about to put the assembled cups on the table when Mum gave a meaningful cough, and I took the hint and carried them out to the kitchen to wipe the dust off first.

Dad was buttering a huge plateful of bread. Mum got busy with the can-opener and the kitchen was suddenly filled with the Sunday afternoon smell of sliced peaches in syrup. 'Dust the small jug for the cream, Janet,' she said, opening a tin of evaporated milk. Posh Mrs Hanbury had once made a terrible fuss in the shop when she'd asked for cream and Dad had offered her a tin of evap, but if you want fresh cream in the country you have to keep your own cow.

Lyndon appeared in the doorway. 'I'm thirsty,' he whined.

Mum called to Brenda to ask what the boys drank, and Brenda said that any kind of orange or lemon squash would do. Mum apologized that we didn't have any. 'How about a nice drink of milk?' she said.

'Milk!' said Darren scornfully. 'We're not kids.'

'All right,' I said patiently, 'I won't bring you any. Do you want some milk, Lyndon?'

Seeing that there wasn't much alternative, he nodded. I gave him some in a cup but he only blew bubbles in it, and when I threatened to take it away he cried indignantly through an innocent milky moustache, so I let him alone and made the tea. Dad switched on the light and drew the curtains, and we all climbed over the furniture to our places and jammed ourselves in elbow to elbow. Samantha took a fancy to Mum and sat on her knee, opening her mouth like a bird to be fed with bread and butter and boiled egg.

'I don't know what to give Darren to drink, I'm sure,' worried Mum. Trust her to revive an awkward subject; he didn't seem bothered except on principle.

'There were bottles and bottles of drink in the shop,' he mourned.

'You should have asked Janet to buy you some, my lovey.'

'I just knew she wouldn't. She wouldn't even buy us any sweets.'

'I thought she was going to hit us,' said Lyndon huskily.

Everybody looked at me accusingly except the little girl, who made cheerful noises to her egg. 'A-goo, a-goo,' said Mum, and I passed round the plate of bread and butter and started to serve out the peaches.

We settled down at last, with Brenda telling Mum how

wonderful it was to have plenty of work at the turkey factory, and to have a telephone and a car. 'Ray drives me to Saintsbury on Saturday mornings when he's not working, and first off I take the washing to the launderette.'

'I thought you'd got a washing-machine?' said Mum.

'So I have, but the launderette's better for towels and bed-linen, everything comes out lovely and dry. None of that old-fashioned nuisance of drying your sheets on a clothes-horse in front of the fire.'

'Did 'oo want a bit more eggy then?' said Mum to Samantha. 'Well, there's a good little girl.'

'And then we go to the supermarket,' Brenda went on, 'and do the week's shopping. Hundreds of bargains, you save no end. And we can park just round the back. No trouble at all, with a car.'

'Eaten it all up? Well, there *is* a good girl,' Mum said. 'Sorry, Bren, what did you say? I wasn't listening.'

The men didn't say a word to each other. I tried to get them started by enquiring about the football match they'd been watching, but Dad said it wasn't bad and Ray said it was bloody terrible, and that was the end of that conversation. I stacked up the empty fruit dishes, climbed out over the back of Lyndon's chair, took away the dishes and refilled the teapot while I was at it.

'Janet's quiet,' said Brenda to Mum when I came back.

I offered her another cup of tea. She refused, but her husband passed his empty cup.

'Janet's going to college, Ray.'

'Oh ar. Going to join the layabouts, then?'

Dad defended me. 'Janet works very hard.'

'And she's a big help in the house,' said Mum.

'I should think so,' said Brenda. 'After all, you're feeding and clothing her for nothing. I don't know how you manage it.'

'Well, she'll have a county grant when she goes to college, and they pay her fares and books and dinner money while she's at school,' said Mum. 'And she's sensible, she doesn't bother us for fancy clothes and make-up and things.'

Brenda's lipsticked mouth was thin with disapproval. 'Funny way of going on at her age.'

'What about your cream cakes?' I said to the boys, offering them the plate.

'I'm not having that one,' said Lyndon disdainfully. 'It's got a finger-hole in it.'

Darren shifted a mouthful of bread and jam to one cheek. 'Well, you needn't think I'm going to have it, you dirty little sod.'

Ray reached across the table and smacked the side of Darren's head. He bawled, and Lyndon howled in sympathy.

'You bad boy, using such language,' cried Brenda. 'I don't know where he gets it from,' she assured Mum.

'Too much bleedin' telly,' growled Ray. 'Shut up, the pair of you, or I'll give you something to yell about.'

The boys subsided into snuffles, which didn't stop them from eating their way through the fancy cakes. Dad made a heroic attempt to talk to Ray about football.

'D'you follow Yarchester?' he asked.

Ray laughed derisively. 'Yarchester! I wouldn't be paid to watch 'em, prancing round the ball like a lot of bloody nancy-boys – '

'Ray!'

'Well!'

'No offence,' said Brenda, placating us as though it was unusual for Ray to swear. She went back to her previous subject: me. 'So what's Janet going to be when she leaves college, Bet?'

'Well,' said Mum cautiously, 'I don't know as she's going to *be* anything.'

'"Cept a BA,' said Dad proudly.

They were all looking at me again. Samantha wriggled off Mum's knee and held out her arms to me. I'm not much interested in small children but she was a sweet little thing, a miniature girl, with a blue ribbon in her hair and tiers of matching nylon frills on the broad seat of her plastic pants. I picked her up and chatted to her, trying to ignore what was being said about me.

'What job's she going to do, though?'

Mum and Dad looked at me uncertainly and I tried to defend myself. 'There are all sorts of jobs,' I said. 'Well . . . journalism. Publishing . . .'

'Ah, but you're not actually going to train for anything, are you?' said Brenda. 'Now that's what I don't hold with. I say nothing against going to college if you're going to train for a

107

teacher, but going when you don't rightly know what you're going for is daft, if you ask me.'

Ray choked indignantly on a fish-paste sandwich. 'It's not daft,' he cried, 'it's bloody criminal. Who pays for students, I'd like to know? Us working men, that's who. What I pay in tax is terrible, and all to keep that long-haired lot in idleness! Marvellous, i'n it, when you can rely on other people to pay for your grown-up kids to do nothing!'

Dad was a fuming red under his ginger hair, obviously longing to say something but not knowing what. I hugged the little girl, wretchedly conscious that Ray had a point, and having no more idea than Dad how to answer it. Then I remembered a game that Dad used to play with me when I was little, and I tried it on Samantha. I opened her small paw, wondering at the completeness of it, fingernails and all, and traced round it with my forefinger.

'Round and round the gar-den, like a ted-dy bear . . .'

'But what I mean is,' went on Brenda, raising her voice above mine, 'you've been keeping yourselves poor for her. If she was out earning, you could live a lot more comfortable than this. And she'll think no more of you for it, you mark my words!'

'. . . one step – ' I tickled Samantha's creased wrist. 'Two steps – ' I tickled the inside of her elbow . . .

'And what good will it all come to? She'll be married before you know where you are – ' Brenda looked me up and down ' – and if she don't get married she'll leave home, so either way you'll get nothing out of her. You're just wasting your money.'

'. . . tickle her under there!' I scrabbled Samantha's woolly cardigan in the approximate region of her armpit and she wriggled with pleasure. "Gen,' she said, "gen.'

Dad was so furious that he went white. His voice rose almost to a squeak. 'I work to earn my money and I shall do as I like with it! Janet deserves the chance to better herself, and I'm going to support her all the way.'

Ray shrugged, draining his teacup and lighting a cigarette. 'Well, you suit yourself, but I reckon you're a bloody fool. It's not even as if she's – '

A pointed shoe stabbed me on the side of the foot, just where the hockey ball had hit me, and I yelped with the sudden pain.

'I'm ever so sorry, Janet,' said Brenda. 'Me foot slipped.'

Dad stood up, breathing quickly. 'If you've *quite* finished,' he said, 'excuse *me*.'

He and Ray looked at each other, and you couldn't tell who despised the other most. Ray got up slowly and moved his chair out of the way, and Dad flounced out and slammed the back door behind him. Samantha slid off my knee, the boys began playing bears with her under the table, and Ray said it was time they got on their way and he'd go out and turn the car round.

'You must all come and see us as soon as you can, Bet,' said Brenda, fiddling about with her compact and lipstick. 'You know we'd be pleased to have you. Only let us know in advance, else we might be out in the car.'

I carried Samantha out to the lav, with the boys following. The path was illuminated by an outside light over the kitchen door, and I could see Dad leaning moodily against the rabbit hutches. 'They're just going,' I whispered to him while I waited for the boys, but he didn't answer.

'Well,' Mum was saying when I got back to the house, 'it's been lovely to see you all. A real nice surprise.' She wrapped a dozen new-laid eggs in individual nests of newspaper and put them in an old carboard box. Brenda protested, but not too much. 'They're lovely, Bet, I do miss a nice fresh egg. And we enjoyed our teas, I hope we didn't put you about too much.'

I carried Samantha out to the car, flourishing a torch to light the way for the boys. Ray wound down the driver's window. 'Sorry, Janet,' he mumbled. 'Didn't mean to be personal. All the best, eh?'

I gave Samantha a big hug before handing her over to her mother. Brenda brushed my cheek with hers and pushed two coins into my hand. 'I know you're grown up, Janet, but I daresay you can spend it. Thanks for looking after the children, Samantha's taken quite a fancy to you. Hope you get on all right at college. It'll be nice to have a BA in the family, we shall be real proud of you.'

Mum and I stood at the gate to watch the lights of the car disappear down the lane. 'You little devil,' she said with vexation, though she was signalling affectionate farewells with the torch, 'you little devil, our Bren,' and I thought it would be tactless of me to mention Brenda's present of four bob.

Chapter Ten

We had a good row after they'd gone.

Dad said what he thought about Mum's relations, and she said what she thought about his mother, and I said I was sick to death of being got at. They agreed that they should never have married, and I pointed out that I hadn't asked to be born. Mum said she'd clear off and leave us, and Dad said if anyone cleared off it would be him, and I said I'd leave school and get a job in town and they could do what they liked. Mum cried with tiredness and vexation, and I sulked with bad temper, and Dad said he hated women anyway and stamped out to brood over the rabbits.

'Let's clear this lot away and have a cup of tea,' said Mum, drying her eyes. So we washed up together and agreed that at least we shouldn't see any more of Brenda and her family for another year, but that Samantha was a dear little girl. Then Mum made the tea and Dad sloped in and we finished off the swiss roll and spent a nice quiet evening, Mum knitting, Dad reading, me reading, and all of us watching the telly.

We had to get up early on Sunday to catch up with the jobs we should have done on Saturday afternoon, including the remainder of the washing. Mum's dream of luxury is a washing-machine. She's saving for a twin tub with a spin-dryer, like Brenda's, but until she gets it she still has to do the washing by hand. At least she's got an electric boiler now, though, so she doesn't have to heat the water in the old copper. And it was a good blowy day, ideal for drying.

While Dad carried water to fill the boiler, Mum began collecting dirty clothes together. She gave me a searching look as I stood at the sink washing up, and I knew why. There are times when she regards me simply in terms of potential dirty washing.

'What shall you wear this afternoon?'

'My best, of course.'

'I thought you might be wearing your school uniform, seeing as how you're going out with a teacher.'

'Oh, for heaven's sake . . .'

'I could wash that blouse if you took it off.'

'I can't wear just the sweater, it scratches.'

'Well, if I'm spending Sunday morning slaving over the wash, I'm not having you filling up the basket again directly after dinner. Give it here.'

We'd quarrelled enough for one weekend, so I sacrificed the blouse and itched for the rest of the morning.

While Mum got on with the washing, I carried the living-room mats out to the garden fence and brushed them in a cloud of dust, then swept the floor and gave the lino a bit of a polish for luck. Dad had the nastiest job, scrubbing out the lavatory and digging a hole in the garden for the contents of the bucket. The youngest Crackjaw kids stood on the other side of the fence goggling at him. Their lav hasn't been scrubbed out in living memory.

By eleven, we were glad to sit down for five minutes. I've tried to persuade Mum to buy Nescafé, but it's not just that it's more expensive, she really prefers bottled Camp coffee essence mixed with hot water and evaporated milk.

'What shall you spend your money on, Janet?' asked Dad as we drank the gluey mixture.

I gave him a quick look, wondering how he knew about Brenda's four bob. But then I remembered the two pounds Miss Massingham had given me. 'Clothes,' I said promptly, feeling rich and happy.

That interested him immediately. He liked clothes, and though he hardly ever bought anything new unless it was essential he was always very particular about his appearance. He polished his shoes every day, and wore a fresh shirt for work three times a week, and regularly sponged and pressed his suit. Mum sometimes called him an old woman, but I was thankful my Dad was like that. It would be disgusting to have someone as slovenly as Ziggy Crackjaw for a father.

'Have you saved enough for your boots yet?' he asked.

'Nearly.'

'What sort shall you get?'

I recalled the enviable boots Mrs Bloomfield had been wearing. 'Tan suede,' I said. 'With about a two-inch heel.'

'Very smart.' He thought about it as he drained his cup. 'Though I prefer the look of the soft black leather ones, meself.'

'Well,' said Mum, 'I don't know why you want to go spending

pounds and pounds on them fancy boots, when you've got a perfectly good pair of wellies.'

You just can't talk to her, she's got about as much clothes-sense as the hens.

We had a hen for dinner that day. If I'd had any occasion to mention it at school afterwards I'd have said we'd had chicken for lunch; I'd learned the idiom. But what we actually had was an old hen, boiled, for our dinner. Mum had killed it on Friday night and plucked and drawn it before she went to bed on Saturday.

'Which one's this?' said Dad, inspecting a yellowish forkful.

'The Old Rhode Island. She was a good layer in her time, but there, no use feeling sorry for fowls. She eats all right, anyway.'

After I'd helped Mum wash up, I gave the bowl a thorough going-over with Vim, poured out a kettleful of hot water, undressed and had a good wash. Then I put on my raincoat for decency and went through the living-room and upstairs to change.

My best wasn't exactly sensational, just a newish skirt and a non-itch sweater. I didn't need Mum to tell me that with over a mile to bike down to the village in all weathers, it was no use hankering after flimsy clothes. Biking doesn't do tights much good either, but I put on a new pair regardless.

I brushed my hair and looked at my face. It was depressingly round and healthy, no character there at all. I'd recently bought a pair of false eyelashes from Woollies for a giggle, but when I finally got them fixed I looked just like a cow, so I pulled them off and did what I could with eyeliner. Finally I put on the dark green poncho that Mum and I had made from a cut-out-and-ready-to-sew offer in her magazine. My school shoes spoiled the effect, it really needed boots, but when I went downstairs Dad looked up from the week's supply of shirts he was ironing and said affectionately, 'You do look nice, our Janet. Hope you have a lovely time.'

Mum, having her feet-up Sunday afternoon treat, kept her eyes on the old film on the telly. She shifted a boiled sweet to the side of her mouth and what she said was, 'Have you got a clean hanky?'

'Oh, *Mum*.'

'And have you remembered your money this time? Mind how you behave, then, and don't miss the last bus.'

Joe Willis was driving. I was quite surprised to see him on a Sunday, and evidently he was surprised to see me. 'Well, well,' he said, looking quite impressed as he took my fare. 'Hardly recognized you, all dressed up. Going to meet your boy-friend?' 'That's right.'

Joe winked. 'Tell him not to do anything I wouldn't – that'll give him plenty of scope!'

I blushed, thinking that chance would be a fine thing. As the bus toured the villages, gradually filling with families who looked as though they were going to Sunday tea with relations in Breckham Market, I longed for an unattached man to come and sit next to me and start a conversation. I'd been hoping that for years, in buses and coffee bars and the public library, but it never happened. There seemed to be a severe shortage of unattached men in my part of Suffolk. Roll on university, and a start to living.

The bus arrived in town just before four, as it was getting dark. There was an hour to fill before I could present myself at Mrs Bloomfield's, and nowhere to go on a Sunday except for a walk. To begin with, I went through the market place, down Bridge Street, and along the riverside to check discreetly where she lived. Then I circled back to the town centre, intending to look at the lighted shops, but the cold wind funnelled through the streets and up my poncho and round the seat of my tights. I had to walk fast to keep warm, so to kill time I had to go further than I'd intended. The main Yarchester road was well-lighted so I stepped briskly out along it, past the police headquarters and the library and on towards the new by-pass.

The wind was making my eyes water. I was also beginning to feel nervous about going to tea with Mrs Bloomfield, and then meeting her friends. I wanted to make a good adult impression, cool and confident, but I had no idea what to talk about and I was afraid that I might come out with some stupid Mum-type remark. Nervousness made my nose feel runny, and I stopped in the shelter of a garden hedge and opened my shoulder bag to find my hanky.

It wasn't there. I searched the bag, but I hadn't got one. I'd snapped at Mum for treating me as though I were a kid by asking if I had a clean hanky, but suddenly I knew perfectly well that I hadn't brought a hanky of any description. I'd been using one of Mum's waste-not-want-not pieces of old sheet that morning, and I'd thrown it on the fire before I had my wash, intending to take a proper hanky from my bedroom drawer. But, like a fool, I'd forgotten.

Turning my back on the street I opened my poncho and searched my clothes, hoping to discover a secret pocket where Mum might have thoughtfully planted an emergency hanky. No such luck. My nose definitely began to run, and sniffing only made it worse. Going to Mrs Bloomfield's suddenly turned into an ordeal. Fine and cool I'd look, with a running nose and a sniff. The evening was ruined in advance.

Then I had an idea. I pelted all the way back to the town centre, and dodged into the public lavatories in the market place, just behind the Town Hall. The first two cubicles didn't have any paper, but my luck changed in the third. The paper was stiff and scratchy, but I gave my nose a thorough blow and folded some of the sheets to put in my bag. I'd never used the public lavatories before and I was surprised to see that the walls of the cubicle were scribbled with messages. I started to read them, and then realized that they were about the kind of thing we didn't mention in the common room at school, so I walked out red-faced as well as sore-nosed.

I thought it was polite to arrive exactly on time for a social occasion, so I did. Mrs Bloomfield lived in a modern block of flats with several communal doorways, and when I'd found the one with her name against one of the bell-pushes I took a deep breath, combed my hair and gave my nose a final scrub.

If I'd been visiting a school friend I could have asked to borrow a hanky, but Mrs Bloomfield was so elegant that I couldn't associate her with problems like running noses. I certainly couldn't imagine that she'd ever be so uncool as to forget her hanky and dash about over the town trying to find some toilet paper to blow into. I felt a real country twit. As I pressed the bell, I wished I were back at home in front of the fire doing the Sunday crossword puzzle with my Dad.

Chapter Eleven

The sight of Mrs Bloomfield, dressed even more elegantly than she always was in school, unnerved me still more. But she gave me a friendly welcome, and by the time she'd left me alone in her sitting-room for a few minutes while she took my coat away I was so captivated by the central heating, soft lighting and furnishings that I couldn't wish myself anywhere else. This was it. This was how I wanted to live, surrounded by warmth and books and pictures, with carpet from wall to wall and curtains and cushions that matched. This was what I was aiming for, and what made it well worth my while to slog on towards university and the eventual well-paid job.

My eyes must have been out on stalks. 'You like my flat?' Mrs Bloomfield said.

'Oh, *yes*. It's very – ' I rejected the first word I thought of and scrabbled round in my head trying to find something less banal. You'd think that after seven years at the grammar school I'd have acquired a reasonably wide vocabulary, but when I'm trying to make a good impression it deserts me. ' – nice,' I finished unavailingly.

'Thank you,' she said, making it sound as though she valued my opinion. 'It suits me well enough, for the time being, but it's too cramped for permanent living. Did I tell you that I'm hoping to move out to a house in Ashthorpe?'

'The village where you grew up? Yes, you told me. I just can't imagine anyone wanting to go back like that, though – I shan't, once I get away from Byland.'

She laughed. 'That's what I once thought, so don't be too sure. Not that I'd want to go back to the living conditions we had when I was young, of course. We lived in a poor old house that was officially condemned as unfit for human habitation.'

'*Really?*' I was astonished, and at the same time highly chuffed. It hardly seemed possible that someone like Mrs Bloomfield could have emerged from a house no better than ours, but it was a liberation to hear it. I began to enjoy myself as we swapped details of rural inconveniences, and I felt relaxed and confident, thinking that there was no reason why I shouldn't do as well for myself in the future as she had done.

'People who've been brought up middle-class don't realize what real country living is like, do they?' she said. 'My husband never did believe it – he thought I was making the whole thing up.'

She spoke lightly, but I sobered out of respect for her widowhood. I'd already noticed a man's photograph, framed, on a writing table, but it had seemed impolite to stare at it. Now I did, and saw that he was very young and handsome, in the uniform of an RAF officer with pilot's wings on his tunic. It seemed desperately sad that he should have been killed.

I said the first thing that came into my head: 'Was he shot down?'

Mrs Bloomfield looked puzzled. 'Shot down? No, he was involved in a mid-air collision.' Her puzzlement changed to a wry smile. 'He wasn't old enough to be in the war, you know.'

Oh, no – what a stupid thing I'd said! I blushed and curled up inside with shame at my tactlessness. Of *course* he wasn't killed in the war – if he had been, all that time ago, his widow would have to be pushing fifty by now. Oh, what a fool I'd made of myself!

Mrs Bloomfield had immediately steered away to the subject of the *War Requiem* we were going to hear that evening and was talking about Benjamin Britten and Wilfred Owen, but I sat dumbfounded by my own folly. I'd been so pleased with myself a few moments ago, imagining that because we shared similar backgrounds I was on the way to becoming as sophisticated as she was. What a hope! Longmire End was about all I was good for. My nose began to run and I fumbled in my bag for a piece of scratchy paper, trying to hold it so as to conceal the perforated edge.

But at least that particular problem had a possible solution. When she went to get tea ready, I asked if I could – er, wash my hands. Her bathroom was a bit cramped but wonderfully warm, with thick towels and luxurious-looking bottles and jars. And as I'd hoped, she went in for soft toilet paper. I had a thankful blow, and helped myself to a few extra sheets to take away. I'd have preferred it to be white rather than that give-away apricot shade, but I knew what Mum would have said about beggars.

I cheered up over tea. I'd had a second helping at dinner, just in case tea turned out to be a polite affair of a cake balanced on a saucer, but Mrs Bloomfield had provided super open sandwiches. At home we only have salads in summer, rabbits' grub really, what lettuces they don't eat we do. This was a winter salad on brown bread, a crisp and fruity mixture with what I thought was probably clotted cream, until she said it was cottage cheese. And afterwards real coffee, hot and strong from a percolator, and a cake with walnuts in it. I'd never had such a delicious, exotic meal.

As we ate, she talked encouragingly about university. She'd been to Oxford, and loved it. Obviously that was where she'd acquired her sophistication, and by the time she'd finished telling me about it I knew that I wanted to go there too. 'Though student life has become a lot more political since my day,' she added. 'Are you planning to join the militants?'

'Certainly not,' I said promptly. 'All I want to do is get a degree.'

I could hear how selfish that sounded. 'It doesn't mean that I don't feel bad about the Vietnam war and everything,' I explained. 'And I suppose I may get involved in politics later on. But what I want at the moment is to join the system, not fight it.'

Mrs Bloomfield understood, as I'd hoped she would. 'I'm sure you're right,' she said. 'Our parents had to make a lot of sacrifices for the sake of our education. It would be most unfair to yours if you spent your time at university being disruptive. Worse still if you turned hippy and dropped out – but I don't imagine you'll be doing that?'

'No chance,' I assured her. 'I don't want to drop out, I've been out all my life. I want to drop in!'

She poured more coffee, and offered me a cigarette from a box of polished wood. I didn't very often get a chance to smoke, but I knew I was practised enough not to cough over it so I accepted, trying to handle the cigarette as elegantly as she did.

'I haven't forgotten the book you lent me,' I said. 'I haven't quite finished it.'

'No hurry. You're enjoying the poems?'

'Especially John Donne.' I was glad I knew how to pronounce the name.

She twitched an eyebrow. 'The erotic ones that don't get into school anthologies?'

117

I blushed. 'I can see why not. They were – a surprise.'
Revelation would have been a more accurate word, but I'd once
made someone snigger by confusing the word with 'relevant'
and mispronouncing it as 'relevation', and I didn't want to risk
it.

I inhaled, trying to give myself the confidence to say what was
on my mind. I didn't want to be indelicate, particularly with a
widow, but I was desperate for some information about sex from
someone articulate who'd had the necessary practical experience. Mrs Bloomfield was the one person I'd been honest with,
who knew all about me, and this was an opportunity I couldn't
afford to miss.

'When I said that all I wanted from university was a degree,' I
began, 'I didn't mean that I didn't want to enjoy life too. You
know what social life's like in a village, practically non-existent.
I'm looking forward to making up for what I've missed.'

'I know the feeling. And it'll be no problem. You'll find as
much social life as you can handle, whichever university you go
to.'

'Yes, well, that was really what I was wondering about.
Because of the poems.' I tapped ash from my cigarette, thankful
to have something to fiddle with. 'In the anthology, there are
those – er, erotic poems. And then there are the poems about
true love, "inter-assured of the mind," and all that.'

'Yes.' She didn't seem to see what I was driving at. 'And there
are of course poems that are both,' she added, obviously trying
to be helpful.

That hadn't occurred to me. 'Both?'

'Of course,' she said lightly. 'They're not mutually exclusive,
are they? Constancy doesn't preclude sexual pleasure.'

I'd honestly thought that it did. That was how I'd got
muddled, thinking that it was a question of True Love versus
Sex. I ought to have had the sense at that point to shut up and
go away and have a re-think, but like the idiot I was I plunged
on.

'But they don't *necessarily* go together, do they? And what I'm
not clear about is whether you – I mean one, not you personally
– can afford to wait to make sure. If one can't find the ideal, the
marriage-of-true-minds bit, does one settle just for pleasure?'

'No, one most certainly does not!' Mrs Bloomfield spoke so
firmly and stubbed out her cigarette so emphatically that I

118

thought for a moment I'd offended her. 'Never, ever "settle for" anything. If you're doubtful about a relationship, don't let yourself be rushed. You've got your whole life ahead of you – for goodness' sake give yourself time.

'Talking of which,' she continued, looking at her watch and then offering me a brisk smile, 'we ought to make a move. It's always difficult to find anywhere in Yarchester to park.'

I stood up clumsily, feeling that I'd been given a verbal rap over the knuckles. The fact that I'd asked for it didn't make me any less sore. Mrs Bloomfield smiled at me again, only this time it was a dazzler. By way of compensation, I suppose.

'Does he live in your village?' she asked.

I couldn't imagine who she was talking about. 'Who?' I said.

'Your boy-friend.'

So *that* was why she'd been so emphatic. I felt myself going red round the ears because she'd misunderstood me. I wanted to tell her the truth, but it was just too difficult. Besides, I was urgently in need of a morale-booster, and she'd reminded me that I had one ready made.

'Well, yes,' I admitted bashfully. 'He's a farmer's son, actually. His name's Andrew, and he's half-Polish so he's very interesting – '

I'd never thought that I would live to be thankful for Andy Crackjaw, but at that moment I was.

As Mrs Bloomfield had anticipated, it was very difficult to find anywhere to park in Yarchester, particularly near the cathedral. The performance of the *War Requiem* was being conducted by the composer, and that had brought in an audience from all over the region. We arrived with less than ten minutes to spare, and I was quite glad because it meant that I didn't have to say much to Mrs Bloomfield's friends.

They'd saved seats for us near the front and she introduced me to them, two couples and an unattached man. They all greeted me in a friendly way, and I was delighted to find myself sitting next to the unattached man until I realized that he really wanted to be next to Mrs Bloomfield. I couldn't blame him for that, but I didn't much like playing gooseberry between them. I began to wonder whether Mrs Bloomfield had invited me just to keep him at a distance.

119

And then the performance began. It was the first live concert I'd ever been to, and although I knew the Wilfred Owen poems I was afraid that I was going to find the music impossibly obscure. But I needn't have worried. There must have been all kinds of fine points that I couldn't possibly appreciate, but I had no difficulty in getting the message. I was overwhelmed by the music, stunned by the violence and beauty and pity of it all.

After the last note died away down the long nave of the cathedral the silence was complete. I sat with my eyes closed, unable to do anything about the tears that slid down the side of my nose.

I felt a sense of almost personal involvement, remembering my visit yesterday to our church and the Massingham memorials I'd seen there. Miss Massingham's brother had been killed in the same war as Wilfred Owen and I wept for him, and for his son, and for the hundreds of unimaginable thousands killed in war.

The emotion was collective. There was no applause and no one spoke. It seemed that everyone was deliberately not looking at everyone else. Mrs Bloomfield and I shuffled with the crowd towards the exit, shoulder to shoulder but carefully avoiding contact.

As we progressed, I noticed an overweight, bespectacled middle-aged man and woman just ahead of us. There was nothing remarkable about them, but I happened to be watching just at a moment when their hands reached blindly, met and clasped.

Ordinarily I'd have thought it comic if not rather disgusting to see such an unprepossessing pair holding hands in public like that. Now, though, I saw them as enviable. Constancy, that was it. Perhaps some pleasure too, even at their age. But what moved me was the simplicity of the gesture, the tenderness. I realized the importance of having a hand to hold, and I felt desperately alone.

Understandably, Mrs Bloomfield's eyes were glistening too. But the unattached man was just behind her, obviously longing to offer her his support. I had no one to turn to, I felt an outsider, conspicuous. I had to get away.

I leaned towards her ear and croaked, 'I'll have to rush for my bus. Thank you, it's been a marvellous evening.'

'Oh, don't go now, Janet,' she protested. 'We're all going to

120

have coffee at the Duke's Head, and then I'll drive you back to Byland. I said I would, remember?'

'I know, and thank you. But Mum's expecting me on the last bus.'

I dodged away without a glance at her friends, escaped through the dimly lit cloisters, and ran as hard as I could out of the cathedral close, up past the castle and on towards the bus station. There were two or four people I knew, at least by sight, waiting there for the bus to Saintsbury via Breckham Market and all the villages between. I suppose they'd been having an evening out in Yarchester. They were all in couples, naturally.

I lurked in the damp ladies' room until the bus arrived, and repaired my eyes with the help of Mrs Bloomfield's apricot-coloured loo paper before I felt able to brave the local faces. Sitting alone on the bus as we jolted on the long journey home I tried to appear cheerful, but really I felt wretched, cold and hard inside, an unwilling listener to the giggling, scuffling couples in the back seats.

There was nothing else to think about, except that I'd made a fool of myself at Mrs Bloomfield's. But then I remembered how wonderful the rest of the evening had been, with music soaring round the high stone tracery of the cathedral roof. With an experience like that to recall, who needs human contact?

I was kidding myself, of course. But when you're lonely you have to.

Chapter Twelve

The letter was waiting for me when I got home from school one evening, muddy and snarling because I'd fallen off my bike in the pitch-dark lane.

'What a mess you've made of that skirt!' said Mum. 'You're worse now than when you were a kid. Give it here.' She hustled me out of it and hung it over the clothes-horse to dry in front of the fire. 'Oh, there's a letter for you from Oxford.'

'What's it say?'

'How do I know?' She was quite indignant but I wouldn't put

121

it past her to have steamed it open, she'd had plenty of time during the day. I would have done if I'd been her.

I was excited but I tried to appear nonchalant as I read it, standing there in my school blouse and cardigan and laddered tights. 'The college wants to interview me,' I said, handing her the letter. She read it slowly, between the lines as well.

'It says you've got to stay the night.'

'That's to see if I snore. They won't take you if you do.'

Mum stared at me suspiciously. 'Go on with you,' she said. 'And make yourself decent, do, before your father gets home.'

Dad was so thrilled when he heard the news that I felt obliged to dampen his enthusiasm. 'It doesn't mean I'll be accepted,' I pointed out. 'They interview no end of people but they only take a few.'

'No reason why you shouldn't be one of them,' said Dad proudly. 'At any rate, you'll go there wearing your new boots.'

'Haven't saved enough money yet.'

'I'll make it up.'

I could have hugged him, but we didn't do that kind of thing in our family.

'And I've thought of something an' all,' said Mum. 'It's time you had a frock to wear, I'm sick of seeing you in skirts and jeans. How about this?' she plonked her magazine in front of me. That week's cut-out-and-ready-to-sew offer was a dress in the latest style and a super choice of colours.

'That'd suit you a treat, our Janet,' said Dad. 'I'd have it in the geranium if I was you.'

I didn't think there'd be time for it to arrive before the interview, let alone for us to sew it up, but as Mum said it was worth a try. She gave me the money, and the next day I got permission to go down town in the dinner hour to buy the postal order and send it off. Then, feeling bold, I fastened my raincoat up to the collar to hide my school tie – at least in the sixth form we were allowed not to wear our school berets – and sloped into a coffee bar.

The coffee was frothy, not nearly as good as Mrs Bloomfield's, but a lot better than Mum's. I had a shock, though, when they charged me one and threepence for it. I'd been going to order a cheese roll as well, but I changed my mind and bought ten of the cheapest cigarettes instead. They cost more than the cheese roll would have done, of course, but they'd last longer. There didn't seem to be any point in buying matches when I could swipe a box from home, so I cadged a light from the nearest unattached man, who looked like a sales rep. He flicked his lighter for me, but went on chewing. I didn't seem to have much luck with men.

Most of the girls in the coffee bar looked as though they were secretaries. I wondered what it would be like to be one of them, working in an office from nine to five, five days a week, with coffee and a roll for lunch at the same time and in the same place every day. I envied them their clothes and pay packets, but what had they got to look forward to? A yearly fortnight on a Spanish beach with a lot of other English people, a white wedding and a bungalow on a new housing estate, two children, and then back to work in town nine to five, five days a week. They probably thought I looked a freak in my navy raincoat, but I knew that I was the lucky one. All the world ahead, and money in my purse to boot.

In the end I bought the soft black leather ones that Dad had said he liked. Well, not actually leather at that price, but they looked as though they were. And what I'd saved on boots I invested in a cheap pair of fashion shoes to go with my dress.

Mum had a wild spending spree on my clothes that week. I was bumping down the lane one evening, home to tea, when I saw a flashlight wavering ahead. 'Is that you, our Janet?' she called, blinding me with her light.

'What are you doing out in the dark? The owls'll catch you,' I said, feeling affectionate for once and getting off my bike to trudge beside her. There was no field work to be had at that time of year, and she didn't usually go down to the village late in the day except for her monthly game of bingo.

'Been to the chapel jumble sale,' she said, sounding pleased with herself. 'Got something for you.'

'Oh ar,' I said cautiously. Mum loves jumble sales, but she does tend to lose her head. We've had many a row over whether I'll be seen dead in some of her bargain buys.

A few of the girls at school loved dressing up in jumble-sale tat, preferably fur coats and trailing skirts and feathered hats. They thought it was a great giggle. But they were the ones with plenty of money and a wardrobe full of clothes. They'd got nothing to aim for, so they did it to express their boredom with the conventional two-car and constant-hot-water way of life. I wasn't so keen on having to wear baggy old jumble-sale clothes because we couldn't afford new ones.

Mum wouldn't tell me what she'd bought until we'd reached home and made up the fire and put the kettle on. 'There,' she said, handing me a crumpled bag. I pulled out a long nylon garment, all lemon-yellow frills and flounces.

'What on earth – ?'

'It's a housecoat,' Mum explained. 'If you're stopping the night at that college there's bound to be a bathroom to go to. Can't wander about in your raincoat like you do at home. Mrs Vernon sent it to the sale,' she added, 'so we know where it's been. You like it, don't you?'

'It's fabulous,' I said, and meant it. Giggling, I tried it on over my clothes and twirled round the room with the frilly hem brushing my shoes. I could just imagine Mrs Vernon swanning about in it up at Longmire Farm, and I practised the gracious wave that she always gave us from her car. 'Thank you, Mother.'

'Stop acting so soft,' said Mum. 'And take it off before you spoil it. It smells clean enough but I'll give it a wash to be on the safe side.'

'How much was it?'

'Never you mind. I'm not asking you to pay for it, am I? Well, five bob if you must know. I reckon it's a real bargain.'

Later that evening I asked Dad to trim my hair. He fancied himself as a hairdresser and always did it for me, tucking a towel round my neck as I sat on a chair in the middle of a newspaper island.

'How about cutting it short, Dad?' I asked, thinking that a shorter style might make me look more sophisticated.

'I shall do nothing of the sort,' he said indignantly. 'It's lovely and thick and I'm not going to spoil it.' And I didn't argue because I knew that he minded that his own hair was beginning to get very thin in front. He did once try brushing it forward to hide the fact that it was receding, but it didn't suit the shape of his face so he had to learn to live with an increasingly high forehead.

'Well,' said Mum, 'I wish you would cut it short. I hate long hair, it's not hygienic.' We took no notice of her.

The cut-out-and-ready-to-sew dress arrived just two days before the interview. I was tremendously pleased with it, the first good dress I'd had for years and my first go at being in the

124

fashion. That evening I stood on a chair trying to be patient while Mum and Dad both fussed round me fitting it, clucking like a couple of old hens.

'What about the length, Janet?' mumbled Dad, pins between his teeth.

'Well it's too short like that, Vincent Thacker,' said Mum. 'Let it down, do.'

If Mum thought it was too short, it was bound to be too long. 'Up a bit,' I said. 'Bit more. How does that look?'

'Just right,' said Dad.

Mum nearly went frantic. 'I'd never have bought it for you if I'd known you were going to wear it as short as that. All the trouble I've taken to bring you up decent – I'd have been ashamed to show so much leg when I was your age. Let it down!'

We ignored her. Mum's so respectable that she'd say 'Pardon' if she burped in private.

And the next night was bath night. There was never a dull moment at our house. We normally had our baths on Saturday night, but it was such a performance that we'd agreed to postpone last Saturday's event until the night before my interview.

After Dad had finished his tea, I helped him to carry water into the house by the bucketful. It was raining, and by the time we'd filled the electric boiler we were so wet that we hardly needed a bath. While the water was heating I vimmed the bowl, and washed my brush and comb and my face and a couple of pairs of tights.

Then we went out to the woodshed, lifted the big zinc bath from its nail on the rafter, shooed a spider out of it and carried it into the kitchen. There wasn't much room left when the bath was in there. I had to edge my way round to the sink to wash my hair, and Dad took his shoes off and stood in the empty bath in his mauve socks while he sloshed a jug of rinsing water over my head.

But at least the tap on the electric boiler fitted over the edge of the bath, so it was easy to fill it. Hot water on tap, a rehearsal for civilization! We all had to use the same bathwater of course, but we played fair. I saved some hot water for Mum to add to hers, then she saved some for Dad. Goodness knows how the Crackjaw tribe would have managed to eke out their hot water on bath night, but as far as we knew they solved the problem by not having baths at all.

Unfortunately, when we'd finished, the bath still had to be emptied. Mum, in her clean nightie, scooped out grey water by the bowlful and poured it down the sink. Dad and I put our raincoats and wellies over our clean pyjamas, and when the bath was liftable we staggered outside with it and emptied it in the ditch at the side of the garden.

'This is what they call the simple life, you know,' I panted. 'Unspoiled rural living . . . Poets write about the joys of it, and people who live in towns really envy us.'

Dad straightened his back and wiped the rain out of his eyes. 'They must need their heads examining,' he said.

Before I went to bed I had a rehearsal with everything I was going to wear and take to Oxford. My new boots were super, and I was glad that the heels weren't quite as high as I'd wanted; my new shoes, bought in a hurry, had higher heels and to be honest they weren't very comfortable. But they looked exactly right with my new dress.

Mum had made up the new dress during the day, with the aid of Gran Bowden's old sewing-machine, and to do her justice she'd resisted any temptation to lower the hem. I was thrilled with it, and so was Dad when I paraded through the living-room. He sounded very proud of me. 'Oh, you do look nice, our Janet. A really smart young woman.'

'Well,' said Mum, tweaking the neckline into a different position and then giving the hem a tug, 'I s'pose you look all right. I don't hold with wearing it so short, but there, it seems to be the fashion on telly. Only you'll have to be careful what you show when you bend down, our Janet. They say there's some goings-on at them colleges.'

'Good grief, I'll only be there one night!'

'One night's plenty,' said Mum darkly.

Chapter Thirteen

I travelled to Oxford on the long-distance bus, taking most of the day to get there. Caroline Adams had been called for an interview too, but at a different college and on a different day. Mrs Bloomfield had sent each of us off with good wishes and a sketch map of the city, so I felt reasonably confident of finding my way round.

My first impression of Oxford, with motels and industrial areas and modern housing estates, and then long Victorian roads and ordinary streets and shops and a windy bus station, wasn't very favourable. The traffic in the narrow streets was worse even than Yarchester's, and walking on the outside of the pavement was like being caught in Gran Thacker's bacon slicer.

But as I approached the centre, I began to see why Mrs Bloomfield had been so enthusiastic about the beauty of Oxford. Not that the spires could possibly dream, with all that traffic thundering through, but they were indisputably there. I peered in medieval college gateways, admiring the honey colour of the stone and the spaciousness of the quadrangles, and I really began to fancy my chances.

Those were the men's colleges, though. When I eventually found my women's college, stuck away in a side road, it was a red-brick Victorian come-down. I was terribly disappointed. Even so, the sight of it gave me apprehensive twinges. Where did I go and who did I see and what did I do? I walked twice round the block to gather courage, and on the second circuit, past the bicycle sheds by the back gate, I found two other uncertain hopefuls to tag along with.

I'd half-expected to be sleeping in a dormitory, and I was very impressed when we were directed to centrally-heated single study bedrooms, empty because the students had gone down for Christmas. This was more like it! A wash-basin with hot and cold water on tap as well! What a wonderful room to be able to call your own . . . It was full of fascinating posters and books and ornaments, and I'd have liked to have a good nose round, but we'd been told that it was almost time for tea and so I

127

washed my face and changed into my new dress and shoes. I was glad to get out of my boots. That soft-looking imitation leather was deceptive, and they pinched. My high-heeled pointed shoes were just as uncomfortable, but at least they hurt in different places.

I made my way to the common room, treading gingerly along polished wooden floors and down the massive staircase. The common room was full of girls of my age, most of them looking not only clever but unfairly attractive as well. We seemed to be divided into two kinds, a few like me on their own and feeling out of place, and the others in groups, knowing each other and talking loudly in posh voices, even more self-assured than the middle-class girls I'd envied in my first years at school. This would be the boarding-school crowd. I'd heard about them, and I didn't see how anyone else could compete.

True, I was more fashionably dressed than most, but that didn't give me any confidence. The glances I got were more amused than admiring, and I realized that I simply looked conspicuous. I wished I'd had the sense to stay in my best skirt and sweater. And in my school shoes.

Before we'd had time to wash down the cake crumbs we were called out individually for interview. I pretended to read a magazine until it was my turn. *Miss* Thacker. I could hardly believe that meant me.

My first interview was with two youngish women who sat on either side of a gas fire looking through what I recognized uncomfortably as my entrance exam papers. The women were cordial but brisk. Every time they invited me to support my written arguments my mind went blank. I said something, heaven knows what, but all I was thinking of was what a poor performance I was giving. I felt as though they'd stood me on my head, shaken out the contents, picked them over, found nothing of interest and shovelled them back. They made encouraging noises as they dismissed me, but I knew that I'd hashed up the interview completely.

There wasn't a lot of time to brood over it before I was called to see the Principal. In a way that was less of an ordeal because she confined herself to general subjects and was clearly trying to be helpful and to understand tongue-tied answers. But her presence over-awed me. I'd never met anyone who was quite so grand. She sat in a great drawing-room of a place and her voice was as deep and rich as her carpet. She was unmistakably a lady, far more so than Miss Dunlop, even gowned in her Speech Day glory, or Mrs Vernon from the farm, or snooty Mrs Hanbury, or poor old Miss Massingham with her barking cough and tribe of cats.

It was the Principal's voice that finished me. 'Just be natural,' Mrs Bloomfield had advised, but now to my horror I found myself doing exactly what Mum would have done in the same circumstances, trying to keep my end up by putting on a posh voice in return. It didn't work, of course. I could hear how stupidly affected it sounded. But the harder I tried to stop myself, the more exquisitely I could hear myself enunciating. The Principal was kind, but I knew I'd blown my chances.

Back to the common room. That was it, then. All over in a couple of hours and no one to blame except me. It wasn't that I'd been set on going to Oxford, but to get as far as an interview and then to be rejected was much worse than not having an interview at all. I felt that I'd really let Dad down. He'd been so proud about it, telling everyone including Mrs Hanbury who would now go out of her way to commiserate, implying at the same time that it was after all a bit much for people like us to aim at Oxford. I only hoped that Mrs Vernon wouldn't get to hear that Mum had bought me her cast-off housecoat for the occasion.

A gong sounded and we all politely after-you'd each other into the dining-room. It would be the first time I'd had evening dinner so I decided that I might as well make the most of it. We sat at huge polished tables, and the cutlery was sized to match. The soup spoons were as big as our table spoons at home. Fortunately, Mum's magazine had occasional articles on etiquette ('Your husband's firm's dinner dance? Remember these few simple rules and you're all set for a happy, carefree evening') so I knew to drink the salt-gravy soup from the side of the spoon without slurping, and to tilt the plate away from me.

My right-hand neighbour was also on her own, a girl with freckles, jutting teeth and wild curly hair. My left-hand neighbour was slim, with long blond hair, and she wore fashionable clothes that made mine look cheap. Which they were. The blonde was laughing with friends on her other side, so I made overtures to the girl on the right who was wearing a skirt and a blouse that were unmistakably home-made.

She said her name was Paula. She had a north-country accent so thick you could cut and butter it, and that cheered me up tremendously. She was ordinary, like me. I could talk to her easily, even if I couldn't always understand her.

She asked where I came from. I knew she wouldn't have heard of Byland so I said Breckham Market, but she hadn't heard of that either.

'All right, then, where are you from?'

'Bratfut.'

I thought about it as we ate grilled fish, and decided that she probably meant Bradford. 'You must be used to seeing Pakistanis about, then,' I said, nodding down the table to where two beautifully composed milky-coffee girls sat in stunning Eastern robes. There aren't any Asians living in my part of Suffolk, and I had to stop myself from staring at them, fascinated.

'Don't be *dafft*,' said Paula scornfully, 'they're Hindu, not Muslim.' I blushed, but at least she didn't seem to hold my ignorance against me. 'D'you fancy coming to this place?' she asked.

I denied it, though I was still feeling sore. 'I shan't get in, anyway, I made a terrible mess of my interview.'

'Oh, that.' She grinned with all her teeth. 'So did I, thank God. Mucked it up good and proper.'

She told me that both her parents were primary-school teachers, and education-mad. Not having been to university themselves, they insisted that their children must. 'And we've all got to go to Oxford, they're Oxford-mad as well. But I hate it down here, it's full of mealy-mouthed southerners. I've got a place at Sheffield University for next October, and that's where I'm going whether Mum and Dad like it or not.'

I didn't much care for the bit about 'mealy-mouthed southerners'. 'I don't see how you can say you hate the place', I said, 'when we've only been here five minutes.'

'Not my first visit,' she said. 'My big sister was here. Got a First, and lost all her character – she's just like a southerner herself now.' Paula said it with a terrible contempt, and I quickly pointed out that I was East Anglian, myself.

'It's not just southern that gets me,' she conceded, 'so much as upper-class. Have you tried talking to any of them? Honestly, it's like trying to communicate with people from another planet. There's one sitting next to you. Go on, have a go.'

130

I looked sideways at the blond girl, and waited for her to stop talking to her friends. Obviously it was going to be a long wait, so I touched her arm. 'Excuse me,' I said in my best voice, and she turned to me immediately, giving me her full attention and the sight of the longest pair of false eyelashes I'd ever seen. 'Could you – er, pass the water, please?'

'Of course.' She not only passed it but poured me half a glass, and I was as charmed as Mum would have been. 'Where are you from?' Her voice was not as grand as the Principal's but it was unmistakably expensive, and I found myself imitating it as I told her Suffolk. I'd come to the conclusion that no one outside the county had ever heard of Breckham Market.

'Suffolk? Oh, soopah – do you know the Hennikers?'

I said I didn't.

'Do you ride?'

At least I was on familiar ground there. 'Oh yes!' I said happily. 'I'm always out and about on my bike.'

I heard Paula snort with laughter, and realized I'd said the wrong thing. The blonde, identifying me as an impostor, raised one quizzical eyebrow. 'Soopah,' she murmured, and turned back to her other neighbour.

'What did I tell you?' said Paula.

'D'you mean your sister made friends with people like that?'

'No chance, if you're an outsider. But she copied them. Got rid of her Yorkshire accent and started being all airy and fanciful. I can't stand that, pretending to be what you're not and denying your origins. I think it's con-temptible, don't you? I mean, you are what you are. This is how I am and I'm not changing my ways to suit anybody. They can take me or leave me.'

I chased some apple crumble ruefully round my plate. Couldn't seem to get the wretched stuff up with just a fork, which I knew was the correct solo implement. Paula shovelled hers in with a spoon, ignoring her fork, and didn't care.

I couldn't help admiring her for her independence. She'd think me completely con-temptible if she knew me, conforming like mad and forever worrying about the impression I was making. And the infuriating thing was that she was probably a lot more successful than I was. I could imagine her talking to the Principal, saying exactly what she thought in her uncompromising accent and probably being given full marks for character, while I got myself rejected as a creep.

At one point during dinner Paula's ears had twitched as she heard a couple of unmistakable north-country voices from further down the table. As soon as we left the dining-room she went in search of them, and I was on my own.

There were plenty of magazines in the common room, some of them women's glossies, and I flipped through them to pass the time before I could decently go to bed. This was another world all right. Impossibly expensive clothes, exotic foods, incomprehensibly enigmatic short stories; no knitting, no cut-out-and-ready-to-sew, no problem page anywhere. Mum wouldn't have enjoyed the magazines, and to be truthful I didn't much either.

One of the glossies specialized in articles on houses and the people who lived in them. The longest article was about a middle-aged professional couple who led a hectic life in London, and decided that they needed a small weekend place in the country where they could recharge their batteries. Exploring unspoiled Suffolk, they had discovered this dilapidated cottage – photograph of a house twice the size of ours and the Crack-jaws' put together, and in much the same condition except that it was older and far more picturesque – and had converted it to a delightful country retreat. Photograph of her in a large comfortable kitchen warmed by an Aga, with decorative plates on a dresser, and a scrubbed pine table on which was arranged a bottle of wine, a trug of apples and what looked like a fancy foreign cheese. Photographs of him in the gardener-tended garden, and of both of them in the chintzy, beamed sitting-room; photograph of amusing rural bathroom, beamed and creeping with potted plants, but of course with a full complement of mod. cons.

It looked delightful. Soopah to live in the country. I curdled inside, socially envious. And then I remembered – I wasn't just a country swede, I was a student for the night. It might be dark and cold and wet outside, but for once I wouldn't have to put on my raincoat and wellies to paddle down to the lav at the bottom of the garden.

Come to that, I could have a bath. Not that I needed one, because I'd come clean, but I hadn't ever bathed in a proper bathroom and so it offered a novel experience.

I went up two flights of stairs and explored my corridor. A room at the end was labelled BATH. One only. Was it, I wondered, for general use? Could I simply help myself, or was I supposed to ask permission? I had a feeling that this bathroom might be for the exclusive use of tutors, and that there would be a whole row of student bathrooms in another corridor. But there seemed to be no one else about and I decided to chance it.

I undressed, put on Mrs Vernon's frilly housecoat, collected my skimpy towel and soap and took guilty possession of the bathroom. I wanted to be quick and quiet, but the pipes groaned and gurgled and the water splashed out so loudly that I nervously turned off the taps when there was still only a lukewarm puddle in the bottom of the bath. I sat in it apologetically and listened. No indignant protests from the corridor so I thought, 'What the hell,' and turned on the taps again. Delicious to feel the water inching hotly up my spine. I relaxed. I was really enjoying myself, for the first time since I'd arrived in Oxford.

And then I heard slip-slap feet coming up the corridor. The door handle turned and rattled. I stopped breathing. 'Anyone there?' said an irritated, superior voice almost certainly a tutor, come to claim her private bathroom. I splashed the water, not wanting to identify myself.

'How long are you going to be?' demanded the voice.

I scrambled to my feet, clutching the towel to me in case she was about to break down the door. 'Just coming out,' I croaked guiltily.

'Fifty-seven,' said the voice, and slip-slapped away.

I didn't dare stay long enough to dry. I simply dragged the housecoat over my wet arms, grabbed my gear and shot out. The corridor was empty. The number of my room was fifty-one, so I hurried along looking for fifty-seven, intending to knock and call out, 'The bath's free,' before scooting back to my room.

Then a girl came round the corner towards me, wearing nothing but a towelling robe so brief that Mum would have died of embarrassment if she'd seen it. I hardly knew where to look myself. I turned away to knock at the door of fifty-seven, and the girl said, 'Well, come in,' in an infuriatingly amused voice.

It was my blond dinner neighbour, blast her. She was about my height, but she managed to give the impression of being at least six inches above me. Her face seemed naked without the false eyelashes, but she obviously felt at no disadvantage and I was suddenly conscious that my fun housecoat must look to her exactly what it was, a serious jumble-sale bargain.

'Was that you wanting the bath?' I said crossly, knowing that she had no more right to it than I had.

She laughed, lightly. Ha ha. 'That was you, was it?'

'Yes. Well, I'm out now.'

'So I see. What kept you?'

I thought she meant it. 'I was as quick as I could be,' I snapped. I turned and swept back to my room, clutching my housecoat so as not to trip over it. It was only when I reached safety that I realized she'd been laughing at my ridiculous haste. But at least she wouldn't find it so amusing when she discovered that I'd forgotten to pull out the unfamiliar bathplug.

Chapter Fourteen

I'd gone to bed so early that I was down to breakfast as soon as the gong sounded. Just as I was finishing, Paula came in and sat beside me.

'What are you doing this morning?' I asked, hoping for company. My bus didn't leave until two and I intended to spend the morning as a tourist, making the most of my first and probably last visit to Oxford.

Paula had no inhibitions about talking with her mouth full. 'What do you think?' She grinned, scrambled egg on her teeth. 'First train back to Yorkshire!'

"Bye, then. Hope you don't get a place here.'

'Thanks. Look us up if ever you're in Bratfut.'

It seemed as unlikely a place to visit as Bombay, so I didn't ask for her address.

I packed my grip and walked out into the streets a free woman, determined to enjoy myself with or without company. A whole day off from school, with the best part of a pound in my purse and four cigarettes left in the packet! It was just after nine o'clock, and not raining all that much. I bought a tourist map, and set off with the enthusiastic intention of seeing as many colleges as possible.

It was disappointing to find that the college grounds weren't open to the public in the mornings, but at least that meant that I could see more of them from the outside. I walked and walked, up and down the streets and along the passages, gazing through gateways and gaping at gables and nearly dislocating my neck to look up at towers and spires. Oxford was splendour in stone, unbelievably handsome.

But three solid hours is a lot of time to spend sightseeing, particularly if you're carrying a grip and it's raining. There was so much time to fill that I made two stops for coffee and cigarettes, and by mid-day I was beginning to feel decidedly queasy.

I was also wet and fed up. My left boot was rubbing painfully against my foot, the same one that had recently been bashed by a hockey ball and kicked by Aunt Brenda. I wanted to sit down and have a rest, but I couldn't face another cup of coffee so I decided to have an early dinner. Lunch, I mean. I'd hardly ever eaten out, so this was going to be another experience.

Coffee-bar food was too expensive, so I knew I couldn't afford most of the other eating-places, even if I'd had the courage to go in on my own. There was always Woolworths, but that was the trouble, because it was bound to be exactly like the one in Yarchester. So I went into the back streets and found an inexpensive-looking café with a menu in the window offering fried eggs with chips, sausages with chips, or beef curry and rice.

I decided to be a devil and have the curry. Yet another experience. It promised an exotic change from Mum's cooking, but I wasn't sure about it when it arrived, a heap of coagulated rice topped with glistening chunks of mustard-coloured gristle. Still, I was committed to paying for it, so I ate as much as I could and washed it down with greasy coffee. My final cigarette tasted rank, and I stubbed it out half-finished.

When I left, with the steamy café filling with men in raincoats and women in headscarves, it was raining steadily. My poncho was far from waterproof, and I decided to shelter in Blackwell's. I'd looked forward to browsing in a big bookshop, but when I got there I found that I couldn't raise much enthusiasm for anything.

I was looking listlessly at a big volume of French Impressionist paintings when my forehead felt suddenly chill. I touched it and found that it was a good deal damper than the rain had made it.

My hair was clinging stickily round my face and my knees seemed to have disconnected themselves from my feet. I didn't feel very well at all. Closing the book, I made for the exit, putting my boots down carefully one after the other, and leaned in the doorway breathing cold rain. Better to stay in the fresh air, I decided. Couldn't get much wetter, anyway.

I would soon have to set out for the bus station, but there was one more place I particularly wanted to see, New College. I turned left out of Blackwell's, in the direction of New College Lane, but I hadn't gone more than a few steps when nausea started to rise in my throat. I swallowed hard, hoping to keep it down by will-power, and walked on gingerly up the lane. A spasm of nausea caught up with me near the college gate, but I tried to keep my mind on medieval architecture. The walls and the tower were blurred and out of focus, though. The harder I stared, the more precariously built it all seemed. And now there was a griping pain in my insides, and it wasn't just nausea I was worried about.

I knew I'd passed a public lavatory somewhere, not too far away if only I could find it. No use trying to hurry, or something desperate might happen. I retraced my wanderings with a slow fixed tread, alternately flushing and shivering as pain and nausea came and went, and I got there with just a whimper to spare.

When I emerged, feeling white in the face, one hand lugging my grip and the other clutching my middle, I had exactly seven minutes to get to the bus station. I don't know how I made it but I did, half-running, half-tottering, with my grip banging against my boots and my feet hurting like hell, desperate to get back home. I'd had Oxford, in more ways than one.

By luck, I got a seat to myself on the bus. I took off my boots and wiggled my toes thankfully. London, here I come!

Mum was resentful when I didn't get a place at Oxford, and Dad was terribly disappointed, but I snapped at her that it was nothing to do with not being posh enough, and explained to him that I'd rather go to London anyway. My only grievance was the waste of time. If Miss Dunlop hadn't insisted on my staying the extra term I could have been in London already,

136

having a go at living. But at least I could now leave school and start to earn some money.

I spent the week before Christmas helping as usual with the mail. A van delivered to outlying houses such as ours, but deliveries in the main part of the village were done by Mrs Howlett, the sub-postmaster's wife, in her postwoman's outfit. The Christmas mail was more than she could cope with single-handed, particularly as her husband needed her help in the office, which was the front room of their house next-door-but-one to Gran Thacker's shop.

The deliveries took me about three hours in the early mornings and two in the afternoons, riding a heavy red post-office bike like Mrs Howlett's. I needed the bike, with its large front carrier, to hold the parcels. There wasn't much actual riding, it was all start and stop and staggering up people's garden paths under the weight of my letter-crammed pouch. I found that my Christmas spirit evaporated rapidly while I was on the job, but with luck and Sunday working I could knock up five or six pounds.

And Gran Thacker was prepared to pay for a little help too, in the week before Christmas when customers went mad and bought enough food for the two-day holiday to last them a fortnight. Dad was run off his feet in the shop, so as soon as I'd finished my morning deliveries I rushed round there and got busy loading up the shelves and filling paraffin cans until it was time to go back to the post office again. We took sandwiches with us and Gran made a pot of tea, as she always did for Dad, and we spent our half-hour dinner break in the store-room with our feet well up, counting off the days until Christmas.

Christmas Day was much as usual, quiet if you didn't count the almighty row the Crackjaws were making on the other side of the wall. I'd decorated the house with the paper chains I'd made when I was a kid, with a bit of holly balanced on top of Gran Bowden's grandfather clock for luck. We didn't have any use for mistletoe. Dad gave me a present of two pounds, and I gave him a lovely flowery tie which he put on straight away. It really suited him. Mum gave me the surprise sweater she'd been knitting every evening for the past month, and I gave her a pound box of Milk Tray. I don't know what they gave each other, they didn't mention it.

While Mum cooked the dinner, with me preparing the spuds

and sprouts, Dad biked down to Gran's, taking our presents: knitted tea-cosy from Mum, tin of tea from me, and a big tin of fancy biscuits from himself. We'd bought the wool and the tea and the biscuits from the shop, of course, so Gran got it both ways, the profit as well as the presents.

As usual, Dad biked back almost as unsteadily as Ziggy Crackjaw does from the White Horse, bringing Gran's present to us. She reckons she doesn't approve of alcohol, but she can't bear to see anything going to waste so she makes it into wine: dandelions, peapods, elderberries, tea-leaves, potato peelings, anything she can lay her hands on. Gran Thacker could make wine out of old boots if she put her mind to it and used enough yeast. Because her wine's home-made she's convinced that it's non-alcoholic, though she might know from Dad's flushed face after one glass that it's got a real kick to it.

This year's present was potato wine; 1968, a good year for potatoes. It tasted earthy, but it went down well with our Christmas cockerel, specially fattened by Mum for the occasion. After we'd stuffed ourselves with bird and veg, followed by Christmas pud, we heated water in the biggest saucepan and washed up together, Mum washing, me drying and Dad putting away. Then we ate once-a-year chocolate mints and watched the telly, and when the Queen came on to wish us a happy Christmas we drank her health, only Mum got hiccups in the middle of it and I had to sober her up with a cup of tea.

Somewhere about five o'clock, we had the traditional family row. While Dad and I were hard at work in the week before Christmas, Mum had gone mad making mince-pies and cakes. Quite apart from the fact that her baking is inedible, we were all too full to eat any tea. But when Dad and I tried to refuse, Mum shouted about our ingratitude after all the trouble she'd taken to please us, and so we ended up as usual eating a heavy tea just to pacify her, and suffering from martyrdom and indigestion for the rest of the evening.

On Boxing Day it snowed, and that night it froze hard. Mrs Howlett, doing her post round solo again next day, slipped on someone's steps and broke her leg.

I wouldn't have wished it on her for the world, but as far as I was concerned it couldn't have happened to a nicer person. The moment I heard the news I rushed down to the post office to volunteer.

For the next three months I was the village postwoman, with an official armband and a big red bike to prove it. It wasn't a full-time job and I didn't qualify for the adult rate, but I had my eighteenth birthday that January and that upped my pay a bit. With overtime, because of the bad weather, I was taking home just over five pounds a week. Fantastic. I gave Mum three pounds, and saved the rest. No expenses; I'd gone off smoking ever since Oxford.

I certainly earned the money, though. It was a very bad winter, snow and ice until the end of March, and once or twice our lane was impassable until Mr Vernon unblocked it with his tractor and snowplough. Dad had to sleep at his mother's during the worst of it, so that he'd be on the spot to open the shop at the proper time. He did offer to ask her if I could sleep there too, but I didn't fancy living in such close proximity to Gran Thacker. I preferred to fight my way through the snow.

I got up at five, every morning except Sunday, and did my best to be at the post office at six, when the mail was due to arrive from Breckham Market. Sometimes it was late getting there, and quite often I was, but whatever the weather and however long it took I managed to complete each day's deliveries somehow. Mr Howlett, the sub-postmaster, had impressed on me that The Mail Must Get Through, and I felt quite heroic about my part in the process.

It's a rotten job in winter, though, setting out from the post office in freezing darkness, back and bike both loaded, to deliver by torchlight. Bike wheels skid on the rutted snow of the roads, legs sink into the roadside drifts, feet slip on icy garden paths, fingers are so numbed that they can't feel the letters. People's letterboxes are either non-existent or sealed up against the draught, so it's trudge round to back doors, 'Good dog, good dog, there's a good boy, shut up you stupid animal,' while the snow crumbles over the tops of your wellies and soaks your socks. I'd have gone on strike, except that no one had asked me to do the job in the first place. So I just thought of the money and ploughed on.

It wasn't quite so bad when daylight came. And there were one or two housewives, Dad's nice regular customers, who would invite me in for a cup of coffee if they happened to see

139

me, and that hope helped to keep me going. I was always careful to stand on their doormats while I drank it, so as not to make a mess on their kitchen floors, and I worked on the principle of never refusing a hot drink, even if I'd just had one elsewhere, in case the offer wasn't made again.

My only exception to that was with old Miss Griggs, who'd been the headmistress when I was at the village school. She lived in a house at the far end of Byland, on the road that led out to where the Hall had once been. Her house was my final delivery point. She had a lot of mail because she belonged to various organizations, most of them to do with wildlife, and she used to watch out for me like a hawk.

I suppose it was a bit mean of me to try to nip up the path, slam the letters through her box and make my getaway before she could open the door. She was retired, and probably lonely, and it was very nice of her to keep on offering me cups of coffee even though I always refused them with the excuse that I was late and had to get back to the post office. But I'd had enough of Miss Griggs when I was at school. By singling me out for her favour she had made my life a misery. If she hadn't been nice to me, I wouldn't have been tormented by Andy Crackjaw, and the memory of that was still so painful that I wasn't prepared to forgive her.

Chapter Fifteen

As the weather improved, so did Mrs Howlett. By the time spring had sprung and the early birds were making a racket in Spirkett's Wood as I rode past in the mornings, I was made redundant. Still, I'd done very well out of the job. Twenty pounds saved, though I'd worn a hole in the seat of my jeans and demolished several pairs of Dad's socks.

Mum said she'd never been richer in her life. With the prospect of field work to come, when all three of us would be out earning, she took it into her head that she'd like to go away for a holiday later in the year. We'd never been away, and Mum fancied going to a Butlin's holiday camp.

'Hope you enjoy it,' said Dad.

'All of us, I mean. A family holiday before our Janet goes to college.'

'I'm not going to a holiday camp,' I said, alarmed.

'Why ever not? There's bingo, competitions, dancing, something for everybody. Enjoy yourself for a change, lovey.'

'I'm saving,' I pointed out. 'I couldn't afford it.'

'I'd help you,' said Mum generously. 'What about you, Vince? You'd come with us, wouldn't you?'

'No, I wouldn't.'

'Well, you miserable devil, Vincent Thacker! Why can't you behave like anybody else's husband?'

'Because I'm not, am I?'

They didn't often take the trouble to have a personal row, so I went to the kitchen and let them get on with it.

'I'm just about sick and tired of you. Just when we get a little extra money and can go out a bit, you won't come with me.'

'I'm not stopping you, am I? You can go by yourself.'

'A fine thing that'd look, having to go on holiday without my husband! You never come out with me. I don't know why I ever married you.'

'You know damn well why you did. You were glad enough to, at the time!'

Dad stamped out and I made a thoughtful pot of tea. This was a new one on me. So I must have been on the way before they got married . . . I'd read some statistics about pregnant brides so I knew it wasn't unusual, but it comes as a bit of a shock when your own parents are involved. Statistics is other people. Besides, it was beyond imagining – Dad and Mum so consumed by passion for each other that they couldn't wait for the wedding ceremony! I decided to ignore it.

'Tea up, Dad,' I yelled, and the Crackjaw mongrel went into hysterics behind their back fence.

Mum clipped the Butlin's coupon from her magazine and sent for the brochure anyway, but when she discovered how much the holiday camp would cost she nearly had a fit. In the end, she decided that she was going to Stopat'um for her holiday, as usual, and put the money towards a washing-machine instead.

Before field work started I spent a few days with Caroline Adams in Breckham Market. It made a change, but I didn't enjoy it much, apart from the use of their plumbing. I bought some new underclothes and dressmaking material in the town, but we spent most of the time mooching about, drinking coffee, and then drifting back to her room to listen to records. Caroline hadn't got a place at Oxford either, so she was going to York. Since leaving school she'd been working for her father, but she'd hated it and had walked out of his office. Her boy-friend Richard was giving trouble, and what with one thing and another she was fed up and couldn't wait to leave home.

The Adamses' house was absolutely luxurious. There were only three of them, but they had a bathroom and a shower room and a downstairs cloakroom as well. Three loos, so they could all go at the same time if they needed to. But it wasn't a happy place. There was a lot of heavy atmosphere when her parents were about, and I was glad to get back to Byland. I found that I was looking forward to spending the summer at home in the country, with no exams to worry about and money to be earned in the open air.

Field work began in May with asparagus cutting. The grower was very particular about having the stalks cut correctly because he sent it to London where it sold for fantastic prices. We were careful, because our pay was docked if we had more than a few rejects, but at least we could take home what we'd been made to pay for. For a couple of weeks we ate asparagus with everything.

After that it was sugar beet hoeing, bring your own hoe. Then the fruit: strawberries, blackcurrants, plums and apples. The work was intermittent but it would keep me busy until term started, and as it was piece work I could earn a useful amount if I really flogged at it.

Between times, I read some of the recommended books and conducted a correspondence with the university lodgings bureau and a list of landladies in order to get a room. Mum knitted like mad for me, and all three of us cut out and pinned and sewed up my new clothes. I couldn't bear to have my hair flopping round my face as I worked out of doors, so I finally persuaded Dad to cut it short for me.

Then it was back to the fields, sometimes on my bike and sometimes on a special bus with Mum and a dozen of the village women. God, how they yackety-yacked! Ribbed me, too, or dropped snide remarks, but I didn't care much. I kept as far away from them as possible when we got to work and they soon started puffing and blowing, bent double with their behinds in the air as they shuffled between the rows, too busy earning to yack any more.

It was hard work, but I enjoyed it. Happiness is a mindless, dirty job. It wasn't much of a life, working throughout the heat of the day and coming home tired and filthy, wanting only a wash and a meal and bed. My face and arms were burned with wind as much as with sun, and my legs and feet were scratched and sore and my hands were stained and my fingernails were broken and the skin on my knuckles was cracked and split, but as I sat at night absorbing an hour's telly and nursing my cuts with ointment, I was happy.

Not madly, sensationally, fantastically, fabulously, groovily happy. Just plain happy. Contented. All my school life I'd been working towards university and now that I was really on my way there I could afford to enjoy my last few months in the country, knowing that I wasn't going to be stuck for life with no plumbing and only my bike for transport, looking forward to making new friends and having great times.

And one reason for my contentment was that, working in the fields, I could be natural. No need to try to make a good impression on anybody, or to pretend that I was what I wasn't. It was a wonderful relief. Remembering Yorkshire Paula, at Oxford, I determined that once I got to university I'd never be con-temptible again. I'd use my own voice, and I'd be proud to tell people that my Dad worked in a shop and my Mum did field work. But I'd be careful not to romanticize our way of life because I know all about the realities of shop and field work. Happiness is a mindless, dirty job *only if you can see an end to it.*

Take strawberries, for example. And please do, because I never want to see another. Strawberry-picking sounds idyllic. But in fact it's muscle-cramping, filthy, nauseating work: creeping at a squat along the rows for hours on end, picking against time to fill your baskets while the season lasts and the weather holds, scrabbling among slug-slime and piercing straws to find the sound, acceptable fruit because you don't get paid for picking anything else, plagued by the flies that cluster on your sweaty skin.

The strawberries rot, slug-nibbled and bird-pecked, on the stalk and the remains squish on your fingers. The strawberry smell is sickening. Individual strawberries are repulsive: mis-shapen, every pore sprouting a whisker, bulbous as an old

143

man's nose. No one works at picking field strawberries for pleasure. If I'd thought that I'd have to spend the rest of my life scratting out on field work just in order to maintain our poor rustic standard of living, I'd have been bitter enough. But that summer, last summer, I was happy, working in the fields while I waited for real life to start.

Then Dad fell out of our apple tree.

Chapter Sixteen

It was a Saturday afternoon towards the end of September, less than two weeks before the beginning of term. I no longer had my Saturday morning job at the shop because Gran Thacker had decided to economize by employing a schoolgirl instead. I didn't mind, because she was a nice willing kid and I knew that Dad would need help when I went to college.

Mum and I had been picking apples all month, and I'd just done my last morning on the job. I wanted to concentrate on getting ready for college, by scrubbing some of the ingrained dirt off my hands for a start. My new second-hand trunk already squatted in one corner of the living-room, partly filled.

Mr Jessup's fish-and-chip van was very late that day. He usually came soon after one, but he still hadn't arrived when Dad got home from the shop at half-past. While we were waiting for our dinner, Dad decided that he might as well make a start on picking our own apples.

The tree in our back garden is a big old Bramley, never been pruned, twenty feet high, needing a ladder. The hard winter had held it back, but in late spring the branches had been smothered with such a fragrant outburst of pink and white blossom that going to and from our lav was a real pleasure. Now the tree was loaded with fruit, enough to keep us in pies throughout the winter. Some of the apples near the top, flushing red in the autumn sunshine, were as big as my two fists, so heavy that I wondered how the crooked twigs could hold them.

Dad had only just climbed up the ladder when the fish-and-chip van arrived. To make the climb worthwhile, he stayed up at the top of the tree to pick a basketful of apples while Mum

144

went to buy the grub. Mr Jessup refused his usual cup of tea on account of being so late, and chugged back down the lane. Mum brought in the steaming parcel, with its mouth-watering fish-in-batter smell, and started to get out the knives and forks and salt and vinegar.

I was at the kitchen sink in bare feet, bra and jeans, having a much-needed wash before we ate, when there was a crack from outside like a gun going off. Then a shout of alarm, more cracking, and an ominous slithering noise. I rushed to the open door in time to see Dad, clutching a broken branch, topple off the ladder and thump down on the grass. The ladder fell with a sickening crash on top of him.

I ran to him just as I was. He lay silent on his back among the apples, his eyes closed, the ladder across his body, leaves and twigs still pattering down. I fell on my knees beside him, fearful that he was dead. 'Dad, Dad,' I urged, and thankfully his eyelids flickered.

Mum arrived panting. 'What shall we do?' she panicked. 'What shall we do?'

'You stay with him, I'll go round to the farm for help.'

I didn't stop to put on my sandals. I dragged my shirt over my wet arms and buttoned it as I ran up the lane, my face stiff with drying soap and fright. I was afraid there'd be no one at home, but Mr Vernon was there in the farmyard, a balding, solid, reliable man doing something to the engine of his Land Rover.

I yammered out my story and he hurried indoors immediately. I heard him calling to his wife in his authoritative middle-class voice: 'Helen! Vincent Thacker's had a bad fall from a tree in his garden. Ring for an ambulance, quickly. I'm going back with Janet.'

I ran back ahead of him, down the lane and through our gate and across the potato patch towards the tree where Mum, and Mrs Crackjaw and two or three of her youngest kids, stood watching over the crumpled figure on the grass.

They had lifted off the ladder. Dad lay flung about, legs and arms anyhow, except for his right knee which was raised in the air, bent as though he were doing a cycling exercise. He was moving his head from side to side, and every now and then he let out a gasping moan.

Mum hurried to meet Mr Vernon, and he assured her that an

145

ambulance would be coming. 'We moved the ladder,' she gabbled, 'but now his knee won't stay down.'

'Shall we carry him indoors?' said Mrs Crackjaw, wanting to be involved. She'd been having trouble again, one of her eyes was discoloured and puffy, but the other was goggling as eagerly as her children's.

Mr Vernon had been bending over Dad, and now he straightened. 'Best not to try anything ourselves,' he decided. 'Might do more harm than good. Best to wait for the ambulance men.'

The Crackjaw kids were hopping round excitedly, stuffing their mouths with handfuls of chips. The smell of fried food was nauseating.

'Clear off,' I told them angrily, not caring whether their mother took umbrage or not. 'Go and eat your dinner at home. And stay there.'

Mrs Crackjaw took no umbrage, but she didn't take the hint either. Her kids went, but she stayed to extract the maximum interest from poor Dad's accident. 'Shall we give him some hot sweet tea?' she suggested.

'Certainly not!' Mr Vernon turned to me. 'Have you got a blanket to put over him, Janet?' I ran to get one from my bed, and on the way back met Mum, followed by Mrs Crackjaw. They'd decided to make a pot of tea anyway.

Dad had begun to shiver and sweat at the same time. Mr Vernon helped me to put the blanket over him, avoiding his raised knee. I crouched beside him, pulled my hanky from the pocket of my jeans and mopped his face as gently as I could, brushing off leaves and twigs at the same time. I felt frightened, especially when he moaned. I was thankful that Mr Vernon was there to take charge, but when he bent to move the splintered branch that was jammed under Dad's back he quickly dropped it muttering, 'Oh God – ' and I knew then that he was frightened too.

Aloud, Mr Vernon tried to reassure me: 'He'll be all right, Janet. The ambulance won't be long.'

He tried to chat to me about going to college, and I gave him distracted, disjointed answers. Then Mum returned, Mrs Crackjaw still following, carrying a tray of tea. Only she hadn't brought it in our everyday mugs, she'd gone and got out the best cups and saucers, unused since Christmas, and poured the sugar into a bowl as well.

'One spoonful or two?' she asked Mr Vernon in her poshest voice, crooking her little finger genteelly. And we stood about drinking tea while we waited in the September sunshine for the ambulance to come, gazing helplessly at Dad as he lay groaning with his knee bent in the air, trying not to notice that from underneath the blanket a dark liquid was steadily seeping out among the apples on the dusty grass.

In the evening, Mr Vernon kindly drove to Yarchester hospital to pick up Mum, who'd gone with Dad in the ambulance. He was having an operation, and we were to ring the hospital next morning to hear how he was.

Mr Vernon said that we could use the telephone at the farm, to save us going all the way down to the village, but I had to go down in the morning – Sunday – anyway, to see Gran Thacker. I'd biked down the previous evening to tell her what had happened. Now, having had time to get over the shock, she was resentful, demanding to know how long Dad was going to be in hospital and how she could be expected to run the shop single-handed. I used her telephone, and the hospital said that Dad was having to have a second operation; I was to ring again in the evening.

When I got home, Mum was cooking the Sunday dinner as usual. It didn't seem right, and I was ashamed of feeling hungry, but I was, so I ate it.

I explained to Mum that Gran Thacker was worried about running the shop single-handed, so I'd told her I would help out for the rest of the week. But evidently Mum had been making plans too.

'I'm glad you're going to be there,' she said. 'I shall need you to give me a start. I'm going to go and serve in the shop meself.'

I was incredulous. 'You, in the shop?'

'Why not?' she said. 'I worked there for two years afore you were born.'

That was news to me, but it seemed irrelevant. 'Things are different now, Mum. And you don't know all the prices.'

'Then I shall have to learn 'em, shan't I? You'll be going away in ten days, and your Dad will take longer than that to get better. Until he does, I've got to keep his job open for him.'

'But you don't get on with Gran Thacker.'

'What's that got to do with it? It's a regular job, and we need the money. Beggars can't be choosers, our Janet.'

The rest of the day seemed interminable. I couldn't stop worrying about Dad, so after we'd washed up the dinner things I set to and scrubbed out the kitchen and the lav to pass the time.

At six, I biked down to the call-box in the village. It was nice of Mr Vernon to say I could phone from the farm, but it's embarrassing to have to use other people's telephones, particularly when you're anxious.

Using a public telephone isn't very pleasant when you're in that state either. I had to wait for a man to finish a long call, and when he left I found that the box stank of cigarette smoke, and the receiver mouthpiece was wet with condensed breath. But at least I could make my call in private.

I'd prayed that the hospital would say that Dad was doing well, or making a good recovery, or something equally hopeful, but all they would tell me was that he was as well as could be expected. It sounded ominous. I had another rough night, tossing and turning and worrying, and at one point I got up and knelt by my bed, this time praying properly. 'Please God,' I said, 'make my Dad better soon, Amen.' I felt that it was probably a bit much of me to ask, considering that I still didn't know whether or not I believed in God. But if he does exist, I suppose he's used to being made a convenience of.

Whether God helped or not, when I rang the hospital on Monday morning Dad's condition was said to be stable. He could have one or two visitors for a short time. I was so relieved; I'd missed him so much. Home just wasn't home without Dad.

I'd biked down with Mum to the shop, and telephoned from there. She hated using the phone, she wasn't used to it and got all flustered. She was very agitated that morning, standing ready for the customers in her respectable skirt and cardigan topped by her best nylon overall. At least Dad had recently managed to persuade his mother to invest in a proper till, and now I'd shown Mum how to use it she wouldn't need to add up in her head, which was just as well.

Hospital visiting-hours were every afternoon between two and four. I wanted to go, desperately, but I felt obliged to give Mum a chance, even though she and Dad never had anything to say to each other. I said I'd mind the shop for her that afternoon, if she liked, but she was too harassed to leave it, and when I asked Gran Thacker she said she'd got enough worries without traipsing off to Yarchester on a weekday, so I gladly went alone.

The bus to Yarchester didn't reach Byland until two, and then it dawdled round every village it could find, wasting precious visiting time. And when we reached Yarchester, there was quite a long way to run from the bus station to the hospital. I knew where it was, but I'd never been there before.

The hospital was a great sprawling place, built in bits over the past hundred-odd years, and I wasn't sure which of the many entrances to use. And once inside, in the old original building, it took me five minutes to find the right ward, up stone stairs and along gloomy corridors, a foreboding clinical smell filling my nostrils.

The Sister in charge of the ward directed me briskly. 'Mr Thacker? Last bed on the left. He's still very weak, so you mustn't stay long.'

I hardly recognized him at first. His orange hair seemed to have thinned and faded, and his face was a dirty grey. His shoulder and chest were heavily bandaged, and one leg was in plaster, held up by a pulley. He was attached by tubes to a bottle hanging above his head, and to another bottle on the floor beside his bed. He lay with his eyes closed, and for one terrible long moment I thought he was dead. But when I whispered, 'Dad,' his eyes flicked open. He blinked, and then smiled his wide gentle smile.

'Janet!' he said hoarsely. 'I'm glad it's you.'

I bent over and kissed him, on the lips as I'd always done when I was little. He smiled again, and I felt warm with relief and happiness, because he was going to get better and everything was going to be all right.

'How are you, Dad?'

'Not too bad. Numb, mostly. They've had to do a lot of patching up. Shan't be out yet awhile.'

'As long as you're doing well, that's all that matters.'

'Good as new in a few weeks.' He shifted painfully. 'How are you all managing?'

'Miss you like anything. But we're keeping going, Mum's helping Gran at the shop.'

'I thought she would.'

149

'That's why they couldn't come. They'll be here either Saturday or Sunday. They sent their love, anyway.' They hadn't mentioned it, actually, but I thought it was the right thing to say.

'But you'll come as often as you can, won't you, Janet? Before you go to college, I mean.'

'Every day,' I promised. 'I've been wondering whether I ought to go to college, though. I don't want to be in London while you're here in hospital.'

'Don't be silly, 'course you must go. Your future's more important than visiting me. Anyway, I'll be doing well by then. Probably be home to see you off.'

'Hope so!'

I took his good hand, and we fell into a loving silence. Holding hands was something else I hadn't done since I was little, because once I'd started school Mum had discouraged what she called 'slopping about'. I'd always admired Dad's hands, with their long cool fingers, and now I recalled what a comfort the contact was, I knew that I was never going to take any notice of Mum's dreary edicts again. Not that I wanted to slop about with her, of course. Dad was the one I loved.

He was obviously very tired. His eyes kept rolling up so that only the whites were showing, and I thought it was probably time for me to leave. But then he focused his eyes on me, gave a long swallow and said, 'I've got something to tell you, Janet.'

He took his hand out of mine, reached for the hoist and eased his position on the bed. 'Been meaning to tell you for long enough,' he said painfully. 'You ought to know. By rights your mother ought to tell you, but she never will. I've been worried you'd find out from village gossip – you must have heard the hints and sneers. Haven't you guessed?'

He was hopeful, wanting me to make it easy for him, and I remembered. 'Oh, that! You mean I was on the way before you and Mum were married? I did guess, but I haven't lost any sleep over it. It doesn't matter, Dad, really it doesn't.'

He moved his head restlessly. 'Yes . . . but it's not only that . . .'

Whatever it was I didn't want to hear it. 'Tell me tomorrow,' I said quickly. 'The Sister said I wasn't to stay long.'

'No, I want to get it over with. I've got to tell you, Janet. Please.' He was upset, pleading with me, and I knew I couldn't

150

walk out on him. His voice was fainter, and I bent my head towards him as he forced himself to talk.

'It's true that your mother was expecting before we got married. That's the only reason why we married. We didn't . . . we didn't love each other.'

No problem so far. I'd never thought of Mum and Dad as a loving couple. Caroline Adams reckoned that her parents hated each other, but I couldn't say that of mine either. Indifferent, perhaps, but certainly not hating.

'That's all *right*, Dad,' I said. 'I mean – I'm sorry, I realize it can't have been much of a life for you. But it doesn't make any difference to me, I've always been very happy at home.'

'I'm glad.'

I thought that was all. 'I really ought to go now,' I said, but he was already struggling to find more words.

'You see – we'd never thought of marrying. Your Mum didn't want to marry me, and I didn't want to get married at all. But you were on the way, and our mothers pushed us into it for the sake of respectability. Your mother and I haven't . . . haven't been husband and wife. Haven't ever been.'

He was agitated, willing me to understand, but I still didn't. Wouldn't. He closed his eyes, and I was glad because it prevented me from seeing the unhappiness in them.

'Janet – ' he said. 'I'm not your real father.'

Once, when I was playing hockey, a rising ball struck me thump in the middle. It didn't hurt badly at the time – that came later – but it left me floundering and breathless. Now I floundered again, sick and bewildered. There was obviously some terrible mistake.

'It's not true,' I said loudly. 'It's not true.'

'"Fraid it is.' He groped for my hand but I was too shocked to touch him. 'I'm sorry, but you had to know. I'd never been interested in girls, you see, and the other lads in the village used to tease me on account of it. That was why I went to sea, to get away from them. But then my father died, and I had to come back to help Mother. Then the teasing and tormenting started all over again, from girls as well, and I couldn't live with it. I had to do something to make them all leave me alone.'

There wasn't anything to say. I just stared at him, dumb with misery. He shifted his position, drew breath and plunged on.

'Betty Bowden – your mother – was working for us in the

shop. A rumour started that she was pregnant, only she wouldn't say who the father was. It was nothing to do with me, but one day I lost my head and told another lad it was, just to shut them all up. Only that got round the village too, of course, and our mothers married us off.

'But it doesn't matter how it happened. That's all in the past. It's worked out real well, that's what I wanted to tell you. I never wanted to marry, never wanted to be a father, but having you as my daughter has made everything worth while. We've had some lovely times together, haven't we? And you'll go on thinking of me as your Dad, you will, won't you, Janet?'

He was feverish, exhausted, his head rolling on the pillow. I knew I ought to leave. I ought to have soothed him and reassured him and said, 'See you tomorrow, Dad,' and then perhaps everything would have been all right. I ought to have tried for once in my life to be tactful and sensitive to the feelings of others but not me, not Janet Thacker.

Because that was the point: I wasn't Janet Thacker at all, and if I wasn't Janet Thacker, who was I?

It was natural enough to want to ask, but I shouldn't have done it then, not when he was so ill and weak. But stupid, selfish Janet had to open her mouth and let the words come right out, thinking only about herself and never mind about Dad. Because he wasn't my Dad at all:

'Who – ' I croaked, 'who is my father, then?'

He closed his eyes. 'I don't know.'

I knew that he knew and didn't want to tell me. 'You must tell me,' I said. 'I've got a right to know. If you don't tell me, I'll ask Mum.'

'No, don't,' he begged. 'Don't let on that I've told you, it'll only upset her.' He put out his hand weakly but I wouldn't take it.

'Who is it, then?' I insisted. I thought quickly of all the men of the village who would have grown up with Mum, and I couldn't bear the thought that any of them might be my real father, but I had to be told. 'Is it someone I know?'

'No – no, truly it's not.'

A passing nurse told me it was time I went. I got up, but I had no intention of leaving until I knew the truth. 'Tell me!' I hissed angrily. 'You've got to tell me!'

Sweat was gathering on his face. He seemed to be drifting

away from me. He opened and closed his lips, trying to get the words out. Eventually he whispered, 'An American. From the airfield. They were all over the village in those days. You mustn't blame your Mum, she was very young – '

'But who was he? What was his name?'

'I don't know.'

'I'll ask her, then.'

'No, don't. She doesn't know.'

'Of course she does. If she had a love affair with him she couldn't forget his name. What was it?'

'She doesn't know . . . It wasn't . . .'

'Wasn't what?'

'It wasn't love – she doesn't know which one . . .'

My arm was suddenly gripped from behind. It was the Sister, sternly pulling me away. 'You *must* leave now. Your father is still very ill, and you've stayed far too long. You've been very inconsiderate.'

She bent to attend to him and I just stood there, lost. ''Bye, Dad,' I whispered, 'see you tomorrow,' but he didn't hear me.

I walked up the ward. It was two miles long and everybody was watching me and I could hear my shoes clumping on the polished floor. I turned at the door to look back at him, but my eyes were so blurred and there was such a confusion of beds and heads and flowers and pulleys that I couldn't see him at all.

When I telephoned the hospital later that night from the village call-box, shaking with remorse, they said that Dad's condition had deteriorated and was giving cause for anxiety, and when we finally got there they told us he was dead.

Chapter Seventeen

'Are you sure you've got everything, lovey?'

Mum and I were standing at the door of the shop, saying goodbye. I knew she'd want to make a scene of it so I'd gone to bed very early the night before, and pretended to be still asleep when she'd come to call me before she went to work. Mr Vernon had said he was going in to Breckham Market, and had offered to drop me at the railway station. I'd felt that I had to ask him to stop for a minute at the shop so that I could say goodbye, and he was now sitting at the wheel of his car looking tactfully at the other side of the street. But it wasn't going to be a sentimental farewell, on my side anyway.

Mum gulped. A single tear detached itself from one eye and slid downwards, leaving a snail's trail on her cheek. 'You'll send your towels and things home for me to wash, won't you, lovey?'

'No, thanks, I'll take everything to a launderette.'

'That'll ruin your clothes.'

'No, it won't, everybody does it. Well – '

Mum produced a pound note from the pocket of her overall. 'Your Gran said to give you this.'

I was surprised and touched. Old Mrs Thacker wasn't my Gran at all. Even if she believed she was, she must have thought that Mum had snared her son into marriage, which would account for the disapproving way she'd always treated us. In the circumstances it was very nice of her to think of giving me anything.

'Thank her for me. I'll have to go now, can't keep Mr Vernon waiting.'

A customer approached and we stood aside to let her pass between us into the shop. 'Be with you in a minute, Edie,' said Mum. 'Just seeing our Janet off to college.'

'Oh ar. Mind what you get up to, then, Janet.' But she spoke kindly, as people had taken to doing ever since Dad's death.

'Well,' I said, anxious to go. I could see more tears washing round in Mum's eyes. She'd want to kiss me, and I couldn't stand it. 'Cheerio, then.'

She lunged towards me but I dodged. And she didn't understand, and the tears spilled over, and they left me cold. I wanted to shout at her that I'd heard all about her and the American airmen, and to ask if she knew which one of them my father was.

'Mind you write regular, Janet. Take care of yourself, lovey.' She wiped her eyes, and I escaped to the car. She didn't know it yet, but I was leaving home for good. I didn't feel in the least sentimental about it, but Mr Vernon put the radio on and as we left the village I found that I was quite glad to listen to the Jimmy Young programme.

At the station, he insisted on carrying my luggage to the platform. With all the emotional upheaval, I hadn't got round to sending my trunk off in advance. I'd just piled some clothes into an old suitcase that had belonged to Dad, and stuffed my grip with as many books as I could carry. I intended to write later to tell Mum that I wasn't ever going back, asking her to fill the trunk with anything I owned and sending a postal order to cover the cost of carriage.

Mr Vernon had been tremendously kind and helpful, taking us on that last futile journey to the hospital, and giving Gran Thacker and Mum a lift in to Breckham Market after the funeral to see Gran's solicitor. I would have liked to tell him, before I left, how grateful I was for his help, but all I could find to say was a lame, 'Thank you very much, Mr Vernon.'

He held out his large hand. 'Good luck, Janet,' he said, and then I was really on my own.

The best thing was to give myself no time to think, so I bought the thickest newspaper, *The Times*, and ten cheap tipped cigarettes to keep me occupied on the journey. I really worked at that newspaper, poring over the lines as though I'd just learned how to read. I read everything: home news, foreign news, business news, leading articles, fashion, sport, advertisements. I couldn't get the hang of the crossword, but I had a go at an eight-page supplement on the oil industry.

Mum had packed me some unasked-for sandwiches before she left for work that morning. They were special sandwiches, fresh, buttery, filled with thick slices of cold chicken, and they tasted like greased cotton wool. I pushed them back into my grip, and took out another cigarette. A man sitting on the opposite side of the table leaned forward with a light. 'I'm just going to the buffet to fetch a cup of coffee,' he said. 'Would you like one?'

I considered the offer. He was youngish, pleasant enough, in fact just the sort of man I'd always hoped would start a conversation in some public place. But now I wasn't interested. I'd have liked a cup of coffee, but to accept it would mean that I had to talk to him, and all I wanted was to be left alone. 'No, thank you,' I said, and he left for the buffet and didn't return.

To stop myself thinking about Dad, I thought about Mum. My feelings about her were so complicated that I didn't know where to start unravelling them. I ought to be grateful to her, I knew. She'd married to give me a name, and she'd always done her best for me. But what nauseated me was the thought that she was so outwardly respectable and proper: shocked because I wore short skirts, when at my age she herself had had the morals of a rabbit. And anyway, getting married and setting up home with Dad hadn't been for my benefit, but for the sake of cheap respectability, to stop the village talking.

I hadn't felt able to tell her what Dad had told me, because she was upset by his death. She'd done a lot of snivelling. Not that she'd loved him, but she'd lived in the same house with him for eighteen years so she was bound to notice his absence. I was too numbed to cry. I'd got through the days by keeping busy and being politely distant to her.

And now here I was, my ambition achieved, a university student on my way to London. Only scared. And miserable. And trying desperately to keep all the horrors buttoned down in the bottom of my mind: Mum, unbelievably, disgustingly, rolling on the grass with so many casual airmen that she couldn't even put a name to the one who made her pregnant; and Dad, dear Dad who wasn't my father at all, lying broken under the apple tree. And most dreadful of all, Dad writhing in the hospital bed because I'd forced him to tell me, making him so ill that he died. If only I hadn't, if only I hadn't, if only I hadn't.

I'd read of people wringing their hands and I thought it was just a figure of speech. But that was exactly what happened to me as I sat in the train with my hands on my lap and the newspaper spread on the table in front of me, reading the pages over and over. As I fought to keep the terrible thoughts from crowding to the surface of my mind, I wrung my hands.

But it was an involuntary action. They wrung themselves, squeezing and pulling and snatching at each other until the half-healed work cuts opened and wept. And all the time I absorbed the world of the personal columns: Winter Cruises to the Bahamas . . . Horses need Holidays . . . Are you a Benefici-ary?. . . Ski-ing Parties for the Under 30s . . . Incontinence?. . . Try Oxfam's Perfect Worry Cure and put your Problems in Perspective.

I'd been to London just once, for my college interview, and afterwards I'd written to the lodgings bureau to find myself a place to live. Obviously I'd hoped to be near my college in

Regent's Park, but what I'd eventually had to settle for was a share in a room in West Kensington, miles away.

It took me a long time to find it, by underground and on foot, dazed by the noise and the traffic. I was wearing my poncho and my boots to save carrying them, but the afternoon was sunny and by the time I arrived I was sweating, my arms nearly pulled out of their sockets by the weight of my luggage.

I'd assumed that I should be living in some squalid back street, but obviously I'd been watching too many television plays. This area was tree-lined and grandly alarming, with rows of tall white-painted houses with pillared doorways. Some of the paint on Number 54 was cracked and peeling, but I was apprehensive as I hauled my gear up the steps to the front door. I wiped my damp forehead before gingerly ringing the bell.

I waited for a long time, then rang it again, and a tall fat woman with her hair in rollers bounced open the door and snapped, 'I heard you the first time! What do you want?' Then she saw my luggage. 'Oh, you must be Miss – er – '

'Thacker,' I said.

She briefly exposed some teeth that would have interested a dentist. 'I'm Mrs Dooley, the housekeeper. I can't help you with your luggage, not with my bad leg. Miss Forbes, the student you're sharing with, is here already. *With* her boy-friend. I daresay he'd give you a hand with your cases if you want to leave them down here.'

I said I could manage. I didn't want to begin by asking favours of a stranger's boy-friend.

Mrs Dooley went up the stairs ahead of me, puffing and grumbling. It was an imposing staircase, with a carpet thick enough to muffle the clop of my boots. I was puffing too by the time we reached the second landing, where the carpet was a good deal thinner.

'Miss Forbes', panted Mrs Dooley, stopping for a rest, 'was here last year so she can tell you anything you want to know. Only one thing I'll tell you myself.' She leaned towards me, gathering breath that filtered back nastily through her teeth. 'Don't you *dare* put them down the pan, or I'll have your guts for garters. I mean it. The trouble I have with blocked drains . . . Do you hear me?'

I nodded, trying not to breathe in, and then we hauled ourselves up another two flights of stairs to what appeared to be the top of the house. The carpet was reduced to a threadbare runner.

'This is as far as I'm coming.' Mrs Dooley opened a door that led to a much narrower staircase with scuffed lino on the treads. 'Miss Forbes!' she bellowed. 'Do you hear me, or do I have to come up?'

'What do you want?' A very cross voice.

'Your new room-mate's here.'

'Oh God . . . All right. Just give me a few minutes – '

'Bloody boy-friends,' grumbled Mrs Dooley. 'If I catch her at it she'll be out on her ear. It's your room as well as hers, Miss – er – , you're paying the same rent, so you'll have to stand up for yourself.'

She nodded at me and lumbered down the stairs. I stood waiting, feeling an intruder. From the corner of my eye I thought I saw a door on the landing open and a little old lady peek out, but when I turned my head she disappeared like a mouse in our living-room wainscot.

'Come on up,' called down the voice at last. The stairs were too narrow for me to carry my luggage all at once, so I heaved the cases up one at a time to a gloomy top hallway. At one end was a sink and a couple of gas rings. There were several doors, one of which stood ajar. I thought I ought to knock.

'Oh, come in,' said the voice impatiently.

Even though it was the middle of the afternoon, the room was as dark as evening. There was one very small window framing a square of sky, but you'd have had to stand on a chair to see out of it. A girl in a mini skirt considerably shorter than mine switched on a fluorescent tube as I went in, and stood blinking in the light. She was dark, small, nice-looking except that her face seemed to be oddly blotched and blurred. I wondered if she were sickening for something. A man with extravagant side-burns sat in an armchair reading a newspaper.

'I'm Libby Forbes, this is Ed Newson.' She didn't sound superior, which was something, but she was confidently middle class. I told them who I was, and Ed said 'Hi,' without lowering his newspaper.

Libby introduced me to the furniture that crowded the room. 'This is your bed, that's your wardrobe, this is your dressing-table. You'll have to use it as a desk as well. We go shares in this

158

food cupboard. There's another on the landing, but if you leave anything out there it's liable to disappear.'

'Wine bar at six?' said Ed to Libby, getting up and putting on his jacket. 'See you,' he told her, then he nodded to me and strolled off.

'I'll make some coffee,' she said, putting Nescafé into mugs and carrying them out to the landing. I moved my luggage to my own patch of territory, took off my poncho and started to unpack. Libby's trunk was open and her things were scattered about the room. She seemed to have a fantastic quantity of clothes. I didn't see where she kept them all, until I opened my wardrobe and found it half filled. But there was plenty of room for what I'd brought, so there was no point in making a fuss.

Libby returned with black coffee. I hadn't drunk it black before. As a friendly gesture I brought out my cigarettes. 'Good God,' she said, inspecting the packet. 'No thanks, I'll smoke my own.'

'Bathroom and loo on the first landing down,' she continued. 'There's never enought hot water and it's wickedly hard, ruins your skin.' Her blotches had subsided completely, so she couldn't be sickening for anything after all. 'Will you be going away at weekends?' she asked hopefully, and looked vexed when I shook my head.

'Haven't you got a boy-friend, then?'

'Oh yes,' I said quickly. I'd intended to tell the truth once I got to university, but I had to keep up my morale somehow. 'His name's Andrew, he's a farmer's son – '

Libby didn't seem impressed. 'Are you a good cook?' she asked.

'Well er – scrambled eggs, that sort of thing. But I've never used gas rings before.'

She sighed. 'Jill, who used to share with me, was a fabulous cook. Great fun, too. I'm going to miss her.'

'Has she graduated?'

'Not exactly. The pill made her feel dizzy, so she stopped taking it – can you believe it?' Libby looked at me. 'Well, yes, you probably can . . .' She sighed again.

I had a feeling that I depressed her, sitting there large and awkward in my boots. I'd hoped that my room-mate would be someone ordinary and sympathetic to whom I could mention in passing that my Dad had just died. None of the details, of course, and not because I wanted to be fussed over, but simply to establish that I needed time to adjust. But Libby was too sophisticated, not at all the sort of person I'd had in mind.

'This is a much bigger house than I thought it would be,' I ventured. 'Is it mostly students' lodgings?'

'Students' lodgings! Don't let Mrs Dooley hear you say that, or she'd throw a fit. This is a *guest house*, if you please. The only reason we're allowed to live up here in these servants' rooms is that the old girls can't manage the stairs.'

'The old girls?'

'The residents, inmates. This is where decaying gentlewomen come to die.'

It sounded a dismal place to start my university life. Recalling the old lady I thought I'd seen on the stairs, I said, 'Aren't there any other young people here?'

'There's a Canadian couple opposite, newly-weds over here on post-graduate scholarships. And there're two Indian medical students at the top of the stairs, and a girl journalist in the single room opposite them. Hardly ever see any of them, but the bathroom's always occupied when you want it. That reminds me, I'd better get ready.'

She disappeared for a few moments with a towel and sponge bag. When she came back, and was changing in to a dolly-rocker dress, I asked her which college she was at. I was pleased when I heard that we were at the same one, because I thought it would give us a common interest. It seemed, though, that Libby had a very poor opinion of college.

'Ghastly place,' she said as she did her face, putting on thick foundation, false eyelashes and some very pale lipstick. 'I never spend any longer there than I have to. It's full of women.'

'But I thought it was mixed.'

'Mixed! Ha! Five women to every man, and most of them are weeds anyway.'

'Is Ed there?'

'Certainly not. He's post-grad at UC.'

'Oh,' I said.

Libby sorted through scattered piles of clothing and chose a coat to wear. I wondered for a moment if it was her year in London that had made her so well-dressed and self-assured, but then I decided it was probably the way she came.

'Sorry about the mess,' she said. 'Lord knows when I'll be

160

back, we're going on to a disco. I'll try not to wake you. There's an Indian grocery on the corner if you need any food tonight, but if you don't want to go out you can borrow my Nescafé. See you.'

A moment later she put her head back behind the door. 'No doubt Mrs Dooley said her piece about the loo?'

'I think so,' I said.

'She does that at the start of every term. It's never been blocked, to my knowledge. Stupid old trout's never heard of Tampax.'

The room seemed very quiet after she had gone. There was no one about on the top landing, though I could hear a Beatles record playing behind one of the closed doors. I found the bathroom but it was a grotty place, with flaking plaster, stained plastic window curtains, a ferocious-looking geyser, grey high and low tidemarks round the bath and permanent brown drools below the taps. The seat-cover of the loo was badly cracked. It was the only room where I was likely to find much privacy, but it wasn't the sort of place you'd want to linger in.

There was no point in going out to buy food when I still had the remains of Mum's sandwiches. This time I was hungry enough to eat them. I experimented with the gas rings, made myself a small mug of Libby's Nescafé, and then set about finishing my unpacking.

In the bottom of my suitcase I found a mysterious wodge of old newspapers. I tore them apart, and discovered that Mum had gone and packed me an unasked-for couple of pots of her blackberry and apple jam.

It's a fiddling jam to make but she does it well and she knows that it's my favourite. I don't know whether the sharpness of the apple sets off the sweetness of the blackberries, or the tartness of the blackberries offsets the sweetness of the apples, but either way the combination is delicious. You can taste the autumn sun in it, and see the blackberries glistening on the bushes at the edge of Spirkett's Wood.

Mum seals each pot with a transparent disc and a cover held down by an elastic band, and she writes a careful label and the date. I lifted the pots out. This year's, made in the middle of September when my dear Dad was alive and we were happy . . . I felt suddenly overwhelmed by a rush of longing, not only for him but for home.

161

And then I realized that one of the pots was only partly filled. The cover had split and the jam had oozed out through the newspapers, spreading itself over the sleeve of the new oatmeal sweater that Mum had knitted for me.

I had to laugh. If once I'd started crying I wouldn't have known where to stop.

Chapter Eighteen

I disliked college from the start. When I first saw it, in the spring, I'd been delighted by its parkland setting because I knew how much I would miss the countryside. Now, the falling leaves and the sharp, earthy smells of autumn induced nothing but melancholy.

Difficult to say whether I'd have enjoyed college in other circumstances, if I hadn't been weighed down by my load of misery and guilt. As it was, everything seemed pointless. I combined my new-girl-up-from-the-country awkwardness with a depressing sense of oldness and experience.

I'd been fed up with school, where you had to be all day whether you wanted to or not, and where they chivvied you into doing something the whole time. What I'd most looked forward to at university was freedom from supervision. But now that I'd got it I didn't want it. There was too much time for thinking.

I didn't like my course, either. I'd chosen Sociology because I thought it would be full of human interest, but all it was full of were statistics. I found it difficult, and the books I needed were always out of the library.

College was crowded with people, but I knew no one outside my fortnightly tutorial group. There were ten of us – including two men, one bumptious, one who sat picking his pimples – and we usually gravitated towards each other at lectures. But as soon as lectures were over we drifted apart again, scattering to our habitations in distant parts of London.

There were plenty of clubs and societies I could have joined, of course, but I didn't feel like joining anything, not that first term. Next term, perhaps, when I'd had time to come to some kind of arrangement with myself, it would be different. Until then, I preferred to be on my own.

Finding my way about London, with an A-Z guide, had to be a priority. It was supposed to be a swinging place, but I found it just crowded and confusing. Everywhere was rush and push, and it didn't take me long to discover that country good manners were out of place. There was no need to stand back to let old ladies on to buses or tubes first, because they were experienced shovers with very sharp elbows who knew all about city survival.

What really dismayed me, in all the noise and hustle, was that London was such a very *foreign* city. The streets were packed with people of every conceivable nationality and colour, and I began to wonder whether any genuine native Londoners existed or whether they had all fled to the country, as Mrs Marks had to Byland, leaving the foreigners in occupation.

I longed for some escape from the traffic and the strangeness, but my shared room was no haven. I knew I'd have to find somewhere else. It was essentially Libby's room, overflowing with her things and her personality even though she was rarely in it. When she had gone out that first evening, apologizing for the mess, I'd assumed that she simply hadn't had time to put her clothes and books away. Then I discovered that she lived in a permanent muddle, and presumably liked it.

Nothing to do with me, except that she used my bed and dressing-table as additional dumping-grounds. It made me furious to come in and find that there wasn't a square inch I could call my own. I remembered Mrs Dooley's remark that I'd have to stand up for myself, but there was no point in having a row with Libby until I'd found somewhere else to live. Certainly no point in sending to Mum for my trunk until I had a room of my own to unpack it in.

And that was clearly going to be difficult to find. I bought the *Evening Standard* and searched the small ads, but single rooms were wildly expensive, their rents geared to the £1,000-a-year secretary market. But at least the search gave me an occupation and a purpose. I set about seeing how little I could live on and how far I could stretch my grant.

I hadn't smoked since I arrived. I didn't much enjoy it anyway. I lived on Nescafé and brown bread and eggs – though I hated paying good money for such small pale objects – and canned

163

soup and baked beans. Fruit was fantastically expensive, eating-apples two-and-something a pound in the street markets, when at home we tripped over them in the grass . . . But apples no longer appealed to me.

Fares for my journeys to and from college were another expense that could be pared. There were several possible routes and I walked for long distances, taking public transport only between the most economical fare stages.

The underground, with its hot stale wind, depressed me. I preferred to walk or ride on buses because there was always something to see and, looking and listening, I could sometimes forget about Dad for a few minutes. And then the desolating facts would come crowding in on me again, worse than ever.

I hadn't realized how physically painful grief would be. It gave me a terrible, persistent ache inside. Once, when I was waiting on an underground platform at Leicester Square, I heard myself cry out loud with the pain: 'Dad, Dad!' But no one took any notice; that sort of thing goes on in London all the time.

Finding a boy-friend, which I'd originally thought of as priority number one, didn't matter any more. Just as well, because there didn't seem much prospect of making friends with anyone, male or female. The Canadian couple who lived in the room opposite were very pleasant and we smiled and said 'Hi,' if we met, and I exchanged a few 'Hallo's with the journalist, and said a polite 'Good evening' to the Indians, but that was all.

I received several letters, redirected from home. The announcement of Dad's death had appeared in the local paper, and the news had evidently circulated. My school friends, Caroline and Sue, wrote to say that they were sorry, and to tell me what great times they were having at York and Essex, and to say they hoped I was having a great time in London. I wrote back to thank them and assured them that I was.

Miss Dunlop used the official school writing-paper to send me a formal letter of sympathy, which I had no reason to keep. Mrs Bloomfield wrote me a sympathetic letter which I would have liked to keep, but I couldn't read it without crying so I tore that up too. I was sorry afterwards, particularly as she'd finished it 'Yours affectionately'. I was deeply in need of whatever affection anyone could spare.

Except from Mum. I simply couldn't fancy it from her. She wrote to me twice a week, first class, her letters overflowing with maternal love. It wasn't what she said, exactly, because she wasn't much of a letter-writer, but I knew what she meant. And she *would* keep sending me things. The regular food parcels were an embarrassment, except that I was very glad of the contents. Having to thank her for them made it difficult to tell her I was never going back, so I postponed the telling and wrote short stiff letters in reply, irregularly, second class.

Dear Mum,
Thank you very much for the cakes. They are very nice. I am still enjoying the jam.
I hope you are getting on well at the shop. I expect the journey is a nuisance in this wet weather.
I am glad the hens are laying well, but please don't try to send me any eggs, they will only get broken in the post.
I have settled down nicely, my room is comfortable and I am sharing it with a very pleasant girl.

I was writing the letter in my usual place in the library at college. The main reading-rooms were always full but I'd discovered the periodicals room in the basement, where a few tables and chairs were jammed in among the racks of back numbers. Very few people ever read down there because it was gloomy, but it suited me. It was the only reasonably private place I'd found since I'd been in London. That was where I spent most of my time in college, reading and writing and thinking about Dad, staying there until the library closed so that by the time I got back to our room Libby would have gone out.

That evening, as I was writing to Mum, the swing-doors swung and a girl from my tutorial group walked to the far end of the room and back. I looked up as she passed. We smiled and nodded, but we had nothing to say. And then I heard her reporting to someone else just outside the door.

'No one there except that Thacker woman. You know.'

'Oh, her. Don't let's go in, then. She's so dull, never stops working.'

'Perhaps someone will give her a medal.'

The door swung behind them. I finished my letter:

College is very interesting and I have made a lot of friends.
I hope you are keeping well, from Janet.

165

I walked almost to Oxford Street, limping a bit in my boots, then caught a bus for Notting Hill Gate. I'd bought an *Evening Standard* (PRINCESS ANNE – SHOCK! the placard had screamed, but I'd already been in London long enough to know that it probably meant she'd got a cold) and skimmed through the To Let columns. Plenty of choice, but nothing I could afford unless I shared, so I might as well stay with the Libby I knew.

I turned to the Sits Vac. I was seriously wondering whether to try to get a job rather than stay at university. It was an uncongenial half-life and I didn't think I could stick it for three long years. Better to give up my place to some eager schoolkid . . .

I was sitting on the sideways seat just inside the bus. A girl got on at Marble Arch and sat opposite. I looked at her without seeing her, and was surprised when she gave me a friendly smile.

'We do know each other,' she said when I didn't respond. 'Kate Bristow – we share a kitchen and bathroom, remember?'

I started, blushing because I hadn't recognized her as the journalist from the single room. 'Sorry,' I said.

'That's all right. You were miles away.'

'Yes.' I looked at her properly for the first time. She was several years older than me, fashion-aware but casual, with a fringe of brown hair that flopped into her eyes, lashes that were definitely her own, a nicotine stain on her thin fingers, and one of her coat buttons hanging from a thread. She looked human and approachable, so I said, 'You're about to lose a button.'

'Oh, Lord – typical . . .' she said ruefully, pulling it off and putting it in her pocket. 'Thanks very much.'

'That's all right,' I said, and we both laughed, radiating goodwill across the bus. I knew that it was stupid of me to sit there with a grin on my face but I'd suddenly realized how lonely I was, how much I needed company.

The bus charged the Bayswater Road traffic and eased into Notting Hill Gate. I stood up reluctantly, not wanting to cut our acquaintance short, but Kate got up as well. 'I always use the delicatessen here,' she said. 'Are you shopping too?'

'No – I walk from here because it's cheaper.'

We paced along together, much of a height though she was thinner than me. The shop fronts we passed were brilliantly

166

lighted, their multi-coloured neon signs reflected on the greasy wet pavements.

'How are things?' she said. 'Are you enjoying being in London?'

I'd have liked to tell her the truth, but we had reached the Italian delicatessen. Half-past eight in the evening and the shop was full. I wondered what Dad would have thought of that.

'Oh yes,' I said. 'It's super.'

'Even sharing a room with Libby?' She laughed. 'Better not answer that. Look, you must come and have a cup of coffee with me some time. Only not tonight I'm afraid – deadline tomorrow.' She hitched a document case under her arm. 'See you.'

'See you,' I said, and we parted.

When I got back to the room, I found that I was humming. Feeling cheerful for the first time since I'd come to London, I stuffed my accumulated dirty clothes into my grip and took them to the coin-op. There was the usual mix of customers: two children in charge of the family washing, a young white woman with a baby in a sling, a black couple folding their sheets, a seedy-looking man reading a paper while he waited, a group of hippies making use of the warmth, an old woman ditto. Unusually, I felt quite benevolent towards them all.

I fed my clothes into a machine and sat watching them churn past the porthole. I could see my life revolving in the suds. There was the big bath towel, colour-fast cotton, that Dad had ordered specially from the drapery traveller; the fun pyjamas I'd made out of some jazzy material, slightly imperfect, that I'd bought from a stall in Brockham Market; the striped hand towel, a mothball-smelling contribution from Mum's bottom drawer; the Snoopy tea-towel that Caroline had given me for my birthday; and my Marks and Spencer underclothes. Almost as good as the telly. I hummed as I sat watching, irrationally pleased because I'd been given an unspecific invitation to drink a cup of coffee with someone.

After I'd returned to the room and put away my clean clothes, unironed because I wouldn't ask to borrow Libby's iron, I decided to make some Nescafé. I hoped I might see Kate Bristow on the landing, but one of the Indian medical students was there, cooking a pungent mixture over a gas ring.

'Ah, Miss Thacker – '

'Good evening.' It seemed discourteous just to say 'Hallo' when he was unfailingly polite. I felt ashamed that I didn't know his name. He was the smaller and darker of the two.

'Miss Thacker, will you please have some of my vegetable curry?'

'No, thank you,' I said, putting the kettle on the other ring. 'I just want some coffee.'

'But I do most honestly and sincerely beg you to share my curry, Miss Thacker. I assure you there is plenty.'

'Thank you, but I don't want it, really.'

He smiled, infinitely sad. 'Ah, Miss Thacker – I had the temerity to hope that you would not be racially prejudiced.'

Damn it all, it wasn't racial prejudice not to want to eat curry at ten-thirty in the evening. Racial prejudice was something we'd often discussed at school, and we'd all condemned it without ever having any opportunity, in deepest Suffolk, to put our beliefs to the test. Now I was caught. I didn't see how I could refuse without offending the man, so I allowed him to spoon a little on a plate for me.

'Would you care to come to my room to eat it, Miss Thacker? It is a very comfortable room and I have a fine collection of Beatles.'

'Yes, I know, I've heard them. But really, I'm just going to bed. Thank you very much, this is delicious.'

Embarrassed, conscious that the unaccustomed spiciness was bringing me out in a sweat, I ate the curry with my teaspoon and then made a mug of Nescafé. The Indian stood watching me, polite but disconcerting.

'Where's your friend?' I asked, feeling obliged to make conversation.

'He is going out. With a nurse from the hospital.'

'There must be a lot of other nurses,' I said, trying to be encouraging.

'Miss Thacker – would you perhaps come to the cinema with me one evening?'

'Thank you,' I said faintly, and retreated to my room. I didn't see that going out together would help either of us. I needed someone to whom I could explain everything, and how could he possibly understand? And whatever he needed in the way of sympathy and understanding, I felt totally inadequate to supply.

Now I should have to try to dodge him as well as Libby. It was a ridiculous situation. And four long weeks to go to the end of term. And then, where could I go for Christmas?

The euphoria I'd felt after speaking to Kate Bristow evaporated. I'd hardly seen her before and I didn't see her again. Her invitation had obviously been a polite formality, and I was as much alone as I had been before. I started room-hunting in earnest, cutting lectures to tramp round agencies and hunt down addresses, but anything I could afford was either unbearably squalid or snapped up before I got there.

Inevitably, I had a row with Libby. One evening I went back to our room early, soon after she had returned from college.

'Yours, I think,' I said, picking up a skirt and a sweater and some unwashed tights from my bed and tossing them on to hers.

'You needn't throw them.'

'You needn't put them on my bed.'

'Why not, for God's sake? What's so special about your bed?'

'I'd like to keep it to myself, thank you.'

Libby laughed. 'Well, nobody seems eager to share it with you! You haven't heard from that rustic boy-friend since you've been here, have you? I'm not surprised. I didn't think you would. You're a real drag, do you know that?'

'I don't get in your way.'

'You just irritate me. I saw you in college today, wandering round looking as though you were a thousand miles from home. Why the hell don't you make some friends, or go out and try to enjoy yourself?'

'I'm looking for somewhere else to live, if you want to know.'

'Thank God for that.'

'Amen,' I snapped, and grabbed my poncho and stamped off, up Holland Park Avenue to Notting Hill Gate, down Church Street, along Kensington High Street, up Addison Road. Bloody Libby, bloody college, bloody London. It was icy cold, and my boots hurt. My feet felt as tortured as though they'd been put through Gran Bowden's great mangle, cast-iron frame and wooden rollers and all.

I went to bed early, and was woken by Libby coming in and putting on a reading lamp. Only she wasn't alone, she was giggling with Ed.

'Ssh,' she whispered. 'Mustn't wake the sleeping beauty.'

'I'd better not stay,' he muttered.

'Come on in, it's all right.'

Libby crept to my bed and leaned over it. I pretended to be asleep. No point in making a fuss if she wanted to bring Ed in for coffee, as long as they weren't too noisy and didn't put on too many lights.

'It's all right, she sleeps like the dead. Come *on*, Eddy – '

They didn't put on any more lights. There was a shuffling and rustling, then a scrunch from her mattress, and lot of heavy breathing. Then a gasp from Libby and a grunt from Ed, and a creaking from the floorboards under her bed. The creaking and breathing intensified, rhythmically, and I suddenly realized what they were doing. The shame and indignity of my being there overwhelmed me. I pulled the blankets over my head and stuffed my fingers into my mouth and wept in bitterness and desolation, while my own bed creaked in time with theirs.

Chapter Nineteen

Tuesday. Letter-from-Mum day. She wrote every Sunday afternoon and posted the letter on her way to the shop on Monday morning, so I knew that when I got back from college every Tuesday it would be waiting for me on the hall table, a square envelope covered with big childish writing, my name half-hidden by the stamp.

No rush to read the letter. I started to cook my supper first, scrambling three eggs because they were small and I was hungry, and at the same time keeping a look-out for Indians.

I opened the envelope while I waited for the eggs to thicken. Mum always wrote on lined paper, and so did I when I wrote to her. It was much cheaper than unlined Basildon Bond which I knew you were supposed to use for polite letters.

'Dear Janet,' Mum wrote, and I recalled how some hang-up from her schooldays made her write with her left hand always cupped over the paper so as to hide her laborious words:

I hope the apples arrived safe I know how much you like them. I rapped them up separate so they should not get brused. I am sending a Parcel with a cake Im afraid it is sad in

170

the middle Im afraid I don't bake like your poor Father. I am glad your getting on so well and I shall look forward to seeing you Xmas. I am doing alright at the Shop your Gran is worried about the new Decimal Money and so am I but I dont let on, we shall have to manage. Well Janet I am sorry to tell you some bad news Miss Massingham died Friday of Lung Cancer poor old soul. Tom Billings found her when he took the milk.

Well no more now I must close.

Your loving Mother.

PS Dont eat the sad bits of the cake you will get indigestion.

The eggs caught on the bottom of the pan. I snatched it away from the gas and stirred conscientiously, concentrating all my attention on what I was doing so that I didn't have to think about Miss Massingham.

Before Dad's death I wouldn't have been affected by Mum's news. Miss Massingham was old and it was natural for old people to die, they were doing it all the time. I hardly knew her. She was just an eccentric old lady who'd once been kind enough to give me two pounds. I'd have thought, 'Poor old Miss Massingham,' felt sad for a minute or two, and then I'd have forgotten her again.

But Dad's death had raised my emotional dew-point. I'd been too shattered to cry over him, but instead I'd started to cry over the most unlikely things, bands playing in the streets and newspaper reports of cruelty to animals. I knew that if I let myself think about Miss Massingham I should cry my eyes out, so I stirred the eggs, scraping the flakes off the bottom of the pan and thinking hard about nothing.

I heard footsteps on the stairs but didn't bother to look up, so I nearly dropped the pan when someone took hold of my shoulder. I jerked my head to see who it was and found myself eye-to-eye with Kate Bristow. Her eyes were green-brown, glassy, and I could see myself reflected in her pupils.

'That shook you,' she said with a lop-sided grin, and she didn't let go, and I realized she was using me for support. Her words were slightly slurred, and though she didn't smell of alcohol I was sure she must be full of either drink or drugs. I felt that I probably ought to do something for her, but I didn't know what.

171

She took the problem out of my hands. 'Food! Marvellous. Come on, let's eat at my place.'

Holding the pan in her other hand, she fended herself off my shoulder and made for the door of her room. Mesmerized, I picked up the plate I'd been warming and followed her. As an afterthought I ran back and turned off the gas.

Kate's room was about the size of mine at home, very small, and not even Libby could have created such a mess. It was difficult to tell whether her bed was made or not. She had a clothes line instead of a wardrobe, and coats and skirts and dresses hung suspended across the room. But drunk or drugged, she parted the clothes accurately to reveal a tallboy and she knew which drawer to rummage in for a couple of forks.

I stood holding my plate like Oliver Twist, except that I hadn't had anything yet. Kate helped me to some egg, and started to eat her own share straight from the pan. 'Mm, this is good. Thanks, love, I was starving. Were you making some coffee?'

I went out and made two mugs of Nescafé, Kate's extra strong. When I returned with it, she was sitting on the floor in front of the gas fire. The single armchair was occupied by folders and a typewriter, with my plate balanced on top. After a moment's hesitation I sat down beside her, ignoring my share of the egg which by now had congealed. After reading Mum's letter I wasn't hungry any more.

'Thanks for the coffee. You're a friend in a million,' Kate said, and I felt absurdly gratified. She took two cigarettes from a packet of Gauloises, lit them both, passed one to me, then leaned back with her head against the side of the chair and closed her eyes.

I puffed at the cigarette, and coughed as the strong foreign smoke hit the back of my throat. I couldn't help thinking of poor old Miss Massingham choking over the cigarettes that were killing her, so after a bit I stubbed it out.

I thought perhaps Kate was asleep, and I ought to leave, but I didn't want to. Sleeping company was better than none. But she stirred and drew on the cigarette she'd been holding in her fingers.

'Do you know where I'd like to be, right now?' she said. She stretched her arms towards the fire, smiling at what she saw in her head, oblivious of me. 'High in the Alps, in a mountain inn with a roaring stove and deep snow outside. Do you know the French Alps?'

I started to tell her that I didn't know any Alps at all, but she wasn't listening.

'French Alps for preference, but in the mountains anyway. I love the mountains – sun and snow and the scent of the pines. The air's like wine and the wine's like wine and you're drunk all day with the joy of it. And instead we're here, stuck in this bloody city, just existing.'

It was depressing to find my view of London confirmed by someone who was older, who had a job and a salary and a room of her own.

'You can get drunk in London,' I pointed out.

She looked at me sideways. 'How very literal of you. Vodka. No smell, no headache, and it doesn't make me weep. Two gins and I'd have been pouring out my life story to you, but when I'm on vodka you don't have to worry.'

'I'm not worried,' I said. I was getting uncomfortably cramped on the floor. I shifted to ease my muscles, and tried not to think about the news in Mum's letter.

Kate was talking about abroad again. She told me about last year when she ('we', she said) had travelled Western Europe in a little car that she described as a corrugated-iron coal scuttle on wheels, working in ski chalets and summer caravan camps. It was interesting, but she smoked too much and the smoke made me cough, and coughing made me think of Miss Massingham, found dead or dying by Tom Billings when he took the milk.

'Cigarette?' she said, for about the third time.

'No, thanks, I ought to be going.'

'Oh. All right, then, push off if you want to. No, don't – I'd like you to stay, if you can bear my talking. I'm sorry, but I want to get it out of my system. That was the most wonderful eight months of my life and it's hard to adjust to reality. I need someone to talk to.'

I wasn't entirely enthusiastic. Despite her assurances about the vodka, it was clear that if I stayed I was going to hear her life story. But I could hardly leave now without being rude, so I stayed.

I offered to make more coffee, but Kate was sober enough to heat some water over a gas ring that was sited perilously close to her bed. I shifted my legs again, refused another cigarette,

173

and heard that the other half of the 'we' she had talked about was a Frenchman. They had been inseparable during those eight months in Europe, working and playing and laughing and making love. Making love in particular. I boggled over the unimaginable details she casually revealed, but she didn't notice my discomfort. Yves was, apparently, a fabulous lover, and Kate was crazy about him.

'Can't you go back to France again?' I said.

'No, because the bastard's dumped me. Being French, damn him, he's under Maman's thumb, and she has now found him a prospective wife. He's buckled down to work in the family business, and he's getting married next month. Oh, he says he still loves me. It's not that he loves the girl – but he says he'd like to get married and she's very suitable and both families are happy. And he has the nerve to say he hopes I'll be happy for him, too!'

I didn't know what to say, except, 'I'm sorry.'

'Sorry to bore you with it. I needed to tell someone, and you're a very patient listener.'

'When did you hear about it?'

'End of last week.'

'You must have had a bad weekend.'

'Bad? I've had a ball – parties every night. Haven't slept in my own bed since, though God knows where or who with – '

I was shocked, though I tried not to show it.

'And now I've shocked you.'

'No, you haven't. I've had a lot of experience, it takes a lot to shock me.'

She looked amused. 'Been reading books, have you? Then you must have learned that life's too short to waste. I'm not going to mope over Yves – I feel better already. And soon there'll be someone else.'

I was shocked again. 'But you said how much you loved him. If I loved someone, I couldn't get over it just like that.'

'Don't be silly, of course you could. You'd be a fool if you didn't. Cigarette?'

'No, thanks. And you'll get lung cancer if you go on smoking like that.'

'My point exactly. We've all got to die, so we might as well make the most of every experience that comes our way. And I've certainly done that . . .'

174

When I'd asked Mrs Bloomfield's opinion on the subject, I hadn't known about Mum and the Americans. I had some views of my own now. 'I think promiscuity is disgusting,' I said.

'That's a loaded word for a start.'

'Well, you said you didn't know whose bed you were in.'

'Exaggeration, love. I knew, but I don't much want to remember.'

'It's still disgusting. And supposing you had a baby – nice for her, not even knowing who her father was!'

'Agreed. But I'm on the pill so it's no problem.'

'Well, anyway – '

I was sickened by the conversation. I closed my eyes, unable to think of anything to say but too lethargic to make the move back to my own room (and poor old Miss Massingham, coughing out her lungs alone).

'God, I'm a selfish bitch, aren't I?' Kate suddenly moved from her patch of floor to mine and knelt beside me, suede skirt and silky shirt and a breath of stale Gauloises.

'I'm sorry, Janet. You've kindly listened to my troubles, and all I've done is nauseate you. I really am sorry. How old are you? Eighteen? You stick to your principles, love, don't take any notice of me. Come on, cheer up. Have a cigarette – no?'

'No. Someone I know just died of it.'

'Of what?'

'Lung cancer. I've just had the letter this evening.'

'Oh, no – I've been boring you with my problems, and all the time you've had this sadness of your own.'

I nodded. Couldn't trust myself to speak.

'And you're not happy here, are you? I knew that when we met on the bus. I really did mean to ask you in for coffee later, but I was too much occupied with my own affairs. I'm hopelessly selfish, I'm afraid. But I did realize that you were lonely – you are, aren't you?'

'Yes.' Any minute I was going to howl and there was no point in trying not to.

'Was it a relation who died? A great friend?'

'No, just an old lady I knew. She didn't mean anything to me. It was just, sort of, the last straw – '

'Tell me.'

Kate sat with her arm round me and I told her everything.

175

And she listened, and she lent me her shoulder, and relief flowed warmly into me as the words came hiccuping out.

'Don't,' she said, when I told her about Mum. 'Don't think too badly of your mother. It's very easily done, you know. Saying "No" is the most difficult thing in the world.'

'But she didn't even love him. She didn't love any of them . . .'

'You don't know that. Perhaps she really did love this particular one, but their relationship didn't work out, so she pretended she didn't just to save her pride. As long as they loved each other at the time, that's all that matters, isn't it?'

'No. No, that's not real love.'

Kate gave me a small shake. 'Oh come on, wake up. What's "real love", for goodness' sake? A magazine concept for disappointed women, that's all. You can't spend your life hanging about waiting for someone to come along labelled Real Love Guaranteed Mothproof. Love comes in all kinds, you know. Sometimes it lasts faithfully for ten days, and sometimes unfaithfully for a lifetime. Who's to say which is the more real?'

I shook my head. I didn't want to believe her.

'You'd better push off, then,' she said, taking away her arm.

I didn't move. I made my own decision, and I decided to stay. She sighed. Uneasy? Reluctant? Just tired? I didn't know, but I stayed.

'Not so lonely now?'

'No . . .'

'No need to be, now.'

I don't remember what conclusion we came to that evening.

Well, I do, of course. But the trouble is that I can only describe it in such corny images: dark tunnels, shafts of sunlight, elusive butterflies.

I could spend half an hour sitting here trying to make up something more original and less like the lyric of a pop song. But what would be the point? Thinking it over, I've decided that the fact that I have a derivative imagination doesn't invalidate the experience, so here goes.

When Kate kissed me that evening, I really felt that I was approaching the end of a long dark tunnel, coming out into a shaft of sunlight. Silhouetted at the end of the tunnel was an intricate wrought-iron gate that opened on to a beautiful garden. A butterfly fluttered ahead through the bars of the gate, just out of my reach, but I knew that I could go through into the garden and catch it if only I could find the key.

I didn't find the key that evening, or enter the garden to catch the butterfly. But at least I'd made the discovery that it was there.

Chapter Twenty

I hitched down to Dover. I'd never hitched a lift before, never thought of doing so, but that was one of the two hundred and fifty-six things Kate had enlightened me on since we'd been together.

I took a Green Line bus to the outskirts of London, as she'd told me, and hung about near a main road filling-station. The first motorist who noticed my bashful thumb was going only as far as Maidstone, but I accepted the lift for practice. Kate was going to join me at Dover after work, so I had all day.

The driver was middle-aged, pale and paunchy. He asked where I was going, and I told him I was on my way to France.

'Lucky you! Student, are you?'

'Sort of.' I didn't quite know whether I was still a student or not, couldn't make up my mind.

The driver sighed. The back of his car was piled with boxes of greetings cards, and slipped down beside his seat was a clip-board with a list of names and addresses. 'Marvellous to be young,' he said enviously.

'Yes, it is,' I said, and I meant it. I didn't know when I'd been so happy. In fact I'd never been this happy before in the whole of my life. It was a cold day in early December and the car heater didn't seem to be working properly, but I was so warm inside that I didn't care.

From Maidstone I got a lift in a timber lorry. The driver was going down to Dover docks, but I asked him to put me off in the town. Hours to wait before Kate would arrive so I holed up in a coffee bar for the afternoon.

There were still two days to go before the end of term but I'd had my last tutorial (my painstaking essay carelessly shredded by the tutor) and no one would know if I were in college or not. I still hadn't got round to telling Mum that I wouldn't ever be going home again, but I hadn't told her the date term ended and she wouldn't be expecting me this early in December. It would be easier to break the news to her from France.

I'd have been perfectly happy to stay in London. London was wonderful, with Kate. But she had a better idea.

'Let's travel! Come on, love, we'll get you fixed up with a passport.'

'But what about your job?'

'The hell with that. There'll be plenty of other jobs when we get back.'

'But I can't afford to go abroad.'

'Of course you can! We're not going to sit in the sun at St Tropez, we're going to clean ski chalets in the French Alps. The pay's terrible, but we'll have a great time.'

'How long for?'

'Does it matter? For as long as we want. We'll hitch down to Chamonix and be in the mountains in time for the start of the Christmas season. I know a couple of chalet owners who'll give us some work.'

'But what about college?'

'There's a month before next term starts, isn't there? That'll give you time to make up your mind whether you want to come back. But once you get to France you're certain to want to stay there. It'll be marvellous fun, being there together. We can move higher up the mountains until April and then find work on a caravan site for the summer. You do speak French?'

'I don't know, I've never really tried.'

'Then it's high time you did. You've been stuck in that Suffolk mud for far too long, young Janet. From now on, you're going to *live*.'

I gave Mrs Dooley a week's notice, as Kate instructed. 'We'll find somewhere to share when we finally come back,' she'd said. 'Don't keep worrying over details, just let things happen.'

Mrs Dooley puffed and grumbled when I told her. Even Libby felt aggrieved. She couldn't afford to pay double for the room

178

and she didn't like the idea of having someone else foisted on her.

'Why don't you get Ed to share with you?' I asked nastily.

'Mrs Dooley would have a fit.'

'You'll have to move in with him, then.'

'How can I? His bed's only two foot six; sleeping with him gives me a terrible crick in my back.'

'Too bad.'

Libby gave me a suspicious look. 'You've been very pleased with yourself lately. What are you up to?'

'Minding my own business,' I said airily. I was so happy that I felt quite sorry for her, lumbered with Ed and his stupid sideburns. I cleared my things out of her room, packing my warmest clothes in my grip and leaving the rest in my suitcase in Kate's room. Kate was going to sub-let, without telling Mrs Dooley, to someone from her office who commuted from Reading and wanted an occasional bed in London.

'Sorry I can't hitch down to Dover with you,' said Kate, 'but there's a hell of a lot to do at the office before I leave. I'll come down on an evening train. Meet me at the central station, and we'll have a meal in the town before catching the night boat. Can't say which train I'll catch, but I should arrive somewhere between eightish and tennish. Mind how you go darling. Take care.'

I'd promised that I would. Now, safely in Dover, I passed the late afternoon and early evening in a cinema, watching a Frank Sinatra thriller. I didn't enjoy it much, he should have stuck to singing. Afterwards I went back to the coffee bar for another cappuccino. At a quarter to eight I was at the station entrance, scanning the times of arrival of the trains from London.

Kate wasn't on the first, nor the second, but I hadn't really expected her to be. To keep warm between trains I walked briskly round the station yard, and up and down the road outside, lugging my grip.

The train I knew she'd be on arrived just after ten. I stood eagerly by the barrier as the passengers streamed through, thinking that every bright brown head was hers. People were meeting people off the train: 'Had a good day?'; 'Frightful journey?'; 'Hallo, darling!' Taxis drove up to the station entrance and away again, cars nosed out of the car-park. The train pulled out, the last car door slammed, and the station went very quiet.

179

The ticket collector left his box, and looked at me through the top half of his bifocals. 'Waiting for somebody?'

'Yes. From London.'

'Last train from London gets in at eleven-thirty.' He motioned me through the barrier. 'Might as well go to the waiting-room, no point in standing about in the cold.'

The waiting-room wasn't a lot warmer, but I was thankful to be able to put down my grip. And at least I could sit down and read. Kate had lent me a French paperback, *Les Fleurs du Mal* by Baudelaire. She said I'd find the poems interesting, but I couldn't make any sense of them even with my pocket dictionary. So I just sat and willed her train towards me, hurtling it along the track as in that speeded-up old film, London to Brighton in five minutes.

The last train came in, crowded with people who'd been to London theatres and concerts. I knew that Kate would be somewhere among them. I stood right by the barrier, standing on tiptoe to search for her face, but she wasn't there.

'Missed it, has he?' said the ticket collector sympathetically. 'Sorry, dear, but that's it. Station's closing now. Try down at the docks, there's a train due there to connect with the night boat.'

Well, of course! That was it. Kate must have been held up so late at the office that she'd decided to go straight to the docks. And she'd expect me to use my common sense and join her there.

The ticket collector directed me and I ran through the dark streets with my grip bumping against my legs. I heard the blare of a diesel engine crossing a viaduct above me and I paused a minute, gasping, to look at the lit-up train snaking through the night, hurrying Kate to the docks before me. But when I got there, with aching feet and a terrible stitch in my side, there was no sign of her. The last passengers were humping their luggage through the gateway marked 'To the Boats', and when they had gone there was no one.

I wandered back up the road, dazed and lost. Perhaps Kate hadn't been able to get away from the office at all. Perhaps she'd had an accident and was lying critically ill in some hospital . . . I didn't know what to do.

It was after midnight, freezing, and everywhere was closed. When I was too tired to walk any further I took shelter in the entrance to a small department store. The windows were decorated for Christmas, their coloured lights and golden metallic fir trees giving an illusion of warmth. The doorway was screened from the road by a showcase of glittering party clothes, so I pitched camp there, sitting on my grip and leaning back against the doors.

I didn't see how I was going to sleep, and in a way I was relieved when I heard a heavy tread on the pavement. A policeman, in cape and helmet, came into view. He looked me over with his torch. 'And what do you think you're doing?' he said in a gravelly voice.

'I'm not doing anything. Just sitting down.'

'Where do you live?'

'I've got no fixed abode.'

'Don't try to be funny with me.'

'I'm not being funny. I don't live anywhere at the moment.'

He took another look at me by torchlight. 'You'd better come with me, then.'

We didn't say anything else to each other. My left foot had pins and needles, and I limped beside him on the frosty pavement to the police station. It was a gloomy old-fashioned place with a slightly ecclesiastical look about the doors and windows. Inside, I stood blinking under the fluorescent lights of a busy office. There were various policemen about, and a couple of drunks giving them trouble. A woman with a lot of make-up and wearing a fur coat was sitting on a bench, smoking. The policemen obviously knew her well because they addressed her as Dolly.

When the drunks had been dealt with, the gravelly policeman introduced me to the sergeant behind the counter.

'This young woman was sitting in Matthews's doorway,'

'She was, was she?' The sergeant, a fat man with a moustache, looked at me with more disapproval than he'd shown the drunks. 'We don't have people sitting in doorways here. What's your name?' He wrote it down. 'And your address?'

'I haven't got an address. I've left home. I'm a student, and I've been living in London, but I've left there too. I'm on my way to France with a friend. We were going on the night boat, but she hasn't arrived.'

'Let's see your boat ticket, then.'

'Er – I haven't got one. My friend is organizing the tickets.'

181

He looked as though he didn't believe me. He pointed at my grip: 'And is that all you've got in the way of belongings?'

'It's all I'm taking to France. We're going to travel light. I left the rest of my things in London.'

'Where?'

I told him, reluctantly, so at last he had an address to write down.

A chunky policewoman appeared and the sergeant showed her what he'd put in his book. She didn't exactly look disapproving, but she wasn't very friendly either.

'How old are you, Janet? Have you been to Dover before?'

'Eighteen, and no I haven't. Look,' I added crossly, 'you've no need to treat me like some kind of suspect. I wasn't doing anything wrong. I didn't want to spend the night in a doorway, but I've nowhere else to go.'

They asked me to open my shoulder bag and my grip, and they had a good rummage round. They weren't very happy about the Baudelaire, I could see them wondering whether it was pornographic, but my creaking-new passport cheered them up.

'You're not destitute,' the sergeant pointed out. 'You've got plenty of money for a room in a private hotel.'

'But I expected to go on the boat. I waited at the Central Station until after eleven-thirty. You can check that, the ticket collector will remember me. Then I went down to the docks to see if my friend was there. By the time I got back to the town everywhere was closed.'

They scratched their ears, disposed to believe me at last. 'Well, you can't sleep on the pavement. You'll have to spend the night here.'

'Anything you say. But look, I'm worried that there might have been an accident. My friend would have been here otherwise. She may be in hospital somewhere.'

They promised to check, and wrote down her name, and the address again. The policewoman took me to a cell. Having decided that I wasn't a suspicious character she became quite friendly.

'It's not designed for comfort,' she said, 'and you'll probably find the neighbours a bit noisy, but it'll be a lot warmer than Matthews's doorway. I shan't lock the door. If we get an influx of customers I may have to turn you out, so get some sleep while you can.'

Everything in the cell smelled of disinfectant, and there were intermittent foul-mouthed shouts, some of them in a female voice, from the other cells. I took off my boots and flopped down on the narrow bed, so bewildered and worried, and disturbed by the noise and the bright light, that I thought sleep would be impossible. I was astonished when the policewoman brought me a mug of tea and told me it was morning.

'We've checked your London address,' she said, 'and your friend spent the night there. Couldn't get away, I expect.'

I didn't understand. If Kate had missed the last train she would surely have tried to get a message through to me at the station. I was thankful she wasn't in hospital, but almost more worried than if she had been.

I'd imagined myself spending the morning at the railway station, waiting, but the police told me I'd do better to go back to London. I had the impression that they still weren't entirely sure about me, and wanted to get me out of Dover. But if Kate was still in London, that was where I wanted to be, so I gladly accepted a lift to the station in a police car, and bought a one-way ticket.

At Charing Cross I made straight for the telephone. Mrs Dooley answered fiercely.

'Who? Listen, I've had the police on to me already this morning. What's going on? Yes, she was here, Miss Forbes saw her going out. How do I know where she was going? Work, I suppose – some of us have to, you know.'

Kate worked for a large public relations agency. I couldn't really believe she'd be there, but the girl on the switchboard was sure she was in the building somewhere, and when I said it was urgent she started to ring round the departments.

I waited anxiously, clutching the receiver. A middle-aged woman, trying to make herself look young by wearing a trendy John Lennon-type cap, came to the next telephone and I could hear quite clearly what she was saying: 'I'm enquiring about an article I sent you three months ago. A travel article under the name of David Warwick. I've heard nothing from you . . . yes, I'll hold on.'

We both waited. And then, on my line, a very brisk voice that I hardly recognized said, 'Kate Bristow.'

I hadn't begun to think what I was going to say to her. I'd imagined that just speaking to her would instantly resolve my problems.

'Kate . . .'

'Yes?'

'It's *me*. Janet.'

There was a pause. 'Oh,' she said, impossibly distant.

'What's happened? Why didn't you meet me last night?'

'Ah, yes. Well. Look, I'm sorry. I ought to have told you I wasn't coming, but I was too much of a coward. Where are you?'

'Charing Cross.'

'Oh no! I thought you'd go on to France without me.'

'How could I?'

'Why not? You're a big girl now.'

'But Kate – '

There was a lot of office clatter and chat in the background. 'Hang on a minute,' she said.

I waited, my eyes staring at nothing, my mouth open and drying fast. The woman in the next call box was explaining to someone else: 'I write travel articles under the name of David Warwick. I sent you one three months ago and I've heard nothing – '

'Janet?' said Kate, and there was no warmth in her voice at all. 'I know I've let you down, and I'm sorry. But I told you I was selfish, I told you that you couldn't rely on me.'

I didn't understand. 'But you love me. You said so.'

'Oh, grow up, do. We helped each other through a bad patch, and it was fun while it lasted, but it couldn't go on indefinitely.'

I refused to understand. 'But I love you – I'll always love you. Please, *please*. You can't just leave me!'

'Why not? I would have done sooner or later. If it's any comfort, I'm quite fond of you. It's a measure of my affection that I couldn't face taking you to France and deserting you there.'

'David Warwick!' The woman in the next booth was almost shrieking in exasperation. 'Morocco. Two thousand words and three photographs.'

I clung to the receiver, my lifeline as long as Kate was on the other end. 'What am I to do?' I babbled.

'Go home for Christmas,' she advised, 'and then make a fresh start next term. You won't see me again, because I'm leaving London for good. I'm going abroad, tonight, on my own. I'll leave your gear in my room, and you must make your own arrangements with Mrs Dooley. Why not ask her to let you rent the room? That'd be better than sharing with Libby. All right? Good luck. "Bye now.'

The line went dead. The woman next door was having similar trouble, still holding the receiver and mouthing her frustration at it: 'Blah blah blah . . . You stupid bloody *little* man.' She went into elaborate, obscene detail, her face old and ugly under the ridiculous cap.

My own reaction was different. I put the receiver carefully on its rest, picked up my grip and wandered away, letting the crowds take me with them. And all the time I held myself together, determined not to cry or to swear or to walk under a bus or do anything equally stupid, because I'd been stupid enough already.

I walked out of Charing Cross and turned right, along the Strand and Fleet Street, up Ludgate Hill to St Paul's, past the Mansion House and the Stock Exchange, and on to Liverpool Street and the train for Suffolk. And either my boots had worn to the shape of my feet, or my feet had become numbed, because they didn't hurt any more, there was no more hurt to be had.

Chapter Twenty-one

I had nowhere else to go, and no one else to go to, so I went back home to Mum.

When my train reached Breckham Market it was four o'clock, dark already. The next bus to Byland didn't leave until six. To pass the time I mooched round the town centre, looking at the Christmas shopping displays. The main streets were hung with necklaces of coloured lights, and there was a big lit-up tree outside the Coney and Thistle in the market place.

As usual, all the town's retailers were trying to get in on the Christmas act. The men's outfitters, where I always went to buy Dad's annual tie, had filled their window with neat displays of socks and ties and gloves and handkerchiefs and scarves, each

185

price card labelled with a sprig of holly and advice for potential buyers: 'Attractive Xmas Gift'; 'Useful Xmas Gift'; 'Acceptable Xmas Gift'. Other items, presumably neither attractive nor useful nor acceptable, were labelled simply 'Xmas Gift'.

It was always the same, every year, ever since I could remember. Always good for a laugh. Except that this year it wasn't the same, and never would be, ever again. An intolerable sense of loss overwhelmed me, and I stood on the pavement weeping.

I couldn't bear the thought of Christmas without Dad. Or home without Dad, because without him it wouldn't be home any more. Might as well go back to London. I wiped my eyes, blew my nose, and began to trudge back towards the station.

But then I thought of London without Kate, and decided that I preferred Suffolk.

There was still almost an hour before my bus went out. At the Corner Bakery and Café I paused for a moment, seduced by their window display of sausage rolls and pastries, and by the smell of warmth and food that wafted out when the door opened. I hadn't eaten all day, except for a cup of coffee and bun at Liverpool Street station. But the café was busy, and I couldn't bear the thought of having to reveal my tear-stained face to strangers at a shared table.

I was just going to move away when a man came out carrying a cake box. He was about my age, going on six feet tall, trendily dressed in a black leather jacket, with thick dark hair and heavy eyebrows that almost met in a straight line above his nose. Hadn't seen him for months, or spoken to him for years.

If I'd stopped to remember how Andy Crackjaw used to torment me, I would have wanted to avoid him. But the fact was that I'd made use of him for so long whenever I needed to describe my imaginary boy-friend that I greeted him without hesitation.

'Hallo, Andy.'

He stared for a moment, then recognized me: 'Well, if it isn't our Janet from Longmire End! What're you doing here?'

'Waiting for the six o'clock bus.'

'Bus, nothing! I'm on the way to see me poor old Mum, it's her birthday. I'll give you a lift in my car.'

He just wanted to show the car off, of course. But I was glad enough to accept his offer. 'Give us your grip,' he said, and I gladly relinquished it. He gave me his cake box to carry in exchange, and held my arm in a neighbourly way as we crossed the street. And I realized then how limp I felt, how all my emotions and energies had drained away leaving me with just a pair of feet that had been mechanically taking me in the direction of home. It was a wonderful relief to be taken charge of, and to think that I wouldn't have to endure the jolting bus journey, the chat of the village passengers, the long plod up the dark lane. However badly Andy had treated me as a child, he was certainly making up for it now.

'I'm parked at the White Hart,' he said. 'Their bar'll be open in ten minutes, so we can have a drink before we leave.'

I'd never been in the White Hart, the best hotel in town. It wasn't the sort of place I'd ever think of going to, though the girls at school who lived in town used to talk about going there for Saturday morning coffee or the Saturday evening dinner-dance. It was a big plain red-brick place, Georgian I'd thought, but inside it turned out to be Tudor, with dark beams and crooked corridors. It was impressive, though, with thick carpets and discreet lighting and antique furniture. I felt very much out of place on account of being both tear- and travel-stained, and I was thankful that at least I was wearing a skirt rather than jeans.

Andy seemed to know his way round. 'You'll find the powder-room down that corridor,' he said. 'I'll be in the lounge bar over there.'

The powder-room was luxurious, with a fitted carpet and coloured loos and basins. There were even two kinds of loo paper to choose from. A box of tissues stood open on the long dressing-table, so I helped myself to a couple. I wished I'd known about those tissues a year ago, when I'd found myself in town with a runny nose and no handkerchief.

There was no one else in the room, so I took a good look at myself in the mirror. I almost expected to find deep lines of experience carved in my face, but it was much the same. Thinner, since I'd been in London, and pale, but there was nothing there that a wash and a good night's sleep wouldn't eradicate. Hard to believe that so much emotional upheaval could leave so little mark.

I washed my face, and the washing released a few more tears. I splashed them off with cold water, combed my hair and put a new face on. Cheer up, Janet. No point in moping, Kate had once said. Just take things as they come, she'd said. Enjoy yourself. Life is for living.

I joined Andy in the lounge bar, all beams and chintz uphol- stery, and he asked me what I'd like to drink. Kate had taught me to drink beer, so I asked for a half of bitter.

'Never!' he protested. 'Go on, have a short. A short, you know, a short drink. Whisky, gin, anything you fancy.'

Amazed by his sophistication, I remembered Kate's recom- mendation and asked for vodka.

'That's more like it,' he approved. 'With lime?'

I'd always thought of lime as a fertilizer, but I didn't show my ignorance. A barman brought us the drinks, mine with a distinct greenish tinge, and also a bowl of crisps. The vodka made me realize how hungry I was, but I didn't like to eat too many of the crisps in case Andy noticed and felt obliged to buy me a meal. He was obviously generous, but that would be taking neigh- bourliness too far. I accepted one of his cigarettes instead.

'Sorry about your old man,' he said gruffly. 'That was a rotten shame.'

'Yes,' I said. 'Thanks.' Andy hadn't said 'Dad' or 'Father', so I felt sure that he knew exactly how shameful the whole situation was. His mother would have known all about it and she must have talked, when Dad died if not before. I hoped Andy wouldn't say any more on the subject, because I was liable to cry again if he did.

'Now if it had been *my* old man,' he went on, 'he'd have been no loss. Bloody good riddance, the bastard. He knocks me Mum about – always has done. Well, you must know that, you'll have seen the evidence.'

Light dawned inside my head. Well, of course! I'd just been too innocent to realize what was going on. Poor Gladys Crackjaw . . .

'The old man thumped us all when we were kids,' Andy continued matter-of-factly. 'But he's afraid of *me* now. I've told him I'll knock his block off if he lays a finger on me Mum again. Trouble is, she won't tell on him. That's why I have to come back every now and then, to keep an eye on the pair of 'em. God knows our house isn't the sort of place I'd choose to spend any time in. Still – ' he downed his drink and grinned at me, 'now you've turned up, things are looking a lot brighter!'

It was nice of him to say so. I was certainly beginning to feel more cheerful. Warm and comfortable, too. I finished my drink thirstily and Andy signalled for some more.

'Cheers, then, Janet,' he said when it came. 'Here's to when we can both get out of Longmire End for good.'

I spluttered with laughter. 'I'll drink to that!'

'So – ' he said, when he'd put his glass down. He moved his chair so that our knees were almost touching, and gave me a boldly appraising look. 'You're a student, eh? I've heard about you students – parties every night, shacking up together . . .'

I saw no reason to disillusion him. 'Something like that,' I agreed.

'You're enjoying yourself? Having a good time?'

'Super.'

'Steady boy-friend?'

I shook my head. 'Don't want to tie myself down,' I explained.

"Course you don't! Fancy-free, eh? And very nice too. I must say you've turned into a looker, our Janet. Funny kid, you were.'

I remembered my grievances. 'You were horrible to me, Andy Crackjaw!'

'I know,' he admitted handsomely. 'I was a rotten little devil – but then, with a Dad like mine, what can you expect? I liked you really, though. Remember that time we went to Spirkett's Wood?'

'I didn't go. That was Lynn Baxter. Or Susan Freeman.'

'So it was. But you were the one I asked first! Anyway – no hard feelings, I hope?'

'Not any more.'

Andy excused himself. The vodka was making me feel quite woozy, so while he was away I finished off the crisps. I put the empty bowl on another table, to make it look as though the barman had removed it, and wiped my greasy fingers on a tissue.

When Andy came back he suggested another drink, but I declined. I knew when I'd had enough. We agreed to go, and he steered me out to the car-park at the back of the hotel, and held open the door of a large car. Obviously it wasn't new, but it seemed luxurious. By way of intelligent conversation, I asked him what make it was.

'Austin Maxi,' he said as he slid behind the wheel. 'Know why I bought this model?' He leaned over, one hand on my knee, and whispered in my ear: 'Because it converts to a double bed . . .'

I giggled, and pushed his hand away. I could imagine that Andy would have plenty of girl-friends who would make full use of the car. He was certainly attractive, and I thought it was very friendly of him to take time off from his conquests to give me a lift home.

'Here we go, then,' he said, doing a tight fast turn in the car-park. He zoomed out of town, but not on the road that led to Byland.

'I've just got to have a word with some of me mates,' he said. 'Promised I'd meet them. You don't mind, do you? Soon have you home.'

He stopped at a small pub on the outskirts of Breckham Market. It was dingy, a real come-down after the White Hart. Andy apologized. 'Sorry – not the sort of pub I reckon to take a girl to. We won't stay long, though.' He led the way inside, holding my arm. I was glad of that because it seemed a very rickety sort of place, the floor kept shifting under my feet.

Two men were leaning on the bar. 'Here he is,' one of them called above the noise of the juke box. They were staring at me, but Andy just waved to them and didn't introduce me.

'Don't want you to meet them,' he said, 'they're not your sort.'

He sat me at a vacant table, gave me a cigarette, and went over to the bar to fetch me a vodka and lime. 'Cheers, Janet,' he said. 'I'll just have a word with them, tell them I shan't be joining them tonight. You all right here? Good girl.'

I hadn't asked for the drink and didn't want it, but it seemed rude not to have a sip or two. Andy joined the men and said something to them. They all laughed, and the two strangers turned their pale, fuzzy faces towards me. I didn't want to seem stand-offish so I raised my glass to them amiably. There seemed to be more in it than there had been in the glasses at the White Hart, so I reduced the level a bit more.

The two men decided to leave. 'See you some time, then, Andy,' they said. I thought that one of them winked at me as they passed, but I wasn't seeing quite straight so I couldn't be sure.

'That's got rid of them,' said Andy, sounding relieved. He came and sat down on the bench beside me. There was plenty of room, but he sat so close that our legs touched. I moved my knees away, keeping them firmly together and wishing that my skirt wasn't quite so short.

'What job are you doing now?' I asked. At least, that was what I meant to ask, but I could hear myself asking it and what I actually said was 'syob'. I corrected myself carefully.

'Pipeline welder,' he said. 'On the gas feeder main from Bacton. Bloody hard work, but the pay's good. Got five days off – but what can you do round here?'

I sipped some more vodka and considered the possibilities. 'Damn all,' I concluded.

'With the two of us, though, it would be different. Have some fun, eh? How about it?'

I drained my glass absent-mindedly as I considered his proposition. I liked the idea of being in Andy's friendly company, but on the other hand I didn't want to take up any more of his time, considering how attractive he was and what a versatile car he had.

'What about your girl-friends?' I was trying to speak naturally, but the lower half of my face seemed numbed and my lips refused to form the words correctly. I knew that I'd said 'Wash' instead of 'What', but it was all a giggle anyway.

'Oh, them,' said Andy. 'Haven't known any of 'em for more'n five minutes.' He leaned towards me with his eyes half-closed, and I could smell whisky and cigarette smoke on his breath. 'But you and me, Janet, we go back a long way, don't we? 'Nother drink?'

'No, thanks. Better be going home. Whish way's the Ladies?'

He piloted me towards a door. It led straight into a damp poky little loo with a cracked seat and a dirty washbasin, but I was happy, beyond caring.

Before going out again, I peered at myself in the mirror. My mouth was curved in a silly smile and I tried to straighten it with my fingers but couldn't. I picked up my cigarette from where I'd parked it on the wooden shelf below the mirror, noticing that I'd left yet another burn mark on the grubby pink paintwork, dropped it into the loo and then opened the door.

I could see Andy waiting for me but the floor between us was an undulating acre, impassable alone. A good friend, he realized my predicament and came over to take my arm. We negotiated the main door, an irresistibly comic obstacle, and then I staggered as the night air hit me. 'Upsy-daisy,' Andy said, catching me and half-carrying me to his car.

It was very comfortable in there. All I wanted was to go to sleep, but once we were on the road Andy reached for my hand and placed it on his thigh. I was a bit surprised but it seemed unfriendly to snatch it away. Besides, I found that I rather liked the contact, and the movement of his leg muscles under my hand as he drove the car.

When we stopped, I roused myself blearily. 'Are we home?'

'Nearly. In the lane, just by Spirkett's Wood. Remember Spirkett's Wood?'

I pointed out that it was an irrevelant question. I tried the word again, but it still wouldn't come out right. I giggled, and when Andy said, 'How about making up for what we missed?' and slid his arm round me, I saw no reason to resist. In fact I enjoyed being drawn into his arms and leaning comfortably against his solid chest while I let my eyelids droop.

'Hey, come on!' he protested. 'Come on, don't go to sleep on me now – ' He leaned across to lower the window on my side of the car. The inrush of night air made me sit up, and then he started to kiss me.

It came as a complete shock. Not just because I hadn't expected it, but because I'd never been kissed by a man before. I was astonished by the emery-paper scrape of his chin, so different from Kate's smoothness. His mouth seemed enormous, engulfing mine so that at first I couldn't breathe.

But then I got the hang of it, and began to like it. It was neither better nor less good than with Kate, just different. It had exactly the same effect on me, though, and that was another surprise, because I'd thought it was the effect of being in love, not just of physical contact.

Anyway, there was no question of my doing anything about it with Andy. Kissing and cuddling was nice, but I didn't intend it to go any further. When he muttered, 'Let's move to the back seat,' I said, 'No, thanks.'

He kissed me again, harder. His hands were roving about, pulling at my tights. I panicked and tried to push him away, but he persisted. 'Oh, come on,' he said, breathing fast. 'Don't play hard to get. You know you want it, just relax and enjoy it.'

It was only then that I realized exactly what I'd been doing:

letting him chat me up and fill me with alcohol, convincing him that I'd be a pushover.

I was horrified by my cheap behaviour, by the sordidness of what I'd led him to expect. A car ride, a few drinks, a few kisses, and he thought I'd be easy. And I very nearly was, because I was to tired and silly and fuddled that it was the hardest thing in the world to say 'No'.

Was that how it had been with Mum and the American who'd fathered me?

'No!' I shouted. And I pushed Andy as hard as I could and wrenched open the door and rolled out of the car, stumbling along the verge of the lane with brambles pulling at me. I heard him following, turned my head, and then my foot caught on a tussock of grass and I fell, Andy pounced.

'Gotcha!' he laughed. 'Want me to play it rough, eh?'

'No,' I gabbled, 'I don't want it at all, don't, please don't – '

I was saved by the three glasses of vodka and lime, drunk on an empty stomach. It rose unstoppably in my throat, and Andy scrambled out of the way just in time.

'Oh God . . .' he said disgustedly, standing over me as I retched and heaved. 'Serves you right, you stupid little bitch,' he added, and then he walked back to his car. He pulled out my grip, and dumped it on the verge. 'And I hope you get pneumonia, an' all.'

I don't know how long I lay there after he'd slammed the car door, reversed and driven back down the lane towards the road. I heard the sound of the engine fade, and then everywhere was quiet.

I looked up at the stars for comfort, but they were no longer the friendly, twinkling eyes that had once guarded Dad's small girl. They were cold and hard and a million miles away, and I was down here on my own.

I wiped my face as best I could, got to my feet and trudged home.

Chapter Twenty-two

The following day. A quiet evening at home.

Mum knitting: clicking, sniffing, coughing, sucking, clucking over the television programme. Me sitting at the table pretending to read, but in reality trying to think rationally about what I've done and what I'm going to do.

I've been a fool of course, no need to tell me that. Letting myself get entangled in emotion and sex, just like the girls I used to despise when I read their letters in the agony columns of Mum's *Woman's Weekly*. And I'm doubly ashamed, because I've had better opportunities than most of them have had, so I should know better. But all the education in the world doesn't help you cope with real life, and with flesh-and-blood people.

Oh, I can find plenty of excuses for myself. Dad's death, for a start. That, and the shock of knowing about Mum, threw me completely. I was so unhappy, so lonely in London, so desperate for affection and human contact that I clung to the first person who was kind to me. And when Kate shook me off, I was only too willing to let Andy pick me up and practise his seduction technique on me.

I've been wondering what would have happened if my stomach hadn't chosen that particular moment last night to throw up. Would I have gone on saying 'No'? I'd like to think so, but to be honest I found Andy so attractive that I might well have let him make use of me.

And wouldn't that have been ironic? A chip off the old block, me. I was so disgusted when I thought about Mum and the Americans, but now I know how easy it is to get carried away I've had to revise my judgement.

Besides, I've never heard Mum's side of it. Perhaps she had some valid excuse. Perhaps she really was in love with the man who was my father, and he loved her, only there was some reason why he couldn't marry her.

But I'd have had no excuse for having sex with Andy Crackjaw. No love, no relationship of any kind. Just a couple of hours together, with too much to drink, a few kisses in his car, and then a squalid tumble in Longmire Lane.

I might even have ended up pregnant, as Mum did. That would have been rich, wouldn't it? Her little mistake – me – following her example a generation later. I can just imagine her outraged respectability and her frantic attempts to marry me off, regardless.

That at least would have been one part of the pattern I wouldn't have dreamed of repeating. But what a lovely juicy scandal for the village women to chew over! And Mrs Vernon and Mrs Hanbury would have been so superior about it, as though my being a fool proves that you can't ever expect anything better from people like us. I would have let poor Dad down so badly. And the other people who encouraged me, Mrs Bloomfield and old Miss Massingham. Mum, too, come to that.

Luckily she was so surprised and pleased to see me last night that she didn't nag too much about the condition I was in. I accounted for my sour breath by saying I'd eaten something that disagreed with me, and for my muddy skirt by saying I'd been tripped by a bramble when I was walking up the lane from the bus. So Mum knows nothing at all about what happened, and things are back to normal – except of course that Dad isn't here.

It's desolating without him. I just can't believe I'll never see him again. I cried myself to sleep last night, missing him so desperately. But at least I can cry now, and that helps a bit.

They say that you get over grief, in time. I didn't believe I ever could, in the first weeks after Dad died, but I think they must be right because I have to admit that when I was obsessed with Kate I sometimes forgot about him for hours. Days, sometimes. And then I'd remember, and the guilt of having forgotten would be sharper than the sadness.

So I know I'll come to terms with it eventually. And things will be better when I go back to college in the New Year. I'll be able to make a fresh start, take an interest, join in. I might even get to like the place, and if I don't it will be my own fault.

I know now that if I want happiness I've got to make it for myself. No use relying on anyone else. I'm not going to be impulsive and get involved with people again, because that way you only get hurt. I'm going to be independent, self-contained, a private person, because that's the only safe way of living. After all, it's not as though I'm alone in the world. If I want human contact, there's Mum.

'Ooh, he's a laugh, that short one! Do you fancy a drink, lovey? I'll put the kettle on as soon as the programme's finished.'
'All right, I can take a hint. What do you want, tea or coffee?'
'Don't mind. Whichever you want.'
'All right, Nescafé then.'
'Oh. Oh, well, if that's what you fancy – '
'You'd rather have tea, wouldn't you? Why on earth couldn't you say so!'
'Sssh, you're spoiling the programme.'

Snarling quietly, I stalked into our perishing cold kitchen. The big enamel water jug was empty. It would be. I pulled on my old anorak and gloves, and went outside and round towards the lane, where the pump is.

I didn't need a torch, because everything was as bright as day. The moon was lodged like a great white dinner plate in the top branches of the elms in Spirkett's Wood, and all the hedges and the winter veg in our front garden were covered with frost. An owl hooted, making me shiver with loneliness and loss.

Then I heard the clink of a bucket. A tall figure appeared on the Crackjaw's path, on a similar course and with a similar purpose. Hadn't set eyes on him since last night and couldn't think what, if anything, to say. But too late now to turn back.

''Lo, Janet.'
''Lo, Andy.'

We converged on the pump. It stood fixed to the front garden wall, muffled in old woollies.

'Give us your jug,' he said.

I handed it over, and stood clapping my gloves together while he filled it. He lowered his voice, although no one but the owls could hear.

'Are you all right?'
''Course I'm all right.'
'I just wondered, considering you'd been sick.'
'I must have a weak stomach. I spent a whole afternoon in Oxford being sick, once.'

He hesitated, still holding my jug. 'Look, Janet, I'm sorry. I

196

mean, I thought you were willing – you know, you being a
student in London an' all . . .'

'My own fault. I shouldn't have drunk so much.'

'I shouldn't have left you like that, though.' He handed over
my jug and began to fill his bucket. 'I s'pose you don't think
very much of me, after what happened?'

'I've hardly thought of you at all,' I said truthfully. 'I've been
too busy thinking badly of myself.'

'Well, I'd like to make it up to you. Don't want you to think I
don't know how to behave myself, just because I was brought
up rough.'

I was quite touched. After all, until he'd started to get randy,
I'd thought of him as a very agreeable companion. Considering
his background, and his brute of a father, he'd turned out a lot
better than anyone would ever have imagined. And he hadn't
had the benefit of my educational express lift, he'd only had his
own bootstraps to pull himself up by.

'That's all right, Andy,' I said. 'You don't have to do any
making up. Let's just forget about it.'

'But I'd rather put it right. Look, how about going out together
tomorrow night? No messing about, honest. Not for a pub
crawl, either. I'll buy you a meal somewhere – tell you what,
let's go back to the White Hart, they do a good dinner there.'

I was staggered by the suggestion. It seemed so unlikely to be
invited out for a meal by anybody, let alone by Andy Crackjaw,
let alone after last night.

'Well – er – '

'I won't muck about, promise. I'm asking you as a friend.
After all, we're both stuck at home for a bit, but I've got the car
so we might as well make use of it. No reason why we shouldn't
have an evening out together in a decent place for once, seeing
how the other half lives.'

It was a handsome offer, but there was no question of my
accepting it, of course. I'd only just decided that I was never
going to act on impulse or get involved with anyone again, so it
would be crazy to go out with Andy Crackjaw, however well he
behaved himself.

On the other hand, I really did appreciate his offer. It seemed
unfair to give him a blunt refusal, but I was too cold to stand
about talking any longer.

197

'Thanks, Andy,' I said. 'D'you mind if I think it over, though? You know, it's all a bit unexpected.'

'Fair enough. Let me know in the morning, then.'

He picked up his bucket, and we parted to make our way up our respective garden paths.

'Hey, Janet,' he called softly across the frosted sprouts.

'What?'

'I'n it marvellous?' he said, pointing upwards. 'They've sent men up there to walk about on that moon – but our families still have to come out to a pump for every drop of water. I reckon something's wrong with their priorities, don't you?'

We laughed and said goodnight. As I stood in the kitchen filling the kettle, I suddenly heard myself humming and realized that I'd quite forgotten how bleak and friendless life had seemed just ten minutes ago. I caught myself wondering instead, in pleasurable panic, what on earth I could wear for being taken out for an evening at the best hotel in Breckham Market.

6

On Thursday 30 March, a week after Ziggy Crackjaw last collected the pensions for himself and his wife from Byland post office, Mrs Thacker senior suffered a stroke.

Ada Thacker was ninety-three years old. Until her stroke she had been in moderately good health; quicker on her feet than her daughter-in-law, as she had enjoyed saying in order to annoy Betty. She had also enjoyed saying that she looked after herself entirely in her part of the house, ignoring the fact that Betty did her washing and ironing and cleaning as well as serving in the shop.

It was some ten years since Ada had handed over the management of the shop to Betty's daughter, with great reluctance and only because her eyesight had grown too poor to do the paperwork. She was not displeased that Janet had become the sub-postmistress, because the post office paid Janet's salary and also brought more customers to the shop. But despite that, Ada had continued to keep a tight grip on all business and domestic finances.

It had begun to seem to Betty and Janet that Ada Thacker was going to live forever. Finding her on that Thursday morning, immobile and mumbling incomprehensibly in her bed, had taken them completely by surprise. Naturally, they did everything they could for her. They didn't pretend to grieve, but as the ambulance took her mother-in-law away to hospital, Betty had shed some stressful tears.

When the news went round Byland, everyone anticipated old Mrs Thacker's death, and with it the ending of an era. But she was tougher than they thought. Within the first twenty-four hours, skilled nursing enabled her to regain some movement and most of her speech. As she told Betty, who had been driven to Yarchester by Janet, after work, to visit her: 'I'm not finished yet, you needn't think it!'

Chief Inspector Quantrill was not a reader of anything except official reports and a limited quantity of the *Daily Telegraph*. He had never read an autobiography in his life, and when Sergeant Lloyd urged Janet Thacker's on him, he told her that he wasn't going to start now. But she insisted that he must at least read the pages she had flagged, because they were relevant to the Crackjaw investigation. And as Gladys Crackjaw's body still hadn't been found, and there had been no sightings of Ziggy, Quantrill stopped complaining and settled down in his office for a quiet read.

'Well, well – ' he said when he finished. 'I see what you mean about the book giving us a different viewpoint on the Crackjaws' disappearance. We've been assuming that Ziggy killed Gladys, when the chances are that Andrew killed Ziggy.'

'It does seem to be more likely that way round,' agreed Hilary. 'I was beginning to wonder how the old man could possibly have managed to dispose of his wife's body, and then disappear himself.'

Quantrill stood up and walked to the window, working it out. 'If Andrew arrived home to find his mother had been ill-treated, he might well have carried out his threat to knock his father down. He wouldn't necesarily have meant to kill him. But when he realized the old man was dead, he could have put him in the boot of his car, wiped up the living-room floor, and then dumped the body miles away . . . Ah, but what about the old lady? What would he have done with her?'

'I'm hoping he's put her in a residential home some-where,' said Hilary. 'He's obviously quite fond of her, but he couldn't look after her himself. Before we convince ourselves that it's Andrew we want, though, there's a big problem with the timing.'

Quantrill rubbed his chin. 'Blast, I'd almost forgotten. Ziggy was last seen on Thursday 23rd, at the post office. By that time, Andrew was back at work on a gas rig in the North Sea . . . That checks out, I suppose?'

'Yes, his company confirms that he returned to the rig from leave on Tuesday 21st. He's been there ever since, apart from the day he came to meet us at Longmire End. Andrew Crackjaw's got a perfect alibi – *if* it's true that his father was alive on Thursday 23rd. That's what I'm begin-ning to doubt. And that's where Janet Thacker comes in, because I think she's the key to this investigation.'

'You mean she's been lying to you? Ziggy didn't collect his pension on the 23rd?'

'Janet's the only person in the village who says she saw him that day. Andrew was recognized by someone the previous Monday, though, going to the post office. Janet says he went to buy some stamps, but I think his father was probably already dead, and what he really wanted was an alibi. He got it by persuading her to date-stamp the pension counterfoils in advance.'

'Fiddling the official date stamp is bound to be against post-office rules,' objected Quantrill. 'If she was found out, she'd lose her job at the very least. Why would she be prepared to take the risk?'

'For old times' sake?' suggested Hilary. 'It's clear from the ending of her book that she and Andrew were on the brink of some kind of relationship. Perhaps she's still half in love with him.'

Quantrill snorted. 'After all this time? There'd have to be more to it than that. Look, there must be some way of checking whether or not Ziggy actually drew those pen-sions on the 23rd. He and his wife would have had to sign for them, wouldn't they? Can't the post office produce the receipts?'

Sergeant Lloyd had already made enquiries. She had found that Janet Thacker would have sent the week's accumulation of receipted pension dockets to the central accounting department on Saturday 25th. The department handled several million items each week, and there was no possibility of any individual docket being identified. The proof that anyone's pension had been paid was provided solely by the date-stamp on the counterfoil of the pension book.

'And anyway,' said Hilary, 'even if their dockets could be found, we couldn't be sure that Janet Thacker hadn't forged the signatures. As long as she persists in her story that Ziggy Crackjaw collected the two pensions on Thursday 23rd, we've no way of disproving it.'

Quantrill and Hilary chose to arrive just after Janet Thacker had closed Byland post office for the day. They wanted to be sure of having her uninterrupted attention. By going round to the back door of the house, they took her by surprise.

'Not again!' she complained, standing square on the doorstep in her fisherman's slop. 'I've already told you, Sergeant Lloyd – '

'This time I've come to apologize,' said Hilary disarmingly. She introduced the chief inspector, and the postmistress gave him a wary nod.

'Brought reinforcements, have you?' she asked the sergeant with a quirk of one eyebrow. 'Well, I suppose you'd better come in. But don't think I'm not busy just because we're closed! When I've finished in the post office, and shifted some goods from the warehouse to the shop, I've got to take Mum to visit Gran in Yarchester hospital.'

Janet led the detectives to her private room and immediately busied herself behind the post-office counter, tidying away the debris of the working day: sorting completed forms, securing them on an array of bulldog clips, tearing up waste paper and tossing it into a plastic rubbish bag. She didn't ask her visitors to sit down, which suited Hilary in view of what she had to say.

'I helped myself to some reading material, last time I was here,' Hilary admitted. 'Sorry I didn't ask your permission. I thought the book looked interesting, and it was.'

She placed the dog-eared typescript on the counter, and waited for Janet Thacker's reaction.

It was some moments in coming. Janet was shocked into temporary speechlessness. When she turned to face the detectives, her red cheeks had paled to pink. Then they reddened more than ever.

'How – how *dare* you?' she said in a furiously indignant voice. 'How bloody dare you take away and read my private papers?'

Hilary answered her pleasantly. 'You told me you hoped to have the book published. You said you'd sent it to half the publishers in London, and if they'd read it I didn't see why I shouldn't.'

'But not *this* version.' Janet snatched up the typescript and riffled through it angrily. 'Look, it's full of alterations! This is just the first draft – it was never intended for publication in this form, and you had no business to read it. Of all the underhand, despicable – '

Quantrill, who had been looming quietly in the low-ceilinged room, awaiting his opportunity, cleared his throat and set about defusing her anger.

'I'm not a great reader myself, Miss Thacker,' he said. 'But I'm interested that you were at Breckham Market grammar school. That's where my daughters went. Mrs Bloomfield was headmistress in their time. Like you, they thought very highly of her.'

He didn't, of course, add that he too had thought highly of Mrs Bloomfield; had been in love with her, until a distressing major aberration had removed her from Breckham Market. But his mention of her had the desired effect.

Janet Thacker was unprepared to talk or listen to Hilary, but she found him more sympathetic.

'I have to tell you', he explained, 'that we're now treating the old Crackjaw couple's disappearance as suspicious. We've found evidence that someone fell heavily against the iron fender in their living-room. Someone else tried to wipe that evidence away. Now, Miss Thacker – '

He paused. She was beginning to look worried.

'Your book makes it clear that Andrew Crackjaw had threatened his father. He had good reason, I agree, and it was a long time ago, but – '

For a moment, Janet had looked even more worried. Then her face cleared; she even chuckled.

'Now hold you hard, Chief Inspector,' she said, lapsing into the Suffolk idiom. 'You can't use my book as evidence of Andrew Crackjaw's relationship with his father! Or with me, if it comes to that. I wasn't writing fact, you know, I was writing fiction. It's a novel, not an autobiography.'

Quantrill was thrown. 'Didn't it actually happen, then?' he said uncertainly.

'Of course it didn't!' Half-amused, half-exasperated, Janet resumed her tidying of the post-office counter. 'Just because a novel's written in the first person, it doesn't mean that it's true. Writing fiction's a bit like economy dressmaking – you take whatever material you can get hold of, whether your own or someone else's and then you make it into something different.'

'But most of this material's your own, isn't it?' said Hilary. 'Longmire Lane, your schools, this shop . . .'

'Well, yes.' Janet spoke with the care of someone who knew she was on the edge of a verbal minefield. 'Yes, most of the first part did actually happen. I wrote it in my first year at college. At the time, in the early 'Seventies, people who lived in towns were enthusing about the importance of keeping the countryside "unspoiled", as they called it. It made me cross, because they hadn't the faintest idea what real country life was like. It wasn't simple and unspoiled for us, it was poor and downright insanitary. So I wrote about it in detail, just to tell 'em.'

'And did they get the message?' said Quantrill.

'No chance. What I'd written didn't amount to more than half a book.' Janet flapped a duster over her counter, fastened the top of the bulging waste-paper bag with an elastic band, and propped the bag by the door ready to be taken out.

'It seemed a pity to waste it, though,' she said. 'Years later, I thought I'd have a go at making it a proper novel. This time it had to be mostly fiction, because the reality of my first year in London was far too dull to write about. The guest house was real enough, but I had to invent most of the characters and incidents, just to make the book more interesting.'

'You didn't invent Andrew Crackjaw,' pointed out Hilary.

'True . . . But I certainly invented the last two chapters! I wanted to round the novel off, you see, and I had the idea of reintroducing Andrew so as to bring it full circle. And that's all I can tell you. Everything I wrote about him in the second half of the book is *fiction*, not fact.'

Unwilling to believe her, the detectives stood frowning at her. A little redder than usual, but otherwise entirely composed, Janet Thacker looked from one to another without a blink

'When Andrew Crackjaw came in here on Monday 20th,' said Hilary, 'did he ask you to put a false date-stamp on his parents' pension books?'

'No, he did not.'

'Did he ask you to say that his father came here to collect their pensions on Thursday 23rd?'

'No, he didn't. And to save you the trouble of asking, Ziggy Crackjaw *did* come in on the 23rd. That's all I have to say – except that I'd be very grateful, Chief Inspector, if you would instruct Sergeant Lloyd to stop wasting my time.'

Quantrill apologized on behalf of his quietly fuming

sergeant, picked up his hat and ushered Hilary out. But then, in an attempt to maintain communication before he left, he turned to Janet and asked if she was still in contact with Mrs Bloomfield.

'We exchange Christmas cards,' she said.

'Does she live anywhere in this area, now?'

'No, in Dorset. She married a prison chaplain; they run a school for disadvantaged children.'

Quantrill thanked her for giving them her time, and joined his sergeant in his car. Hilary was too cross about Janet Thacker to talk, and he drove back to Breckham Market in unaccustomed silence.

He felt decidedly miffed. It had nothing to do with the frustrating interview they had just had; nothing to do with Janet Thacker at all. Puzzled, he analysed his emotions and came to the conclusion that what miffed him was the news that Jean Bloomfield had remarried. So much for the last lingerings of his one-time dream . . .

He shook his head, surprised at himself. He wouldn't have believed that his former love for the woman could still affect him. It hadn't even been an affair, they'd got no further than holding hands across a restaurant table. He hadn't set eyes on her for years, and what's more he'd since gone through an infatution with Hilary. Astonishing, he acknowledged, how an old love could persist.

Instructive, too.

If long-forgotten love possessed so much staying power, perhaps Hilary was right about Janet Thacker. The events in her book might be fictitious, but even so it was possible that she'd once had an affair with Andrew Crackjaw. And if she was still half in love with him after all these years, she might well be prepared to lie for him; and to go on lying because she was sure she couldn't be disproved.

7

At home in Breckham Market, Douglas Quantrill was still trying to come to terms with the aftermath of the March gales.

His wife Molly, intent on replacing their well-worn furniture, was having a lovely time looking through samples of floral fabric to cover the hand-made suite she wanted. Which design would he prefer, she kept asking. But as the prices were uniformly horrendous, it was a matter of complete indifference to him whether he ended up sitting on the peonies or the cabbage roses.

What added insult to his financial injury was the fact that the walnut tree, whose fall had flooded their living-room with revealing light, was still lying stricken in full view. The tree's downfall was not only a vexation to Quantrill but almost like the loss of a family friend. He hated to see it lying there, with its great pad of roots up-ended and a gaping hole in the grass at its base. The best thing to do, he decided, was to dispose of it as soon as possible.

The following day, he called for petrol at a garage that also hired out agricultural machinery. He served himself at the pumps, and went inside to pay. Half an hour later, after obtaining some basic instruction, he emerged carrying a hard hat with a safety visor, and a heavy-duty chainsaw.

Like a boy with a new bike, he went home early in the lengthening spring evening, eager to try the chainsaw out.

Molly was less enthusiastic when she saw what he was carrying.

'I hope you know what you're doing with that dangerous thing,' she said.

Quantrill bit back the reply he would have liked to make. His son was at the kitchen table munching a pizza, and he didn't want to set him a bad example. 'Of *course* I know what I'm doing,' he said with dignity.

'Well don't start doing it now. Your supper will be ready in twenty minutes.'

'I'm just going to try the saw, that's all. Coming to watch, Peter?'

He realized too late that it wasn't the most tactful of invitations. Having previously refused to allow Peter to touch a chainsaw because of the risk it involved, he could hardly expect him to take kindly to being instructed in the use of the machine.

Peter gave him a dirty look, but otherwise ignored him. With any luck, though, Quantrill thought as he donned his hard hat, the boy would watch from the window and pick up a few tips from a distance.

Carrying the heavy chainsaw in both hands, Quantrill walked respectfully round the fallen tree. The walnut was all of thirty feet long, from roots to topmost branches, and the trunk was a good two feet thick. Cutting up the tree was going to be a very big job he realized – much bigger than he'd imagined. In fact he wasn't sure how he was going to tackle the trunk at all.

No sense in even thinking about that problem this evening, though. The thing to do was to get in some practice with the saw, starting at the easy end of the tree. He surveyed the spread of the branches, in never-to-open-bud, and chose where to make his first cut. Then he lowered his visor, and went through the routine the hirer had recommended: hold the chainsaw well away from you as you pull the starter, brace the feet wide, grip the saw firmly, cut *away* from yourself, and never lose your concentration.

It worked even better than he'd anticipated. The saw slid easily through the first branch and Quantrill selected a thicker one. Simple, really, and not at all dangerous if you were sensible and took the right precautions. Fancying himself as a lumberjack, he cut through another branch. And another. Just five more, he decided, and then perhaps he'd better pack it in and go and have his supper before Molly got annoyed.

Afterwards, he couldn't be sure what it was that had warned him that the tree was about to move. There was a bit of a creak, and a bit of a shudder; that was all, but it made him lift his saw out of the way and jump back to safety. Almost to safety.

He had made the mistake of assuming, because the walnut had fallen, that it was inert. In fact it was still partly anchored to the earth by some of its roots, and very much alive. The tree was like a spring under tension, held down only by the weight of its branches.

Anyone who knew anything about forestry would have taken the precaution of first severing the trunk, just above the roots, so as to render the walnut harmless. In his ignorance, by relieving it of the weight of some of its branches instead, Quantrill had done a very dangerous thing.

The tree was released. With a prolonged creak it sprang majestically upwards, almost to its full height. As it rose, one of its remaining branches snatched Quantrill's chainsaw from his hands and tossed it away like a toy. Had he not moved in time, he too would have been caught up and catapulted, very probably to his death.

What saved him was the fact that the minor branch that hit him was the one he had just severed almost through. It swept his legs from under him and began to carry him upwards. Then it broke, and deposited him with a bonejarring thump on the ground.

For a few moments Quantrill lay quite still, shocked and winded. His body ached all over. Then he moved his limbs, experimentally. The thigh that was particularly painful was gashed and bleeding, but he didn't think he'd broken any bones, thank God. Relieved to be whole, he almost hoped that Molly and Peter hadn't seen what happened. It was going to be humiliating, to know that they knew that he hadn't known what he was doing.

But as his wife and son hurried towards him, he took a detective's comfort from the event. Despite his pain, he couldn't help marvelling at the way in which the risen tree's roots had fitted themselves back into the gaping hole from which the gale had torn them.

At least he now had the satisfaction of knowing the probable hiding-place of Ziggy Crackjaw's body.

While Douglas Quantrill was being taken by ambulance to Yarchester hospital, for stiches to his leg and a precautionary X-ray, Janet Thacker and her mother were driving to the same destination to visit Gran Thacker.

At the same time, taking advantage of the Thackers' absence from Byland, Sergeant Lloyd was about to enter the yard behind their shop. She had with her a uniformed police constable, in case any observant neighbour should suspect a break-in.

What she wanted was access to Janet Thacker's sack of waste paper. It was easy enough to find where Janet kept it, awaiting collection in an open shed next to the garage. Unfortunately, there wasn't just one bulging black plastic sack there, but four of them, all fastened neatly at the neck with elastic bands.

Hilary wasn't even going to try to guess which sack she wanted. She and the constable carried the lot of them out to her car, and took them back to Breckham Market divisional police headquarters. There, in an empty office, she shook the contents of the first sack on to the floor and began her search.

*

Stitched up and badly bruised, but with no bones broken, Douglas Quantrill sat in his living-room the following morning resting his injured leg. So far, Molly and Peter had spared his pride by making no reference to his own culpability. Their unaccustomed solicitude wouldn't last, of course, but while it did Quantrill intended to make the most of it.

He had telephoned his sergeant on his return from hospital the previous evening, asking her to take the scenes-of-crime team back to Longmire End first thing in the morning. He was eager to know the result, and just before eleven-thirty he heard a ring at the doorbell, followed by Hilary's voice. 'Hallo, Mrs Quantrill, how's the patient this time?'

'He's a very lucky man,' he heard Molly say thankfully. 'Come in, Hilary – you'll stay for coffee, won't you? When I think of what might have happened . . . Go on through, he's making the most of his last opportunity to put his feet up on our old furniture.'

Quantrill greeted his sergeant with pleasure. She told him that she was glad to see him in one piece, but her attention wasn't on him. It had been caught, as soon as she entered the living-room, by the fact that the walnut tree was back in place outside the window, a bit lop-sided in the branches and not standing quite straight, but even so, miraculously there.

'Wow,' she said. 'Isn't that amazing?'

'I wouldn't have believed it could happen', said Quantrill, 'if I hadn't seen it with my own eyes.'

'Can the tree be saved?'

'Hope so, but I'm afraid it's lost too many roots. We'll probably still have to fell it and replant. A man's coming tomorrow to take a look.'

'Not just a man, dear, an *expert*,' Molly corrected him as she brought in a tray of coffee. 'A proper forester – which is who we should have had in the first place.'

But she said it cheerfully; having decided on the peony design for the loose covers, she was about to order her new furniture. She anticipated no trouble at all in persuading Douglas to write a cheque for the deposit, but a bit of wifely praise would do no harm, she thought. 'Was my husband right, Hilary, about a body being hidden under the roots of a tree out at Byland?'

'Oh, yes,' said Hilary. 'He was absolutely right.'

'I thought he would be.' Molly patted him affectionately on the head in passing. 'Douglas may not be an expert with trees, but I've always known that he's a very good detective.'

She made her exit, leaving him attempting to cover his excruciated face with one hand.

'You can stop being embarrassed,' Hilary told him. 'What I said about the body under the tree wasn't true.'

'Wasn't it?' Quantrill sat up, dismayed. He was appreciative of her loyalty, but undeniably disappointed. 'Blast, I was so sure that's where you'd find Ziggy Crackjaw – '

'I didn't say we didn't find him,' said Hilary. 'You weren't absolutely right, though. There wasn't just the one body, there were two.'

'Ah – poor old Gladys as well?'

"Fraid so. I'm having Andrew brought in, and he'll have to identify his mother. That won't be easy because the pathologist says she's been dead a lot longer than Ziggy, and they've both been crushed by the weight of the tree. I don't think there can be much doubt, though. Her body had been roughly wrapped in an old sheet, and then put inside a couple of plastic fertilizer sacks.'

'Sounds as though the old man did that,' said Quantrill. 'We were trying to work out how he disposed of her, but he probably didn't even attempt it. Chances are that he just wrapped the body up and stowed it away.'

'And then Andrew came home,' said Hilary, 'found out what had happened and killed his father. But that would have left him with two bodies to dispose of. He must have thought he was in luck when he found the apple tree had been blown over, leaving a large hole where its roots had been.'

212

'A ready-made grave,' agreed Quantrill. 'A brilliant hiding-place, if you happen to know anything about fallen trees. All Andrew would've had to do was tip the bodies inside, and lop off a few branches so that it would set itself upright again.'

'I did see an axe in the old man's shed,' said Hilary.

'Yes – and when I was there I saw some chopped-off branches lying on the ground, too. They didn't seem significant at the time, but I remembered them as soon as I'd been felled by my own walnut tree . . .' He shifted his injured leg uncomfortably.

'It all fits, Hilary,' he said. 'Except for the fact that we can't pin his father's death on Andrew Crackjaw. We can't shake the witness who says she last saw Ziggy on the 23rd of March, and we know that Andrew was then working in the North Sea.'

'Oh, but we can shake her now,' said Hilary with satisfaction. 'She thought she'd outwitted me, but she hasn't. I've found evidence to prove that Janet Thacker *didn't* pay the Crackjaws' pensions on the 23rd.'

She produced from her briefcase the pension books that had belonged to the old couple, and also a card on which two pieces of torn-up paper had been painstakingly reassembled and stuck. The pieces of paper were pension dockets, each printed with an amount of money due, and both carrying the printed date 23rd March. Neither docket had been signed, nor date-stamped. Each carried a number corresponding with the numbers on the two pension books.

'So Janet Thacker didn't forge the Crackjaws' signatures, then?' said Quantrill.

'There was no need for it, once she'd date-stamped the counterfoils in the pension books. In fact, if she'd gone to the trouble of forging the signatures and putting the receipted dockets through the system, she would only have complicated things for herself.

'Post-office accounts have to be balanced at the end of each week against customers' receipts. Receipted dockets

213

represent cash paid out, so if Janet had signed these dockets and included them, her accounts would have shown an unexplainable surplus.'

'Couldn't she have solved that by taking the cash herself?' said Quantrill.

'Of course she could,' said Hilary rather sharply. 'But I didn't believe she'd stoop to it. I know she's prepared to lie – and in fact that was a point she made several times in her book; she prided herself on being a good liar – but I feel quite sure that she isn't dishonest. I thought it was much more likely that when she date-stamped the counterfoils, she simply tore up the dockets and threw them in her waste-paper sack. She should have had the sense to burn them, of course.'

'Just as well for us she didn't,' said Quantrill. 'Though come to think of it, when Andrew Crackjaw knows we've found his parents' bodies he may well be prepared to admit what happened. He'll be only too anxious to assure us that his father's death was an accident. So that's it, Hilary – you've got it all wrapped up, haven't you?'

But his sergeant shook her head, frowning. 'Not to my satisfaction. It's still a mystery to me why Janet Thacker should have been prepared to lie to us on Andrew Crackjaw's behalf.'

'I thought you said it was love,' said Quantrill.

'I know I did. But I've been thinking about that book of hers and somehow, now, I doubt it.'

8

Sergeant Lloyd had intended to go to Byland to bring in Janet Thacker at lunch time, when the post office would be closed. To her surprise, on her return to police headquarters after seeing Douglas Quantrill, she found that Janet had forestalled her and was waiting for her in the front office.

An additional surprise was that Janet looked unusually well dressed; not stylish, because her navy-blue suit was of the never-in and therefore never-out of fashion kind, but as smart as though she were applying for a job.

'How come you're not behind the post-office counter this morning?' Hilary enquired as she led her to an interview room. 'Would you like a cup of coffee, by the way?'

'Thanks, I'd love one.' Janet Thacker paused, then said: 'We've closed the shop and post office for the day. Mum and I had to go to Yarchester again this morning. After we got back from hospital last night, we had a telephone call to say that Gran Thacker had had another stroke. She didn't survive it.'

Hilary said how sorry she was, hating the necessity of pursuing a criminal charge against a woman whose grandmother had just died. But Janet shrugged off her sympathy.

'That's all right, I'm not grieving. The old girl was ninety-three, for heaven's sake, she'd had a very good innings. And she wasn't really my grandmother – but you've read my book, you already know that.'

A police constable brought in two mugs of coffee. Janet reached for hers gratefully, at the same time looking about her at the bleak room as though trying to accustom herself to surroundings she was likely to see more of in the future.

'I've come to tell you', she said abruptly, 'that I've been lying to you all along. Ziggy Crackjaw *didn't* draw his pension on the 23rd March.'

'I know he didn't,' said Hilary, trying not to feel vexed because she hadn't got in first. She produced the reassembled pension dockets. 'I raided your waste-paper collection while you were away last night.'

For a moment, Janet looked furious. Redder than usual, she scowled her displeasure from under her fringe. Then, deciding not to make an issue of it, she relaxed. 'God, you're persistent, aren't you?' she commented.

'All part of the job,' said Hilary. 'We've found the bodies of the old couple, by the way. They'd been hidden under the roots of a fallen tree.'

'I wondered where Andy had put them . . . He wouldn't tell me.'

'What did he tell you, when he came to see you?'

'Oh, that he'd gone home that morning and found his mother missing. Ziggy swore that he hadn't killed Gladys, though. He told Andy she'd died in her bed a couple of months earlier. The old man had kept it secret because he knew there'd be a lot of fuss and trouble. He showed Andy the body, wrapped in plastic sacks and hidden in a cupboard in our old house next door.'

'So Ziggy had been collecting his wife's pension when she was already dead?'

'Yes. Well he'd have had to, wouldn't he? He had to keep up the pretence that Gladys was still alive. I'd noticed that the signature on her pension dockets was unusual, lately. It doesn't do to be too officious about these things, though – old people may have arthritis in their hands, or rheumatism, and their signatures do sometimes change.'

'Did you ask Ziggy about it?'

'No, we never spoke to each other about anything. Anyway, he would simply have made some excuse, and I'd have had to accept it.'

'Did Andrew tell you that he'd killed his father?'

'He said he was responsible for his death, but that he hadn't *meant* to kill him.'

'And you believed that?'

'Yes. That's why I agreed to cover for him.'

Hilary gave her a come-off-it look. 'That's not sufficient reason for you to give false evidence on his behalf,' she said. 'When Andrew Crackjaw goes to court, he can plead mitigating circumstances. He's not likely to get a heavy sentence, so why on earth should you agree to be involved? You must have known you were committing a criminal offence.'

For the first time, Janet looked downcast. She nodded slowly. 'Yes, of course I knew. . . All right, what are you going to charge me with? Conspiring to pervert the course of justice?'

'Very probably,' said Hilary.

'First offence, though,' said Janet, sounding brighter. 'And don't forget that I came here voluntarily to make a full confession, I want that noted in my favour!'

'It will be. But what I don't understand is *why* you decided to confess. I mean, why now? What brings you here this morning, when you've been holding out so firmly all week?'

'Gran Thacker's death,' said Janet simply. 'I had to stand firm as long as she was alive, but now – ' she sighed with relief – 'now the poor old girl's dead, Andy Crackjaw doesn't have a hold over me any more.'

Ada Thacker, Janet explained, had died a wealthy woman. Many of the properties she owned in Byland were in a poor state of repair, but most of them were picturesque and correspondingly valuable. The shop formed only a small part of her estate.

Originally, despite her disapproval of his marriage, she had bequeathed everything to her son Vincent. When Vincent died, Ada had reluctantly remade her will in favour of her daughter-in-law.

Betty had never before had any financial security, and the thought that she would one day be a property-owner had delighted her. The only snag was that Ada Thacker had made the bequest conditional: Betty would inherit only if she was still working in the shop, full-time, when Ada died.

The condition hadn't worried Betty when the will was drawn up. She was then in her middle forties, active and a hard worker. Gran Thacker was in her seventies, and no one had imagined that she would still be alive twenty years later. But as the years passed, and Gran Thacker's need for attention increased, Betty's own health had begun to suffer. She reached the stage when she knew she couldn't keep the shop going single-handed for very much longer.

It was then that Janet had moved back to Byland to join forces with her mother. Janet's interest in the bequest was of course as great as Betty's, and she was determined to prop up her mother for as long as was necessary to meet Gran Thacker's conditions.

Their one fear was that the old lady might take against them and change her will. When vexed, which was often, she would talk darkly about selling the shop and leaving everything to a dogs' home. As long as she was alive they couldn't feel secure. They didn't discuss the problem, but Janet knew that if Gran Thacker ever found out that she wasn't Vincent's daughter, her mother would be disinherited. And the one other person who had that information, and knew how vital the secret was, was Andrew Crackjaw.

'How come?' said Hilary. 'How did Andrew get to know?'

'Because Mum told the two of us, years ago,' said Janet reluctantly.

'It never worried me that he knew, because there was no reason why he should use the information. But then he came to see me last week in the post office, told me what had happened to his parents and asked me, as an old friend, to cover for him. I said I was sorry, but I wasn't going to abuse my official position. So he said he was sorry too, but if I didn't help him he'd have to tell Gran who my real father was. I'm not sure that he would've, but I couldn't take the risk.'

'Andrew went to you as a friend, then?' said Hilary. 'Is that how you'd describe your relationship?'

Janet hesitated. 'Yes, I suppose so. We go back a long way, after all.'

'Were you ever lovers?'

She reddened. 'I don't see what business that is of yours.'

'It isn't,' Hilary admitted. 'I'd just like to tie up the loose ends you left in your book. You weren't *in* love with Andrew, were you?'

'Certainly not. But if you must know – yes, we did eventually have a very brief affair.

'I came back home for a visit, when I was in my first job in London, and I happened to meet Andy in Breckham Market. He insisted on buying me a meal, to make up for being so rotten to me when we were kids. We found that we liked each other's company, particularly as we were both involved in unsatisfactory relationships at the time. There was no question of love. It just seemed the most natural thing in the world to get together. It was very satisfactory, too. We'd probably have remained lovers for some time, on and off, if Mum hadn't interfered.'

'What happened?'

'She caught us in Andy's car, parked in Longmire Lane. She'd been suspicious all weekend, and she was determined to find us. She was absolutely *furious* . . .'

'Because she didn't approve of him?' asked Hilary. 'Or

because she felt guilty about the fling she'd had with American airmen in her own youth?'

Janet frowned, uncertain how to proceed. 'Have you got such a thing as a cigarette?' she asked abruptly. 'I haven't smoked for years, but it might help – '

Hilary found a packet, and a box of matches, in the table drawer. Janet lit a cigarette, drew on it, then grimaced and spluttered a protest. 'God, it's disgusting! No thanks, I'll stick to being a non-smoker.'

She screwed out the cigarette on the ashtray, finding the words she wanted as she did so.

'My real father wasn't an American airman,' she said matter-of-factly. 'Dad told me so, before he died, simply because he knew I couldn't have borne the truth. What Mum was raving about when she caught me and Andy was that we're too closely related to be lovers. We're brother and sister, you see. My real father was Ziggy Crackjaw.'

For a moment, Hilary was deprived of words.

'Oh, no – ' she protested eventually.

'It came as a nasty shock, I can tell you,' said Janet ruefully. 'D'you wonder I wanted to keep it from Gran Thacker? She'd have thrown Mum and me out on the street if ever she'd got to hear of it.'

'Yes . . . Now I understand. But it really wasn't a good idea to commit a criminal offence in order to be sure of your grandmother's money. If you're convicted, you're going to find it very difficult to live down, in a small village like Byland.'

'Oh, I'm not worried about what Byland thinks!' said Janet, cheerful again. 'I'm used to being disapproved of. Mum will be able to retire, that's the main thing. She wants to stay in the village; in fact she's already got her eye on one of Gran's smaller properties. But I'm going to move out and start living.'

'And if you're given a prison sentence?' warned Hilary.

'I've taken that into account. I knew I was doing wrong, and I'm prepared for the consequences. As long as there's time for me to sort things out for Mum first, I really don't mind. After all, just think what rich material for a new book a prison sentence would give me . . .'

Janet Thacker paused, and met Hilary's eyes. 'Fiction, of course,' she added with a twitch of amusement, 'not autobiography.'

9

At home, later that day, Douglas Quantrill was anticipating trouble from his son.

Molly was out at work, doing the early evening shift on the reception desk at the town's Health Centre. Peter had arrived home from Yarchester City College rather earlier than usual, having been given a lift instead of coming by train, and the two of them were alone together for the first time since Quantrill had had his accident with the walnut tree. Temporarily immobilized, he knew that he was a sitting target.

'Hi, Dad. How's the pore ol' leg?'

It was Peter's ususal practice to ignore his father, unless of course there was something he wanted. Quantrill declined to be disarmed by the boy's air of innocent solicitude. He muttered, 'Fine, thanks,' turned up the volume of the remote television control and pretended to be absorbed in a programme about the habits of ants.

'Not watching this rubbish, are you?' said Peter jovially. He switched the set off and then, mimicking his father to perfection, took a stand with his back to the fireplace and his hands in his trouser pockets. 'Don't often get the chance of a father-and-son chat, do we? Might as well make the most of it.'

Quantrill tried a diversionary tactic, and asked who had provided the lift from Yarchester. When he heard that it was the father of Peter's friend Matthew Pike he knew exactly what was coming; Pike senior was a smallholder, and the possessor of more than one chainsaw.

'I happened to mention to him that somebody I know had had a bit of an argument with a fallen tree,' said Peter, enjoying himself hugely. 'Mr Pike said he wasn't surprised. He says it's always the way after trees are felled in a gale. He says idiots who know nothing about the job rush out and hire chainsaws, thinking they're lumberjacks, and all they do is damage themselves.'

Quantrill hunched his shoulders and pretended he was somewhere else.

'Mr Pike says it's not just the chainsaws that are dangerous, either. You've gotter understand the trees themselves. Mr Pike says the stupidest thing anybody can do is to – '

But Quantrill had had enough.

'Get out of here!' he roared.

'All right, I'm going,' smirked Peter. 'No need to lose your temper, Dad, just because you did something stupid and nearly killed yourself.' He moved towards the door, with a grossly exaggerated limp in imitation of his father's.

'Out!' Quantrill hollered, flinging a cushion at the boy's head.

Such unfamiliar paternal levity took Peter completely by surprise. Rubbing his head in mock discomfort, he turned to stare at his father.

For a moment, the two of them exchanged self-conscious grins of acknowledgement, suggesting that honours might be even. Then Peter, reinforcing the hint of family affection, picked up the cushion and hurled it back.